Murder on Drake Street

by

Ellen Shapiro

INDIES UNITED PUBLISHING HOUSE, LLC

ISBN: 978-1-64456-681-7 [Paperback]
ISBN: 978-1-64456-682-4 [Mobi]
ISBN: 978-1-64456-683-1 [ePub]

Library of Congress Control Number: 2023949089

INDIES UNITED PUBLISHING HOUSE, LLC
P.O. BOX 3071
QUINCY, IL 62305-3071

Other Novels by Ellen Shapiro

TRACEY MARKS MYSTERY SERIES

Looking for Laura

Secrets Can Kill

Missing or Dead

Memory of Murder

MADDIE LANDON MYSTERY SERIES

Buried in the Attic

In loving memory of my grandmother, Sally Beberman

CHAPTER 1

I was sitting at the bar, my hands tightly wrapped around the stem of my wineglass. My name is Maddie Landon. I'm a private investigator, thirty-seven years old, single, and living in New York City. Six years ago, I was a New York City Police Officer. Leaving the police force was something I grappled with for a long time. I finally left since I didn't see a future in an old-boy network.

A few weeks ago, I got a surprise visit from my ex-police partner, Greg Martin, who is now an attorney. His friend's wife was recently murdered and he wanted me to investigate her death. If it weren't for the fact that we were once lovers that ended badly, my decision would have been easy.

At the same time I was debating whether to work with Greg, I was also struggling with the decision to locate my birth parents. It was a subject I have always avoided since I believed they never wanted me.

My thoughts were interrupted when I saw Greg walk in. Our eyes met as he approached me.

"I'll have whatever beer is on tap," Greg said to the bartender. "Should we get a table?" he asked.

We were at The Dead Poet, a bar on the Upper West Side of Manhattan. The bar was designed to celebrate the lives and spirits of famous writers and poets with black and white portraits that hung on the mahogany-paneled walls.

"Sure." Though I had made my decision to work with Greg, I still had my doubts. It didn't go unnoticed that Greg's hand was lightly pressed against my back as we took our drinks to a table and sat down.

"I'm glad you called, Maddie," Greg said.

Greg looked damn good. Unfortunately, that's what drew me to him in the first place. He was tall, solidly built, with wavy brown hair and a killer smile.

"How is Howie doing?" I met Howie through Greg when Greg and I were partners on the police force.

"What do you think? He's a mess. The police have been questioning him and he's scared. I feel bad for the guy."

"Well, where are we now on the case?"

"Unfortunately, since Howie hasn't been arrested yet, I'm not entitled to any information the police have on him. They're only saying that his wife died under suspicious circumstances. Howie told me Claire had a heart condition that wasn't serious, but she did take heart medication every day."

"Do we know if she was raped?"

"As I said, at this point we don't know anything."

"Where was Howie when his wife died?"

"He told me he was showing several houses that day, and afterward he had drinks with his partner at a bar. Howie owns a very successful real estate agency."

"What do you know about his relationship with his wife?"

"Only what he's told me; that everything was fine, no problems. I hadn't spoken to him in a while."

"Did you know Claire?" I said.

"I met her a few times over the years but just to say hello. I never spent any time with her."

"Do you think Howie's a suspect?"

"It's usually the husband they look at first. Howie did admit that all his credit cards were maxed out and they each had a large life insurance policy on each other."

"Is that it?"

"There was a neighbor who saw them outside in a heated argument a few days before she died. The police brought him in for questioning but haven't charged him yet."

"How did you find out about the neighbor?"

"I still have friends on the force."

"Give me a day or two to settle some things."

"Okay, but don't take any longer. I need you to start investigating right away. Talk with Howie first."

"Let's be clear. Our working together is strictly business," I said, before getting up from the table. I wondered if my words were for his benefit or mine.

"No problem."

I still haven't mentioned it to my boyfriend Jesse, who I've been seeing for the past year and a half. I wasn't sure how he would feel about the fact that I was working with someone who I had an affair with, even if it was more than five years ago.

Walking back home, I called Annie. "Any chance you can meet for an early breakfast before work tomorrow?"

"How about the French Café at 8:00 a.m. Everything alright?"

"Yeah. See you in the morning."

Annie and I met when I was twelve years old. My adoptive parents had recently died in an automobile accident. I had no friends, mostly of my own choice. Annie is everything I'm not, positive, energetic, funny, and always looking at the glass half-full. Annie is the first person I go to when I just want to talk or have a problem. Her husband Doug is a sweetheart. Though he sometimes jokes around and tells me he's jealous of my relationship with Annie, I know Annie is crazy about him.

***

The next day I was up early. The air was chilly as I walked to meet Annie so I hugged my scarf closely around my neck. It was the last day of March and the cold air was still hanging around. The café where we usually met for breakfast is only a few blocks from my apartment building. Annie was already seated at a booth when I arrived. The smell of the dark, rich aroma of the coffee hit me as soon as I walked in. I slid in and reached across to give Annie a peck on the cheek. I love coming here, not only for their scrumptious waffles and pancakes, but also for the décor. The motif is black and white. The French posters on the walls are light and gay with men and women dancing joyously.

"I took the liberty of ordering coffee for both of us," Annie said.

After I left the police force, I didn't know what I was going to do. It was Annie who encouraged me to become a private investigator.

When the waitress brought our coffee, we ordered.

"Greg and I met late yesterday afternoon. At this point, we only know Claire died under suspicious circumstances, which probably means she was murdered. Greg wants me to investigate and get ahead of it in case they're looking at the husband."

I had already briefed Annie about Claire when Greg originally asked me to work on the case.

"So what are you thinking?"

"It's too early to have any thoughts on the case yet."

"I was talking about Greg. If Greg still has feelings for you, it might get sticky. I don't want to see you jeopardize your relationship with Jesse."

When Greg and I began our affair, he was separated at the time, but he went back to his wife when he found out she was pregnant. Subsequently, they divorced after she lost the baby. I hadn't seen or heard from Greg in five years until he knocked on my door a few weeks ago, wanting my help to prove that his friend had nothing to do with his wife's death.

"I know you're skeptical about my relationship with Greg, but I can handle myself. Besides, Greg told me he's in a relationship."

"When does that ever stop anyone? You haven't even mentioned it to Jesse yet."

"When he's here this weekend, I'll tell him. I'm just not sure how much I'll tell him."

"Somehow it will eventually come out. It always does."

"I know you're only looking out for me, but everything will be okay."

"Here you go, ladies," our waitress said as she set down our plates. "More coffee?"

"Yes, please," we said in unison.

"How is work going?" I said, as I crunched on a piece of crispy bacon. Recently, Annie opened up a matrimonial practice with another attorney.

"We're moderately busy. I think Matt and I make a good team, at least so far. What's on tap for this weekend?"

"Let's see how it goes when I tell Jesse about joining forces with Greg."

"Are you still planning to search for your birth parents?"

"I am. It's just a matter of making the time while I'm working on this case."

"I'm glad. You've been keeping the past buried for too long."

"Thanks for the reminder," I said facetiously.

"You're welcome," Annie said, smiling.

When my adoptive parents died in an automobile accident, my Aunt Jenny, my mother's sister, came to live with me. I hated most of the world during that period in my life, including my poor aunt who was stuck raising a rebellious teenager. When I was nineteen, Aunt Jenny died of a massive heart attack and I was completely on my own.

At that point, I was still living in Forest Hills, in the apartment where I grew up. Thankfully, my aunt left me money, and I also had a settlement from my parents' automobile accident. There was enough money to pay my college tuition and to buy the apartment I now live in. When my aunt died, I was in my second year at John Jay

College of Criminal Justice in Manhattan. The commute was easy since I only had to take the subway into the city. After college, I applied to the police academy where I was eventually accepted.

"Well, some of us have to get to work. If you need moral support, call me," Annie said.

We paid the bill and went our separate ways. As I was walking to my office, I thought about what Annie said. I knew she was right about the past, but even though I made the decision to search for my birth parents, it still scared the hell out of me.

CHAPTER 2

My office is located in a brownstone on the Upper West Side. There are three offices on the ground floor: mine, my cousin Will's insurance business, and a criminal attorney occupies the third office.

Since my last case, which I wrapped up a few weeks ago, things have been fairly quiet. I had no intention of turning away any cases that walked in my door, but I also knew working with Greg was going to take up a lot of my time.

Jesse, who's also a private investigator, has a lot of experience with murder trials since he works for two criminal attorneys. He might be able to help if he's still talking to me after I spill the beans. I haven't quite figured out what to tell him. Though he's not the jealous type, working with a former lover might tip the scales in the wrong direction. Who could blame him? I'm not sure I would be thrilled if he was working with a former girlfriend, even though I'm not the clingy type.

When I looked at the time, it was almost two o'clock. I grabbed a yogurt from the small refrigerator I kept in my office. Jesse was the first guy I could see myself being with for the long haul, but the thought of living together frightened me. I've never been in a long-term relationship. I started therapy a few months back, hoping it would help settle my fears. The jury is still out.

I finished up some administrative paperwork that I had been ignoring for as long as possible. Then, I locked up and walked the fifteen blocks to my apartment building on the Upper West Side. I waved to my doorman Louis as I was approaching the entrance. His welcoming smile lifted my spirits.

"Hi, Ms. Maddie. You're home early."

"Guilty as charged. I thought I would go for a run to clear out the cobwebs."

"I hope you're feeling alright."

"I am. Just have a lot on my mind, nothing I can't handle. If I don't see you later, have a nice weekend."

Louis has been my doorman since I moved into the building about twelve years ago. Though he must be around seventy, you would never know it with his smooth, unlined face. Any time I've been sick or have gotten myself in trouble, Louis checks in on me to make sure I'm still breathing. I've already told him he can never retire. He just laughs.

I opened my apartment door and set my keys down on the antique table I have in the foyer. It was originally in the apartment I grew up in. My mother loved antiques but we couldn't afford them. On Saturdays, she would drag me to estate sales in the wealthy towns in Westchester and Long Island. We would drive up to their palatial homes and poke around, looking for bargains. My mother knew I wasn't exactly thrilled with being schlepped along, so she always promised to take me for lunch at a restaurant in a nearby town. Though my taste is more modern, I couldn't part with some of the antiques that my mother collected on those Saturdays.

Before going for a run, I thought I'd do a quick search on Howie Stevenson and his wife, Claire. The report listed their current address in Scarsdale, New York; Howie was thirty-nine and Claire, thirty-five. Greg had already told me that the couple had no children. They own a colonial-style brick house worth about three million dollars, and have two late-model cars, both high-end, a Volvo and a BMW. I wondered about the life insurance policies and what was going on in Howie's life that all his credit cards were maxed out.

I changed into my running clothes, grabbed a few gulps of water from the refrigerator, and jogged a couple of blocks to the park. I did my usual three-mile loop around and stopped to sit on one of the benches. I watched as a little boy was having a temper tantrum when his mother said it was time to leave. She won the battle, dragging him out of the park kicking and screaming.

On my way back, I picked up some Chinese food at a local takeout place that knows me all too well. After a quick shower, I slipped on a pair of boxer shorts and a T-shirt. Though I love to eat, my 5'8" body is lean, probably from running and working out with weights. I sat down on one of the stools in my kitchen, turned on the little TV that sits on the counter, and poured myself a glass of wine. I dug into my shrimp and broccoli using chopsticks, which I'm proficient with. The six o'clock news was on, but I was barely listening, as my mind was on Claire Stevenson's death. I thrive on murder cases. Not that I wish anyone dead, but it gets my juices flowing. Before going to bed, I called Howie and told him I would meet him at his house at 9:00 a.m.

***

In the morning, I took the Bronx River Parkway up to Howie's place. The Westchester section of the Bronx River Parkway was completed in 1925, making it the first modern, multi-lane, limited access parkway in North America. I exited in Scarsdale and followed the lady's instructions on my GPS to Drake Street. I turned onto a tree-lined street with beautiful colonial-style homes and parked in the Stevensons' driveway.

I sat for a moment wondering why I was there. Why was I drawn into working with someone who turned his back on our relationship? I put those thoughts aside and got out of the car.

When Howie opened the door, he was as I remembered him: tall, attractive, square chin, and a full head of very dark brown hair. I always got the sense from the way he spoke that Howie was a player, someone who was always looking for action.

"Maddie, I'm glad you're going to help. It's like I've been in a fog ever since Claire died. I still can't believe it."

I walked through a large foyer with gleaming dark stained hardwood floors into the living room where we sat. The room had two oversized white couches facing each other with a huge glass rectangle coffee table in between that sat on a gray and white handwoven rug. The starkness of the room was offset by large colorful paintings on the walls.

"What has Greg told you?" I said.

"Not much, though I'm probably a suspect. I swear to you I had nothing to do with Claire's death. You have to believe me."

Whether Howie was guilty or innocent didn't matter to my investigation. I ignored his comment.

"I was told that you were the one who found your wife on the bedroom floor. Let's start from there."

"I came home around 9:00 p.m. I called out to Claire when I walked in but there was no answer. As I walked into the bedroom and saw her lying on the floor next to our bed, I quickly ran over to her, leaned down to check for a pulse but there was none. Over and over I kept calling her name hoping I was wrong and she would answer me. At that point, I called 911."

"Greg mentioned that Claire had a heart condition?"

"She did. It wasn't serious but she needed to take medication every day. She was very careful about her meds. There was no way she would have accidentally killed herself."

"Do you know the exact cause of death?"

"I don't. I can't understand who would want to hurt Claire. None of this makes any sense."

"Were there problems in your marriage?"

"No! Did you hear that from her friend Sarah who has never liked me? I wouldn't put it past her to make up stuff."

"I haven't spoken to Sarah yet. Are you telling me that everything was fine?"

I was curious about what was going on between Sarah and Howie.

"Well, all marriages have their ups and downs. Ours was not perfect, but it was a good marriage and we loved each other."

If I had a dime for every time I heard someone say that.

"How is business?"

"The real estate market is doing well. A lot of movement. No complaints."

"So how come your credit cards are maxed out?"

"We lived high, probably too high. It wasn't a problem." Howie seemed to have an answer for everything.

"Is there a reason you took out a large life insurance policy on your wife?"

"We had life insurance policies on each of us. We were just being prudent."

"I have to ask you this Howie, are you having an affair?"

He had a surprised look on his face, as though he wasn't expecting the question.

"No, of course not."

"Howie, I want to trust you, but some things don't seem to add up, and I'm trying to understand what's going on. Somebody most likely wanted your wife dead. Your credit cards were maxed out and you recently took out a life insurance policy on your wife. And you want me to take your word for it that everything was okay?"

"I know you're having a hard time believing me, but it's true."

"Look, Howie, I'm the good guy here. I'm trying to help you. Give me something to work with. The police are going to question everyone in your life. If they haven't found anything yet, they will."

"Are you trying to scare me, because if you are, you're doing a good job."

"I'm just being honest. You have to know what you're up against. Right now, they don't have enough to arrest you. Let's try and get ahead of this. What can you tell me about Claire?"

"I think she may have been having an affair," he said in a quiet tone.

So much for the happy marriage.

"I once saw her holding a burner phone. I'm pretty sure she didn't realize that I noticed it. One day when she was in the shower, I looked for the phone but I couldn't find it."

"Did you ask her about the phone?"

"I didn't. I can't tell you why. Maybe I didn't want to know."

"Anything else?"

"Claire seemed anxious lately. I asked her if anything was wrong but she just made light of it."

"Did Claire work?"

"Yes. She managed a women's clothing shop in Scarsdale."

"Could her stress have been related to her job?"

"I doubt it. She enjoyed working at the shop."

"Is there any direction I should be looking?"

"Not that I can think of."

"Can you think of anyone who would want to harm your wife?"

"Not that I'm aware of. I'm sorry I'm not being more helpful."

"And what about you? Anyone you can think of that would want to harm you?"

I thought I saw a strange look on his face for one quick moment.

"No, of course not."

He was hiding something.

"Greg mentioned that your partner was your alibi."

"Yes, Gavin Stone."

"I'd like his number." I gave Howie a pad and pen. "Write down everyone I should contact, friends, relatives, and anyone else you can think of, including where Claire worked."

I sat there waiting for him to finish. We shook hands goodbye, and I told him I'd be in touch. Did I think Howie was telling me everything, no I did not. Now it was up to me to find out what he was hiding.

I still had some doubts about working with Greg, though I was glad I took the case. When Greg and I were partners, I can't deny that I had feelings for him, but that was a long time ago. I suspect being partners and spending so much time together might have had something to do with how I felt back then. At least that's what I told myself.

CHAPTER 3

I called Greg when I got into the office and gave him my take on my conversation with Howie.

"I have a feeling Howie wasn't being completely honest with me. There was something about his demeanor that I couldn't quite figure out. Time will tell. Listen, I'm going to start interviewing people who knew Howie and Claire. Also, maybe someone in their neighborhood, besides the woman across the street, saw something."

"Some good news," Greg said. "Though I'm not entitled to the police reports since Howie hasn't been arrested, I know someone in the police department who was able to get me copies. I think we should look through the reports before you start interviewing anyone."

"I can be at your office in about an hour."

"I'm in the middle of looking for space. For now, everything is at my apartment."

"How about if I take the copies and bring them back to my office?"

"I don't think that's a good idea since I had to obtain these reports in an unofficial manner, and I don't think they should leave my possession. Besides, we should go through the files together."

Great, I thought to myself. I wasn't too happy that I had to work at Greg's apartment. Was I afraid something was going to happen or was I afraid I wanted something to happen?

Greg lived on the fringes of Greenwich Village in Manhattan. I thought taking the subway would be faster than driving. It turned out I was wrong. I was sitting on the train but it wasn't moving. When the conductor finally spoke, I couldn't understand a word he was saying. I hate being in enclosed spaces. It makes me extremely anxious and I start to sweat. Though I blocked out most of the night of my parents' car accident, the terrifying feelings of being trapped, not knowing if someone was coming to rescue me, continue to haunt me. Whenever I'm in a small space, like an elevator or a subway train, and have no control of the situation, I start to panic.

I was trying to keep my anxiety level to a minimum by closing my eyes and concentrating on my breathing. I was staring at an old ad on the train for the 2017 Super Bowl. Thankfully, ten minutes later, we started to move. I breathed a sigh of relief when the doors to my train stop opened.

I rang the bell to Greg's apartment and a few seconds later, he buzzed me in. It was a three-story walk-up. Greg was on the second floor. He was waiting by his apartment door.

"Can I get you something to drink?" he said as I walked in.

"Coffee, if you're having."

"Black, no sugar, if I recall correctly." Was he trying to impress me that he remembered?

The police files were sitting on the kitchen table.

"Have you gone through any of these reports yet?" I said, as Greg poured our coffee into mugs.

"Not all of them. I thought we would start with the crime scene photos."

Greg placed the mug next to me before he sat down.

"I want to show you a photo of Claire before you look at the crime scene."

I took the photo from Greg and stared at it. Claire was beautiful, with straight jet-black hair down to her shoulders, large dark brown eyes with long eyelashes, and lips that any woman would die to have.

"She's a real knockout," I said. "Do you think she was having an affair?"

"I don't know."

"According to the police report, how did the person get into the house?"

"It looks like there was no forced entry, so most likely she knew her killer. I doubt if she would have let a stranger in."

"Who's in charge of the case?"

"Detective John Vaughn." I vaguely remembered his name from my days on the police force.

I placed the crime scene photos on the table. Claire was lying on the floor next to her bed.

"There was no forensic evidence found," Greg said, as I was studying the photos. "According to what my source said, she died of arsenic poisoning."

"I wonder if her heart condition contributed to her death."

"I guess it's possible."

"Does Howie know?"

"I called him before you got here. He couldn't believe it."

"You know Howie fairly well. Do you think he would kill his wife?"

"They may have had their share of problems, but I can't imagine he would harm Claire."

"Doesn't her hair look wet?" I asked, studying the photo of Claire lying on the floor. I wondered if she had just showered. Could she have been getting ready to meet someone or was that person already in the house? She was wearing a black lace bra and matching bikini underwear.

As Greg leaned in closer to get a look at Claire's photo, his body pressed against mine. I moved, but not as fast as I could have.

"It does look wet," Greg said. "According to their findings, Claire wasn't raped and there was no semen found inside her."

"Maybe he was wearing a condom."

I was reading through the interview with the neighbor across the street from the Stevensons. Her name was Janice Levy. According to Mrs. Levy's statement, she had been living across from the Stevensons for seven years. Her husband died a few years ago. Mrs. Levy witnessed a heated argument between Howie and Claire two days before she was killed. She couldn't hear what was said, but Claire pushed her husband right before she got into her car and drove away.

According to the report, it was after 11:00 p.m. when they were finished with the crime scene. Officer Crane went back the following day and spoke to some of the neighbors, but no one heard or saw anything out of the ordinary on the day or evening of the crime. The couple who lived next door to the Stevensons were friendly with them and socialized on several occasions. As far as they knew, everything was fine with the couple.

"What about the cell phone records? Was there anything that stood out?"

"Not according to the police. If she was having an affair, maybe she used a burner phone."

"Howie thought that Claire may have had a burner phone."

"I'm getting hungry, Greg said. "Why don't we get sandwiches. There's a great kosher delicatessen a few blocks from here. I remember you like a good corned beef sandwich."

I was getting hungry. I couldn't see the harm in having lunch, though I wasn't going to give Greg the satisfaction of acknowledging that he remembered what I liked.

"I'll go to the deli and bring sandwiches back, and you can continue looking through the reports," Greg said.

When he left, I got up and stretched. I wandered around the apartment but I didn't see any photos or any personal items lying around. The place looked basically the same since the last time I was here, more than six years ago. He still had the same brown leather furniture and chrome chairs in the living room. We had just begun our affair. I remember that day vividly. It was the first time we were going to have sex. I recalled being nervous. I had never been with someone like Greg, so self-assured and in control. Was I afraid I was still attracted to him? Could I be playing with fire like Annie said?

CHAPTER 4

I went back into Greg's kitchen, wondering if he was still harboring feelings for me when I heard him come in.

"I got french fries and those sour pickles you like. What's wrong?" he said when he looked at me.

"Nothing, it's just the case," I quickly babbled.

"How about a glass of wine?" he said, while he handed me a plate with my sandwich, fries, and a couple of pickles.

"I'll pass." Greg took out a bottle of beer for himself. "I was looking for the toxicology report. Do you know where it is?"

"Here you go."

Reading through it, there was no alcohol in Claire's system, or if there was, it was an insignificant amount. The cause of death was acute arsenic poisoning.

I went through the rest of the reports, not learning anything more that could assist me with my investigation. I made notes of what I needed to follow up with. When I looked at the time, it was after five o'clock.

"I have to get going. Please tell Howie I'll meet him at his house tomorrow morning before he goes to work so he can let me in. I'll keep you posted on what I find out."

"Maddie, what's the rush. I thought we could get some dinner later."

"I'm sorry, I have to meet a friend." Why did I have to lie? Why couldn't I just tell him the truth? I said to myself as I ran down the stairs and out of the building.

I called Annie before I got on the subway. "You got a moment?"

"Sure. Shoot."

"I'm on my way back from Greg's place."

"What were you doing there?"

"Apparently, he doesn't have an office yet and he was able to get copies of the police reports from a source inside the department. Since the reports were gotten through improper channels, he wanted them to remain in his possession, or that was his excuse. At some point, he went to get us lunch. I started remembering the times we were together. Now I'm doubting myself. Is it possible I still have feelings for Greg?"

"Even if you do, you don't have to act on them. Remember, you're in control."

"I hope Jesse is going to be as perceptive as you are."

"Jesse isn't going anywhere. An old affair isn't going to scare him away even if you're working with the guy. By the way, I need your help on a case. One of my clients has no idea where the marital assets are. We need to locate them," Annie said.

"No problem. I'll get on it first thing tomorrow morning. Send me the information."

"Love you."

"Right back at you."

I was mulling over what Annie said. I wanted to believe she was right, and that I was in control, but what if she was wrong?

***

I was having trouble sleeping. By 6:00 a.m. I was up and showered. I was meeting Howie Stevenson at his house before he left for work. First, I quickly sent an email to my source that locates bank accounts. People seem to have memory lapses when it comes to divulging all their assets when completing their net worth statement. I gave him the information he needed and hit the send button.

What appeared to be a very quiet neighborhood now had the full attention of this sleepy town. A murder in Scarsdale is rare. There was a famous case in Scarsdale where a woman by the name of Carolyn Warmus killed her lover's wife in 1989. She was convicted in 1991 and was paroled in 2019.

"Please lock up after you finish," Howie said as he was leaving for work.

I did a cursory walk through the house before I started an in-depth search. As I was going room by room, I marveled at the décor. The master bedroom, which was on the second floor, was done in shades of gray and white. It had clean lines. I started opening drawers when I heard a voice from below.

"Hello, anyone here?"

I went downstairs and saw a woman standing in the hallway.

"The door was unlocked," the woman said.

"Who are you?" I asked.

"I'm Janice Levy. I live across the street. Sorry to barge in. I saw someone going into the house, and they didn't look like they were with the police."

I remembered her name from the police reports.

"You're the lady who saw the Stevensons arguing."

Janice Levy was probably in her late fifties, maybe early sixties. Hard to tell nowadays. She was slightly taller than me and on the hefty side. She came across as the nosy next-door neighbor.

"Why yes. How did you know?"

"My name's Maddie Landon. I'm a private investigator. It's nice to know someone's watching the house." I hope she didn't catch the sarcasm, though having a neighbor like Janice Levy could be very helpful to my investigation.

"It's so horrible what happened to Claire. Do you think it was the husband?"

I didn't answer her. "Did you know her well?" I said.

"No, not well, only to say hi to."

"How long have you lived here?"

"About seven years. Unfortunately, my dear husband died two years ago."

"I'm very sorry. Can you tell me about the argument you witnessed?"

"I was just coming back from the market. As I was getting out of the car, I heard shouting."

"Could you hear what they were saying?"

"To tell you the truth, I can't be sure, but I thought I heard Mr. Stevenson call Claire a liar. That's when she pushed him and got into her car." I didn't recall from the police report that Howie called Claire a liar. Did Janice Levy just make that up?

"Is that the only time you saw or heard them arguing?"

"Well, unless they were arguing outside, I wouldn't be able to hear them."

"I heard Mrs. Stevenson worked. Do you know what she did?" I was curious how much this woman knew about Claire.

"She worked at a very classy women's boutique in Scarsdale. I've never been there myself, but I heard it's very expensive."

"Is there anything else you can tell me about the Stevensons?"

"Well, I hate to gossip, especially about someone who's dead."

"And what would that gossip be?" I was getting a little annoyed at Mrs. Levy. I didn't know if she was making stuff up or just wanted the attention.

"Like I said, it was just a rumor that Claire was having an affair."

"And do you know who she was having the affair with?"

"I'm sorry, I don't."

"Do you know where you heard the rumor from?"

"As I said it was just gossip. I don't remember where I heard it."

Gossip you obviously wanted me to know, I thought to myself.

"Did you ever see Mrs. Stevenson with someone other than her husband?"

"*Uhh*, no, not personally, but that doesn't mean it's not true."

"Thank you for all your help. If you think of anything else, here's my card."

She looked at it for a moment. I watched her leave and I locked the front door behind her. It seems as if Mrs. Levy might have too much time on her hands, but could there be any truth to the rumors? I went back upstairs to continue with my search.

I found Howie's office upstairs and started going through desk drawers. Nothing caught my attention. I knew his computer had been searched and wondered if they had gone through his office computer.

I went into the garage and started poking around. It was fairly neat, just like the house. All the tools were hanging up against a wall. There was a metal toolbox sitting on a wooden shelf. I reached for it and took it down. I opened it up but there was nothing in it but nails, a screwdriver, and other small tools. While putting it back, I knocked something on the floor. When I went to retrieve it, I saw a covered wall outlet. Standing up, I noticed cords from power tools that I followed to an outlet. I ducked back under and sat on the floor thinking it was odd that this outlet was covered up. Having no luck taking off the cover, I grabbed the screwdriver and pried the cover off. There was a fairly large hole. I maneuvered myself so I could take a look inside. It was too dark to see anything. I wriggled my hand through, my fingers reaching around until I felt something. I managed to get a grip on whatever was in there and pulled my hand out. Was I staring at Claire's burner phone?

I turned it on but there was nothing; the phone was dead. The SIM card gone. Could this be the phone Claire used when she spoke to her lover?

CHAPTER 5

When I got back to the office, I put on a pot of coffee. I was still thinking about my conversation with Howie when I picked up my phone and called Jesse.

"How's my handsome guy?"

"Are you buttering me up for something?"

"I'm hurt," I said playfully. "You got a minute?"

"Go!" Jesse said.

I relayed the conversation I had with Howie Stevenson.

"He's definitely hiding something," I said.

"Even innocent people have reasons why they don't always tell the truth."

"You may be right. By the way, I got tickets for the four of us for the first weekend the Mets are playing at home. Annie and Doug are going to be ecstatic."

"You know I'm a Boston Red Sox fan." I could picture the grin on his face.

"I won't hold that against you. But since they're in different leagues, maybe you can root for my team while we're at the game."

"What's in it for me?"

"I guess we can work something out," I said.

"I'll see you Friday night."

"Be safe."

"Always."

Looking through my emails, I had a job from an attorney who needed to locate a dirtbag who was trying to get away without paying his alimony and child support. In my line of work, I see too many cases of men trying to get out of paying their fair share. Most of these guys already have someone else they're looking to start a new life with. They've already moved on and aren't interested in splitting their salary between the ex-wife and the soon-to-be new wife. Searching through my databases and after many calls, I was finally able to locate the creep. I was delighted to email the attorney my report and invoice. If it was me, I'd put the ex-husband's sorry ass in jail, but unfortunately, these women most likely need the money.

***

In the morning, I got up early, showered, dressed, and went straight to my office. As I was opening my office door, my phone buzzed.

"Hi there," I answered, seeing it was Jesse calling.

"Anything wrong?" I said, since I had just spoken to him last night.

"Hey, babe, bad news. We have a trial that is scheduled for next week and all hands are on deck. So, unfortunately, I have to work this weekend."

"I'm so disappointed since I was looking forward to jumping your bones."

"You're killing me. I promise I'll make it up to you. Maybe I'll stay an extra day next weekend."

"Sounds good. Listen, there's something I want to talk to you about but not on the phone. Maybe I could drive up late Friday and leave early Saturday morning."

"Are you ditching me?"

"You wish. You're not getting rid of me that easily."

"I'll see you on Friday."

"Love you."

"Love you. Stay out of trouble."

I wasn't looking forward to telling Jesse about my affair with Greg, but I knew it was the right thing to do. I was trusting this wasn't going to bite me in the ass.

CHAPTER 6

After hanging up with Jesse, I called Claire's friend, hoping to connect with her this afternoon.

A woman's voice answered.

"Is this Sarah James?"

"Who is this?"

"My name's Maddie Landon. I'm a private investigator hired to look into Claire Stevenson's death. Would you have some time to meet with me today? I'd like to ask you a few questions."

"Whose side are you on?" she said in an abrupt manner.

"I'm not on anyone's side. I'm just trying to find out what happened to Claire. Wouldn't you want her killer found and punished?" I could envision her thinking it over.

"I live in Bronxville. Can you come by at three o'clock?"

"Yes." Before hanging up, Mrs. James gave me her address.

Since I had some time to kill before going up to Bronxville, I decided to look up acute arsenic poisoning. Apparently, less than 1/8 teaspoon can be fatal to a healthy adult. Lethal doses resulting in death typically occur within one to four days of injection. As I had mentioned to Greg, her mild heart condition could have quickened her death.

I wondered if Howie had noticed anything wrong with his wife that day. According to what I was reading,

Claire would have had abdominal pain, possibly vomiting and diarrhea. If she died within twenty-four hours of being poisoned, there had to have been some symptoms. I needed to call Howie and ask him if Claire was complaining about feeling ill. I left a message in Howie's voice mail asking him to call me as soon as possible.

Before going to speak with Sarah James, I wanted to see what information was available on her through my databases. The report I pulled up listed her age as thirty-four and her husband Jonathan as forty-four. They lived in a four-million-dollar house in Bronxville, New York. I must be doing something wrong. How do people acquire so much money?

It listed that Mr. James was a financial advisor. Maybe I could use his expertise, though I think you need money in order to invest. There didn't appear to be anything unusual in the report. My phone rang.

"What's up, Greg?" I said, when I saw the number.

"Did you find anything at the house?"

"I found a burner cell in Howie's garage completely by accident, but I can see how the cops missed it. It's no longer working."

"There's something else I just found out from someone in the coroner's office. Claire was two months pregnant when she died."

"Holy shit! Do you know if it's Howie's baby?"

"It's too early to know. The police took a mouth swab from Howie when they originally questioned him. The lead detective requested the coroner to extract a DNA sample from the fetus."

"I think you need to tell him about the baby right away," I said.

"I'm going to call him now. Also, I know someone who might be able to get information off the phone. Could you bring it by my place?" Greg asked.

"I can drop it off tomorrow morning at some point. I'm going to meet with Claire's friend who lives in Bronxville in a little while. Maybe Claire confided in her."

As soon as I clicked off, my phone rang again.

"Howie, thanks for getting back to me. I have a question. The morning of Claire's death, did she complain that she wasn't feeling well?"

"Let me think. I believe she may have mentioned she was having some stomach cramps."

"Was there anything else?"

"Not that I can recall. Why?"

"If she had been poisoned the day before, she may have been starting to show symptoms. Do you remember if anyone had been in your house around that time or anyone she was with that day or the day before?"

"I'm sorry, I wish I did."

"One other question. The evening prior to the day she died, did Claire go out?"

"Again, I just don't remember."

"Okay, thanks. If you do remember anything, please call me."

I was feeling antsy. I decided to head up to Scarsdale to the boutique where Claire worked before my appointment with Sarah James.

"Can I help you?" the woman said when I walked into a very upscale women's shop in the middle of Scarsdale Village.

"I hope so. My name's Maddie, and I'm a private investigator looking into Claire Stevenson's death."

The young woman looked nervous. She probably never talked to a PI before. It could be intimidating.

"I feel so bad for Claire. I loved working with her."

"What's your name?"

"Dana."

"What's your last name, Dana?"

"I'm so sorry," she said, turning red. "It's Thomas."

I pegged Dana Thomas for no more than thirty, if that. She had blonde soft curls to her shoulders, framing her heart shaped face. Though you wouldn't say she was pretty in the conventional sense, she was very attractive.

"I see you're here by yourself. Who's the owner?"

"Mrs. Crawford, but she rarely comes in. Mostly, it was just me and Claire. She managed the store for Mrs. Crawford."

"How well did you know Mrs. Stevenson?"

"Not very. I mean, she didn't share anything personal with me, if that's what you're getting at."

"Did she seem distracted or anxious in the weeks before she died?"

"I don't think so. You should talk with Mrs. Crawford."

"Did you know that Mrs. Stevenson had a heart condition?"

"Yes. It wasn't a secret. I believe she took medication every day."

"Did you ever meet Mrs. Stevenson's husband?"

She hesitated. "A few times when he came to pick up Claire."

"Well, thank you for your time."

I left with the telephone number of the store owner, Linda Crawford. I may have been mistaken but I thought Dana Thomas seemed a little flustered when I mentioned Claire's husband.

CHAPTER 7

High bushes made it impossible to see Sarah James's house from the street. I drove into a long circular driveway leading up to a huge center hall colonial. A woman with blonde hair pulled back in a ponytail, wearing jeans and a button-down blue denim shirt, opened the door.

"Ms. Landon, please come in. I'm Sarah."

"Your house is beautiful."

"We completely renovated before moving in. We left the structure of the house since we wanted to keep it in the tradition of the other colonial homes on the street, but we wanted to modernize the inside." She led me into a sitting room that had natural light from the outside. Hanging plants hung down from the ceiling. "Can I offer you anything to drink?"

"If you're having."

"I just made a fresh pot of coffee. Is that okay?"

"I rarely turn down coffee."

Sarah brought in two mugs of coffee, and she sat down opposite me on a white wicker chair with a flowered print cushion.

"I still can't believe Claire is gone."

"We learned that Claire was poisoned. Do you know if she had any enemies?"

"Poisoned! Oh my god! Poor Claire. I don't know anybody who would want to kill her."

"How do you know her?"

"We met in foster care. We were both taken in by the same foster family. They were a nice couple but there were other kids under their watch, and basically they didn't have much time for us. Most of the kids only stayed for a few months but we stayed for years. We had each other. Claire and I were very close."

It was a total surprise to me that Claire grew up in foster care. No one had told me.

"Do you know if Howie and Claire were having marital problems?"

"She thought Howie was gambling again and may have owed people a lot of money."

I noticed Sarah had a habit of twirling her finger around the loose strands of hair that escaped the ponytail. I wondered if that was a habit from childhood.

"Can you be more specific?"

"She came over one day and I could tell she was frightened. She said that Howie had received a few phone calls late at night. When she asked him who had called, he shrugged it off and said it was nothing, but clearly, he was upset."

"Why do you think those calls were related to gambling?"

"Claire knew Howie had a gambling problem in the past but he told her he had stopped. She became suspicious and thought he had started again. One day she had gone to the ATM to withdraw some money but the account was overdrawn. Howie had some sort of excuse. He told her not to worry, that he had forgotten to deposit a commission check from the sale of a house."

"Did she believe him?"

"I think she wanted to."

"Was there anything else she told you?"

"Nothing specific. I just got the feeling things were not going well between them."

"Did you know Claire was two months pregnant when she died?"

Her mouth flew open. "She never said anything to me. Does Howie know?"

"I'm not sure. Do you know if Claire was having an affair?"

"Not that I'm aware of. I can't believe she didn't tell me she was pregnant."

"Are you sure she didn't say anything to you, maybe something you didn't think was important at the time?"

"Nothing I can recall. Is it Howie's?"

"We don't know yet. What do you know about Howie's partner, Gavin Stone?"

"I've met him once or twice. Seemed like a nice guy, but other than that, I can't say I know him at all."

"Would you happen to know any of Claire's friends that I could talk with?"

"A woman named Paula Frankel. They've known each other since college."

I knew the name since it was on Howie's list of people to contact.

"I only know Paula through Claire. We've never met," she said. I thought I picked up a bit of jealousy in her voice.

"Does Howie deny that he had anything to do with Claire's death?" she asked.

"He does."

"Do you believe him?" Sarah said.

"I would like to, but I believe in facts. So far, there's no evidence that he had anything to do with Claire's death. I'm not sure I've answered your question but that's the best I can say."

"I understand."

"By the way, have the police spoken to you yet?"

"No. Will they?"

"I'm assuming so. Well, thank you for your time, and if you think of anything else, please call me."

"I would appreciate it if you would keep me informed."

Driving back to the city, I rehashed the conversation I had with Sarah James. It took me by surprise when Sarah told me that Claire had been in foster care. If I didn't have my aunt after my parents died, I could have wound up in foster care, too. The thought made me shiver. Though Sarah and Claire were very close, it seemed she was as much in the dark about Claire as I was. Could there be any truth to the gambling problem Sarah mentioned? If Howie was in heavy debt to a loan shark, was it possible Claire was collateral damage?

CHAPTER 8

After dinner, instead of watching television, I thought I would start looking into my biological parents. Since the case started, I had pushed those thoughts aside.

My parents told me from early on that I was adopted. I was never curious enough to ask any questions even though they encouraged it. Growing up, it didn't occur to me there was a reason I shied away from getting close to people. And because it wasn't an issue for me until Jesse, it never dawned on me it was a problem. There were very few people that I have allowed into my inner sanctum.

I realized now, through therapy, that adopted children, even if they had loving parents growing up, could have abandonment issues. They might be afraid to get close to people for fear they'll leave.

I opened the box and sifted through the photos. Though I've looked through them a million times, I never get tired of seeing pictures of me with my parents. Both my parents were teachers. My father, no matter how tired he was, always had time for me. We lived in a garden apartment in Queens, so we had access to a backyard. You could say I was a tomboy. Even as a little kid, I never liked playing with dolls. I'd rather build something or play with the boys in my neighborhood.

My father taught me how to throw a ball. He took me to a ton of Mets games where I learned all the players' names, their batting averages, and kept a record of what each player did when they got up to bat. At night, I would dream of being the first female baseball player.

I took out the envelope that contained my birth certificate. My parents were not privy to my original birth certificate. When I decided to look for my birth parents a few weeks ago, I opened up the envelope. Though I knew it contained my birth certificate, I was totally surprised when I saw the letter that was written to me when I was only one year old. I opened it up and read it again.

Dearest Maddie,

Thank you for the joy you have brought into our lives. The day we brought you home was the best day imaginable. You were only two weeks old, yet when we looked into your big, beautiful green eyes, we knew you were meant to be with us.

Though we will always be your parents, we hope one day you will search for your birth parents. Your mother had you at such a young age she couldn't give you what you needed and thought she was doing what was best for you. We were lucky that she had chosen us.

Our wish for you is that you will grow up and have a wonderful life filled with joy and surrounded by people who love you.

Your loving parents,
Mom and Dad

The tears poured out of me as I thought about my parents and how much I missed them.

About a half-hour later, I opened up my laptop and conducted a search for the attorney who handled my adoption. All I had was a name. It's been thirty-seven years. For all I knew, he could be dead.

According to my Google search, Thomas Logan, Adoption Attorney, was still practicing. I wrote down his telephone number and address in Queens.

***

In the morning, I called and spoke to Mr. Logan's receptionist. She gave me the next available appointment, which was for the following Monday at 10:00 a.m.

Now that I made the appointment, I was freaking out a little. I was still uncertain whether I wanted to go down this path. What if my birth mother was dead? What if she was a junkie? What if she had a family and I had brothers and sisters? I had to stop obsessing or I would go crazy.

CHAPTER 9

Since I was going to have most of my weekend free after seeing Jesse, I thought I would take advantage of my time and speak with Howie's partner. I was hoping he could shed some light on Howie's life. I heard my phone ring as I was about to indulge in my second cup of coffee.

"Maddie, it's Greg," he said, when I answered the phone. "I spoke with Howie. He said he had no idea Claire was pregnant. I told him the police might pull him in for questioning again but not to say anything without me."

"I met with Claire's friend Sarah James. She told me that Claire was worried that Howie had started gambling again. It could be Howie racked up a sizable debt. If it was through a loan shark, it's possible they killed Claire to teach Howie a lesson. It may be a long shot, but I'll see what I can find out."

I packed an overnight bag and drove up to Jesse's place in Chester, Connecticut. It's about a two-hour drive from the city. Chester is a small rural town that runs along the Connecticut River. Though the town is small, it has some art galleries, antique shops, boutiques, and a handful of restaurants. While I was driving, I was thinking of what I was going to tell Jesse.

I saw his car in the driveway and parked right behind him. Jesse lives in a small stone house that he recently renovated. The first floor has a living room with a fireplace, a kitchen, and powder room. There's a staircase leading up to the loft area that has a huge bedroom, office area, and bathroom. The front door was unlocked.

"Jesse," I called out. "I'm here."

As he came toward me, I walked into his arms and hugged him tightly. Jesse is a good five inches taller than me, with broad shoulders and a hard body. His eyes are dark chocolate brown. Though his nose is slightly off-centered from a childhood fight, it only makes him more handsome.

"Something smells delicious," I said.

"It's a secret family recipe. It's a fish stew my mother taught me how to make."

"I wish I could have met her. From what you've told me about her, she seemed like a great mom."

"She was. Do you want to tell me what's going on?"

"Do you mind if we talk over dinner? Right now, I want to take you up to the bedroom and have my way with you."

"That's hard to say no to."

I was watching Jesse as he was dishing out the fish stew. I was sipping on a glass of wine, thinking it would ease the tension I was feeling.

"Wow, this stew is wonderful," I said, as a clam slid down my throat.

"So, what's on your mind?"

"I told you that Greg and I were partners when I was on the police force. Actually, I was a rookie when we hooked up and he was the senior partner. A year after we became partners, Greg told me he was having marital problems and had split up with his wife." I took a gulp of my wine before I continued. "During that time, Greg and I had an affair." I was trying not to look at Jesse, since I was afraid to see his reaction.

"Go on."

"It turned out his wife was pregnant and they got back together. Our affair ended. It wasn't a relationship, it was just sex. I want you to know you can trust me. I love you and I would never do anything to jeopardize our relationship."

"What would have happened if his wife didn't get pregnant?"

"I can't answer that since I don't know."

"Did you have feelings for him?"

"He was my partner. He knew a lot about me, but the feelings I have for you are different from the feelings I had for Greg."

"I'm not sure what that means."

"I've never felt the way I feel about you with anyone else."

"Why did you agree to help him?"

"I didn't see any reason not to."

"I'm not sure that's a good enough answer."

"I don't have any other. I can handle myself. Nothing is going to happen between us. It was more than five years ago."

"I still think it's a bad idea."

"So you don't trust me?"

"That's not what I'm saying."

"Then what are you saying?"

"I just think when two people were involved and work together again, things can happen that we don't intend to."

"Are you talking from experience?"

"Let's just say I've been in similar situations, and it doesn't always work out how you wanted it to."

"I can only tell you again that I wouldn't do anything to jeopardize our relationship. I don't want this thing with Greg to change our relationship."

"I trust you. That's all I have to say on the subject at the moment."

Neither one of us brought it up again that night.

CHAPTER 10

Jesse walked me to my car early Saturday morning. We held each other for a few moments and then I drove away. I felt uneasy that Jesse wasn't okay that I was working with Greg, but there wasn't anything I could do about it. Hopefully, he would come around.

As soon as I got into my office, I contacted Howie's real estate firm. I figured realtors are busy showing houses on weekends to people who work during the week. The receptionist at his office told me Gavin Stone had an appointment to show a house at noon at an address in Rockland County. I grabbed a water bottle and rushed out. I made a quick stop at Greg's place and gave him the burner phone. Having to rush up to meet Gavin Stone was a good excuse for why I couldn't take Greg up on his invitation to stay a while.

When I arrived at the house in Rockland County, I waited in my car until I saw a couple leaving. I walked to the front door and knocked. A very attractive man about 6′2″ tall, medium built, dressed in a blue dress shirt, a gray cashmere sweater, light beige slacks, and wearing very polished black loafers opened the door.

"Mr. Stone, my name is Maddie Landon. I'm investigating the death of Claire Stevenson. I was wondering if we could talk somewhere?"

"Are you with the police?"

"No, I was hired by Mr. Stevenson's attorney."

"In that case, I'll be glad to talk with you. Anything to help Howie. There's a place a few blocks from here where we can get coffee and something to eat. I just have to lock up and we can go."

While we were walking, Mr. Stone told me he met Howie at an open house several years ago and they hit it off right away. I can see how people would gravitate to Gavin Stone since he had an easy way about him. I imagine he's a great salesman.

The place had a few tables. We ordered at the counter and one of the workers brought our food over. We both ordered eggs, toast, and coffee.

"So how long have you been partners with Howie?"

"It's going on five years. It's turned out really well. Though we have different selling styles, we're both really good salesmen."

"Did you know Claire?"

"Of course. The three of us got together periodically. Sometimes I brought a date."

"Did you know she had a heart problem?"

"Yes. Why do you ask?"

"No reason. How did they get along?" I said, as I took a bite out of my toast.

"They seemed happy as far as I could tell. If you're even thinking Howie had anything to do with Claire's death, you're wrong."

"Why is that."

"He was crazy about her."

"So, no problems that you knew about?"

"Absolutely not."

"When was the last time you saw Claire?"

"Let me think a second," he said as he rubbed his chin. "I can't be sure, but it may have been a month before she died."

"How did that come about?"

"I believe she stopped by the office for a few minutes to speak with Howie."

"Did you talk to her?"

"Not really, just to say hello and goodbye."

"Look, I know you don't want to say anything bad about your partner or his wife, but you're not doing him any favors. The more I know about them, the more I can help Howie. If you have anything to say, now's the time."

Gavin Stone tilted his head slightly away from me. I could tell he wanted to say something. I waited him out.

"Howie was having some financial problems."

"Why would you say that?"

"He wanted to borrow money. Of course, I asked him what he needed it for. He told me he had gotten into some trouble and owed people money."

"Did he tell you who these people were?"

"No. Howie was nervous, so I got the feeling it was quite a bit. Do you think he owed the money to loan sharks?"

"I don't know, but I plan to find out," I said.

"Could they have killed Claire?"

"I can't speculate, but at this point, I have no idea if he was even involved with loan sharks. Do you know if his wife was having an affair?"

"If she was, I doubted Howie would have shared that with me."

"Why do you say that?"

"I just think it's very personal and maybe he wouldn't want me to know if she was cheating on him."

I thought I noticed a slight tic in Gavin's right eye. I wondered if he knew something but didn't want to say.

"Did you know that his wife was pregnant?"

"No," he said, in a surprised voice. "Howie never said anything to me. I wonder if he knew about the baby?"

Gavin Stone was moving his eggs around with his fork. Was there something bothering him?

"Are you sure he never mentioned that his wife was having an affair?"

"I think I would remember if that was the case."

"You were Howie's alibi. Can you tell me exactly where both of you were that day?"

"Like I told the police, Howie and I were out showing houses and then we met afterward for a drink."

"What time did you go for a drink?"

"It was around 7:00 p.m."

"Do you usually meet for a drink after work?"

"We were celebrating the sale of a five-million-dollar house. It was a large commission."

"What time did you leave the bar?"

"I'd say around 8:30 p.m., maybe a little later."

"Do you remember how many drinks Howie had?"

"I think maybe two, but I can't be positive."

"Do you know if the police checked the bar you went to?"

"I have no idea."

"If they had checked, would they have found out you were there?"

"I'm not sure what you're getting at, but the bar was very busy that night and we paid for our drinks in cash. I don't know if anyone would remember us." How convenient, I thought to myself.

"By the way, what's the name of the bar?"

"It's called The Irish Bank in Hartsdale."

"How did Howie get home?"

"We had driven over to the bar separately, so Howie drove home by himself."

"Here's my card. If you think of anything else that might be relevant, please call me."

On the walk back to my car, we didn't talk much. I had my doubts that Gavin Stone was telling me everything he knew.

As I was driving back to the city, I wondered if Gavin Stone would lie for his friend. Was Howie really with his partner at the time his wife was murdered? These were all questions I needed answers to.

CHAPTER 11

I changed when I got home and went for a quick run. On the way back, I stopped at a coffee bar and picked up a cappuccino to go. I was going through the case in my mind when my phone rang. It was a number I didn't recognize.

"Hello."

"Ms. Landon, this is Janice Levy. I think I may have some information that could be very helpful to your case. I was wondering if you could stop by today?"

"Can't you tell me on the phone?"

"I'd rather tell you in person. It could be important."

Did she really have something to tell me or was she just a lonely lady who wanted attention? I couldn't take the chance that she might know something.

"I can stop by tomorrow."

"Oh, not today?" she said, sounding disappointed.

I had no intentions of going back up to Westchester today.

"I'm sorry I can't make it. Let me know what time tomorrow is convenient for you?"

"How about noon?"

"I'll see you then."

Since I was going up to Scarsdale tomorrow, I thought I would contact Claire's friend, Paula Frankel. I knew she lived up in the area.

I dialed the number Howie had given me.

"Hello."

"Is this Paula Frankel?"

"Who's asking?"

"My name's Maddie Landon. I'm a private investigator looking into the death of Claire Stevenson. Claire's friend Sarah James said you were very good friends with Claire."

"We are. I mean, we were. We've been friends since college. I can't believe she's dead. I keep waking up hoping it's just a dream."

"I have some questions I'd like to ask you. I'm going to be in Westchester tomorrow and I thought if you had time we could meet?"

"I'm busy until 11:30 a.m. but any time after that I'm free. Do you know where I live?"

"I have your address. I should be there sometime around 2:00 p.m. I'll see you then."

The rest of the day went quickly. I caught up on my Saturday house cleaning and wound up watching a thriller on Netflix in the evening. I hadn't heard from Jesse and was feeling a little anxious. Did he tell me everything was okay between us, but it really wasn't? Jesse always spoke his mind, so maybe I was reading too much into this.

***

Sunday morning I woke up to a drizzling rain. While I was having breakfast, I took out a notepad and wrote down what I knew so far about the case, which wasn't much. It was very early on in the investigation, but after speaking with Claire's friend Sarah, and Howie's partner, Gavin, I learned that Howie was in financial trouble. *I have to press Howie on the issue. There's also a possibility Claire was having an affair. Maybe I'll find out more today.*

Driving up to Scarsdale, the rain was coming down pretty heavy. I had my windshield wipers on full speed. As soon as I got out of my car, I could see Janice Levy peeking out from her living room window. Before I even had the chance to knock, the door opened.

"Please come in. I just put on a fresh pot of coffee and I made zucchini bread. It's an old family recipe. Do you need a towel to dry yourself off?"

"No, I'm okay, thank you."

I can see this was not going to be a quick visit. I followed Janice into the kitchen. Though it looked like it hadn't been remodeled lately, with edges of the brown linoleum floor covering coming up on the sides, the kitchen was spotless.

"Sit. I'll just be a moment."

I sat down at a yellow Formica table. It brought back memories of my parents' kitchen in Forest Hills. Our Formica table was gray. While sitting at the table doing my homework, my father cooked dinner. I was always trying to trick him into giving me the answers to my homework assignments, but somehow, it never worked. I think he found my devious behavior very amusing.

I waited patiently while Janice poured each of us a cup of coffee and placed a slice of zucchini bread on each of our plates.

"So you had something you wanted to tell me," I said, trying to move this along.

Seeing the annoyed look on Janice Levy's face, I knew she had no intention of being rushed.

"Yes, of course. I remembered it yesterday. I was watching Wheel of Fortune. It's one of my favorite shows."

It took everything in me not to scream at this woman. I had to bite my tongue.

"When the show starts, the three contestants introduce themselves."

Janice stopped to take a bite of her zucchini bread. My frustrations were mounting.

"Go on," I prodded.

"One of the contestants mentioned that she had met her husband-to-be at a bar in the area where they both lived. That's when it hit me. I was meeting a friend for dinner at a restaurant in Mt. Kisco and there was Mr. Stevenson sitting at the bar. At first, I thought he was with his wife but then I realized his wife had very dark, straight hair while this woman had blonde hair. Now that must mean something."

"Before we jump to any conclusions, how do you know he didn't just meet this woman at the bar?"

"I'm not stupid. I could tell by their body language. They definitely knew each other."

I wasn't going to argue the point with her.

"How long ago did you see Mr. Stevenson with this woman?"

"Well, now, let me think. It might have been a few weeks before Mrs. Stevenson was killed."

"Did you happen to see the woman's face?"

"When I went to the ladies' room, I tried to sneak a glance, but I couldn't get a good enough look at her."

"Why didn't you go up to Mr. Stevenson and say hello?"

"Well, that would be plain rude. And besides, if he was with someone other than his wife, that's really none of my business."

You've got to be kidding, I thought to myself. Instead, I tried to remain calm.

"So besides having blonde hair, that's all you know?"

"I may not have seen her face, but it probably means he was seeing someone else. This could be why he murdered his wife. Maybe he wanted to get rid of her in order to marry this woman."

"Did you mention any of this to the police?"

"No. I just remembered the incident before I called you."

"I would suggest you don't say anything to the police."

"Why?"

"For one thing, you have no idea why he was meeting this person. To accuse someone is a very serious matter. I wouldn't want you to be responsible for getting him in trouble when there could be a very simple explanation."

"I see your point. Well, now that you know, you can check into it."

"I certainly will, and I appreciate that you came to me with this information. This information could be very invaluable."

I wanted to make sure Janice Levy didn't say anything to the police. I was hoping if she thought I was thrilled that she had confided in me, it wouldn't go any further. I got the impression Mrs. Levy liked playing detective.

After another half-hour of hearing her life story, I was able to extricate myself from her house. I guess I should be grateful that Janice Levy is a busybody since she might have accidentally come upon information that could be very helpful to my investigation. If she was right and Howie was having an affair, maybe he did have a motive to kill his wife.

CHAPTER 12

I arrived at Paula Frankel's house a little after two. Mrs. Frankel lived in Armonk, slightly northwest of Scarsdale. The house looked more like a cottage. Sitting on the porch were two white wicker rocking chairs.

Paula Frankel greeted me with a warm handshake. Appearance-wise, Paula was the complete opposite of Claire. While Claire was beautiful, there was nothing about Paula that was attractive. She was on the short side and probably carried twenty extra pounds. Though the inside of the house was small, it was cozy. The furniture was old but comfortable looking. We sat down in the living room.

"I want to say how sorry I am about your friend. I know you were very close."

"Thank you. I miss her so much," Paula said, tears running down her face. "I just don't understand why anyone would want to hurt Claire. Do you have any idea who could have killed her?"

"At this moment, unfortunately, no. Do you know if she had any enemies?"

"Of course not. I still can't believe she's dead. I know people thought that she had a charmed life mainly because she was beautiful, but that could not be further from the truth. When Claire was seven years old, her parents died in a tragic plane crash. Claire was placed in foster care where she was taken in by a very nice foster family, but unfortunately, there were other children. Needless to say,

Claire had to fend for herself. Besides trust issues, Claire had trouble forming attachments. When I met Claire in college, she had only one friend, Sarah James, who she lived with in the foster home. Though millions of guys would have given anything to go out with her, Claire basically kept to herself.

"She met Howie by chance at a Starbucks of all places. They were both in line getting coffee. It took a lot of persistence on Howie's part, but Claire finally relented and went out on a date with him. She didn't know about Howie's gambling problem until a few years into the marriage. He swore to her that he had stopped gambling but that wasn't true. She loved him but it was destroying their marriage. She begged him to go for help, but he insisted he had it under control."

"Was Claire having an affair?"

I could see the hesitation on her face.

"I need to know. It could be very important."

"She was, but she wouldn't tell me with whom. That made me wonder if I knew the person."

"Did she tell you she was pregnant?"

"About a week before she died, she told me. She said she wasn't sure if it was Howie's baby."

"Did Howie know she was pregnant?"

"If he did, Claire didn't say anything to me, and I never asked."

"Do you know if she was planning to divorce Howie?"

"She hadn't come to any decision but she knew time was running out."

"Did she ever mention to you her concerns that Howie was having an affair?"

"Not that I can recall."

"Claire's friend, Sarah James, told me that Claire was worried because Howie had been receiving some late-night calls. She thought it had to do with his gambling. Though Howie said it was nothing, she knew he was probably lying. Did she mention the calls to you?"

"No, but she hinted several times that she thought Howie might be gambling again."

"Why do you think she was having an affair?"

"Whatever I tell you would just be a guess."

"That's okay. The more I know, the better, even if it's only an educated guess."

"Claire wasn't the most secure person. If she thought their relationship was rocky, she may have looked to someone else to fulfill whatever needs she thought were missing in her marriage. It might not be logical, but to Claire, it was."

"One more thing; do you think her husband killed her?"

"If I had to take a guess, I would say no. But then again, I'm not the greatest judge of character."

"Here's my card. If you think of anything else, no matter how small or insignificant, please give me a call."

Walking to my car, I realized the more I learned about Claire's past, the more I identified with her. Because of our pasts, we both had trust and attachment issues. Maybe we were both searching for answers at this point in our lives. Unfortunately, Claire didn't get the chance to find her answers. Though I took the case without knowing anything about Claire, I was now more motivated to find out who took Claire's life.

I still had my doubts whether my past was a place I should be searching. What I did know from what I've learned so far was that Claire had demons that had haunted her. But did those demons get Claire killed?

CHAPTER 13

On Monday morning, as I was getting ready to see the lawyer who handled my adoption, I started to think of reasons why this wasn't such a good idea. I tried to push those thoughts aside.

I arrived at Thomas Logan's office a few minutes before 10:00 a.m. His receptionist, Tina, brought me right into Mr. Logan's office.

"Ms. Landon, nice to meet you," he said, shaking my hand. "Please sit."

Thomas Logan must have been close to seventy, if not older. He had a trusting face and a few gray hairs left on his bald head. I imagined the suspenders he had attached to his pants had been part of his wardrobe for a very long time.

"So what can I do for you, my dear?"

"You handled my adoption." He took a long look at me. "I was adopted thirty-seven years ago by Mark and Cindy Landon."

"Yes, I do remember. If I recall, they were both schoolteachers."

"You have a very good memory. I recently have an interest in finding my biological parents."

"May I ask why you waited so long?"

"My parents were wonderful and I loved them very much, so I didn't feel the need to look for people who didn't want me."

"I see. So what brings you here today?"

"A few reasons. When I was twelve, my parents died in an automobile accident."

"I'm so sorry."

"As I mentioned, I never felt the need to search out my birth parents, even though my adoptive parents always encouraged me to look for them. Recently, I opened up a letter written by my parents to me when I was one year old. In it, they said my birth mother was very young when she gave me up." I decided there was no reason to go into other issues with Mr. Logan.

"You know those records are sealed."

"I do, but I also know that when it comes to private adoptions, things have loosened up. I was hoping you could help me."

Mr. Logan sat contemplating what he should do for what seemed like an eternity.

"Jennifer, would you please go into the storage room and bring me the Landon file. The year is 1982, I believe."

"It's a shame your parents didn't get a chance to see what a lovely young woman you've become. Without getting too personal, are you married?"

"No. Maybe one day. Can I ask you a question?"

"Of course."

"In the letter my parents wrote to me, they said my birth mother chose them. Can you remember why?"

"I believe she liked the fact that both your parents were teachers."

"I see. Can I ask you another question?" I didn't give him a chance to answer. "Obviously you've handled many adoptions. I'm just curious; what's your sense of children who are adopted?"

"I can only tell you from my own personal experience. I have a son that my wife and I adopted. I think children always wonder why their birth parents abandoned them and because of that, they may have doubts about their self-worth. Unfortunately, adopted children imagine it's about them. Of course that's not true. Thank you, Jennifer," he said, as she handed him my file.

I noticed my leg started to shake as he was looking through it.

He looked up through his half glasses. "It appears that about five years ago, a family member contacted my office and we were informed that your birth mother had passed away. I'm so sorry, Maddie."

I was totally caught off guard by what he just said. "How did she die? She must have been fairly young," I said, feeling blindsided.

"I don't have that information."

"What about my father?"

"There was no father listed. I'm sorry."

"Is that unusual that a family member would call to let you know about the death of a birth parent?"

"I'd have to say it's not the norm."

"Do you have any information on the person who called?"

"I don't see a name in the file."

"Do you have any explanation why my mother never looked for me?"

"That would be difficult for me to say. It's possible if she married she wanted to keep that secret from her spouse. She could have been afraid of his reaction and what it might do to the marriage. Of course, there may be other explanations."

"Do you think you can tell me my mother's name since she's no longer living?"

He looked at me in a fatherly way, debating whether he should tell me. A moment later, he said, "Her name was Lydia Peterson."

"Do you know if she ever married?"

"I don't. I can tell you she was from West Philadelphia."

"I appreciate the information. Thank you," I said as I got up.

"You're welcome. Good luck to you," he said, resting his hand on my shoulder.

Maybe it was better this way, I thought to myself as I headed to my office. *Now I don't have to search for my birth mother.* Then another thought occurred to me. There must have been a reason a family member contacted Thomas Logan. Maybe my birth mother wanted me to locate family members now that she was dead. Was it possible something or someone from my mother's past could lead me to locate my biological father? Probably a long shot. *The question is, do I want to go down that road at all?*

CHAPTER 14

Before going into my office, I went across the hall to see Cousin Will.

"Hi, Mary. How's tricks?" Mary has been Will's secretary/receptionist for years. I'm not sure the office would function without her.

"Everything's calm at the moment. Go ahead in."

"Hey, Maddie, what brings you to this side of the world? Everything okay?"

"Can't I see my favorite cousin?"

"I thought Noah was your favorite." Noah is Will and Sophie's two-year-old son.

"You got me there. I was looking through old photos the other day. You know, you were a pretty handsome dude when you were younger."

"I'm going to take that as a compliment."

"I went to see the lawyer that handled my adoption."

"Wow. That's a big step. How'd it go?"

"My birth mother died a few years ago."

"I'm so sorry, Maddie."

"It's probably for the best. I wasn't relishing the idea of looking for her. It's obvious she didn't want me."

"We don't know the circumstances. How did the attorney know she died?"

"Apparently a relative contacted his office. The attorney gave me my birth mother's name at the time I was adopted. He also said she was from Philadelphia. There was no father listed on the original birth certificate."

"Do you want to look into it further?"

"Right now, I'm not sure of anything."

"You sound out of sorts, which is not like you."

"I'm just feeling a bit overwhelmed at the moment. It'll pass."

"Both Sophie and I are here for you."

"I miss the little guy. I'll call Sophie and set up a playdate."

"Be careful."

"Always."

Cousin Will is my only family besides his wife Sophie and their son Noah. My mother and his father were siblings. When my parents died in the automobile accident, I had very little memory of what happened. When I woke up in the hospital, Will's parents were standing over my bed. When I was allowed to leave, I stayed with them until Aunt Jenny was able to leave Chicago and come to New York. Will has always been like a big brother to me.

I called Annie as I walked across the hall to my office. "Call me back when you get a chance."

My phone rang as I was pouring myself a cup of coffee.

"Hey, Annie." I gave her the lowdown of everything that transpired since I last saw her.

"I'm so sorry you won't have a chance to meet your mother."

"Don't be. I'm not."

"Maybe you can find this family member and talk to them?"

"There's no hurry. Which reminds me, the game starts at 1:40 p.m. on Sunday. It might be easier if we take the subway to the stadium."

"Sounds like a plan. Also, don't be so quick to dismiss the idea of trying to find a relative of your mother."

"Aye, aye, captain. Talk soon."

"Love you."

"Right back at you."

Annie is the eternal optimist. About two years ago, she was pregnant, but lost the baby when she was in a car accident. Though I know the effect it has on her, she still views life with a half-full attitude. I'm not sure where I would be now if it wasn't for Annie always there for me.

I was feeling a little impatient. I wanted to talk with Howie Stevenson and push him on some of the answers he gave me. They didn't match what other people were telling me.

I went directly to his real estate office, located in a strip mall in the town of Greenburgh in Westchester County. If he wasn't there, I had all intentions of finding out where he was. When I got to his office, Barbara, Howie's receptionist, picked up the phone and told Howie that I was here to see him. Two minutes later, he came out.

"What's going on," he said.

"Why don't we go outside where we can have some privacy."

Once outside I said: "I spoke with friends of Claire's. They both told me that you were gambling again and were in debt for a lot of money." That wasn't exactly true but he didn't have to know that.

"Whose side are you on exactly? I thought Greg hired you to find out who killed Claire, not to interrogate me."

"That's exactly what I'm doing, but I have to go wherever my investigation leads me. Let's suppose you owed some bad people money, and you were having a hard time paying them back; maybe they would take it out on your wife."

Howie's face drained of color.

"You see where I'm going with this, Howie? I'm not saying that's what happened, but I have to look into all possibilities or I wouldn't be doing my job."

"I'm sorry, I have nothing to say."

"Are you scared of someone? Did someone threaten you? I really am on your side, but I can't help you if you don't let me."

Howie didn't say anything.

"Did you know your wife was pregnant?"

"No. I already told Greg I didn't. Why all the questions? Besides, I have an alibi."

"Unfortunately, your alibi might not hold up. There's a lot of circumstantial evidence against you." I wanted to rattle Howie. He was lying but I didn't know why.

I could tell by the look on Howie's face that what I just said had him worried.

"Someone saw you at a restaurant sitting at a bar with a woman a couple of weeks before Claire died. Were you cheating on Claire?"

"No! I think this person saw me talking to Dana Thomas. She worked with Claire at the boutique in Scarsdale."

"Why were you with her?"

"I wasn't with her. I mean, I'm not having an affair. I was trying to find out why Claire had been distant in the last few months, and I thought Claire might have said something to Dana."

"Did she?"

"No. She told me Claire never talked about any personal problems with her."

"So that was it. You've never had any other contact with Dana Thomas?"

"Just to say hello and goodbye, that sort of thing when I had picked up Claire from the store."

I was curious why Dana Thomas never mentioned that she met Howie other than at the boutique. But you could bet I was going to ask her.

"One other thing. Your neighbor across the street said she saw you and Claire arguing outside of your house one morning. It appeared to be pretty contentious."

"Are you talking about that nosy neighbor, Janice Levy? The woman's crazy. She had nothing better to do than bother us. She came over constantly asking to borrow a cup of sugar or something else. Claire used to tell me that she would come by when Claire got home from work and invite herself in for coffee. The woman just wants attention."

"So you're telling me that Mrs. Levy didn't see you and Claire arguing?"

"She may have, but I don't remember what the argument was about."

"She saw Claire push you before she got into her car."

"I'm sure it was nothing. Sometimes Claire can be dramatic."

"Howie, I hope you're not keeping anything from me."

When I left Howie, I wasn't hopeful that he would smarten up.

As soon as I got home, I emailed my source who obtains telephone records. I gave him the information he needed on Howie in order to access his cell phone bills for the two months prior to Claire's death. I was hoping there would be calls listed to the number of the person Howie owed money to.

I changed into my sweats, poured myself a glass of wine, and called Jesse.

"Hey, you home?" I said when he answered.

"Just got in."

"I miss you."

"Oh yeah!"

"That was your cue to tell me that you miss me madly."

"I see. I guess your subtle approach is wasted on me."

"That's too bad. By the way, I have my baseball mitt ready for the game."

"Wow, it must be pretty old."

"Well, since my dad gave it to me when I was nine, you're right."

"Are you really taking it with you?"

"I most definitely am. Is that going to embarrass you?"

"Not at all. I can't wait." I could envision the amused look on Jesse's face.

"I'm going to have the last laugh when I catch a ball with my mitt."

"I look forward to it. What's been going on?"

I went through the conversation I had with the attorney who handled my adoption.

"I'm not sure I believe you when you say you're fine with the fact that your birth mother is dead. Not after all these years it took you to finally decide to look for her. You had nothing to lose and everything to gain. You may have a sibling out there. It may wind up to be more complicated for you, but life is messy, as you already know. I don't want you to have any regrets later on."

Though I knew Jesse was right, his remark about life being messy was not lost on me.

CHAPTER 15

Instead of going into the office the next day, I decided to work from home. I was hoping the cell phone records I ordered would come in by the end of the day. In the meantime, I wanted to do some research into my birth mother and her family.

First, I searched for an obituary on a Lydia Peterson who had once lived in West Philadelphia. I had an approximate year of death within two or three years. Nothing. She probably married and had a different last name. Maybe I could track her through her parents. How many Petersons could there be in Philadelphia? It turns out there were quite a few with that last name. Now what? Without knowing her parents' first names, this wasn't going to be easy. I looked on the social security death index under the name Lydia Peterson, but there were no matches with her approximate year of birth.

This was getting frustrating. I picked up the phone and dialed Thomas Logan's office. His assistant answered.

"Hello, this is Maddie Landon. I was in to see Mr. Logan on Monday."

"Oh yes, I remember."

"Mr. Logan mentioned a relative of my birth mother who had called to inform the office that my mother had passed away. Did that person speak with you?"

"Why yes."

"Would you happen to remember if this person gave you their name?"

"They may have, but I don't recall."

"Wouldn't you have noted it in the file with the information on her death?"

"I'm sure I would have, though I do remember it was a woman's voice."

"Thank you," I said, and hung up.

Maybe this person didn't want to furnish their name for whatever reason. Then I realized I should go into my databases, inputting the name Peterson and West Philadelphia. I had to go through several reports to see if there was someone with the last name of Peterson with the approximate age of Lydia's parents. There was a Martha and James Peterson, both deceased, that had lived on Green Street. They seem to be about the right age.

I then did a search for an obituary on both Martha and James. Bingo! There was an obituary for a Martha Peterson who passed away seven years ago. It listed her beloved husband, James, who was deceased, and two daughters, Lydia Reed, living in Bella Vista, and Lucy Grainger, living in Chestnut Hill.

I found a Scott Reed living in Bella Vista. Could this be my birth mother's husband? And could he be my father? Did this man know of my existence? If not, do I call him up and say: "This is your wife's daughter that she abandoned thirty-seven years ago?" I picked up the phone and called Annie.

"You got a second?" I said, when Annie answered.

"I'm just eating my lunch in the office. What's up?"

"I was able to locate my birth mother's husband. What am I supposed to say if he doesn't even know I exist? I don't want to freak him out."

"Let's think for a minute. You certainly don't want to give this man a heart attack. He's probably in his sixties. Could he have been the person who called the attorney?"

"No. The assistant said it was a woman."

"Okay. Now that you have your birth mother's sister's name, you can track her. Maybe there's other extended family out there."

"That's a good idea just in case Lydia Reed's husband has no clue who I am."

"Keep me posted."

"Will do."

I found an obituary for Lydia Reed. It was strange knowing I was looking at my birth mother's obituary. It said she was survived by her husband Scott and a sister, Lucy Grainger from Chestnut Hill in Philadelphia. Why was there no mention of children? Could it be that I was her only child?

Lucy Grainger was fairly easy to locate. Now what? Should I call her and ask why my mother abandoned me? I couldn't do it. I wasn't ready to face any answers. Instead, I went for a run.

Besides a running path, my neighborhood park has a playground and a basketball court. On the weekends, you can find adults and teenagers shooting hoops and playing basketball.

My phone was vibrating as I was beginning my second loop around the park. I saw it was Greg.

"What's up?"

"The police want Howie to come in for questioning. You got anything for me?"

"Nothing concrete. Claire's friend had no idea if Howie knew about the baby. His partner is still sticking by their alibi, that he and Howie were out celebrating the sale of a five-million-dollar house."

"Anything else?"

"None of the people I spoke with believed Howie killed his wife. One other thing, I think Howie is having an affair, but I don't have any proof at the moment, and he denies it. I'll check into it. All of this is still circumstantial unless they have any forensics tying him to the murder."

"If they think they have enough circumstantial evidence, they can poke holes in his alibi, which might be enough. I wonder if they dug up any info on his gambling problem. I see that as a motive," Greg said.

"I spoke with Howie about it. He clammed up. I'm looking into it. When do they want to question him?"

"Tomorrow morning. I'll let you know what happens."

When we hung up, my mind went back to my aunt, Lucy Grainger. If she was the one who called the law office, there must have been a reason. Maybe she was hoping that I would one day contact the attorney. But why not leave her name? I didn't have an answer.

CHAPTER 16

The next day, I drove up to Scarsdale to speak with Dana Thomas. I wanted to know why she lied to me when she knew she had met Howie at a restaurant bar.

When I walked in, Dana was helping a customer. When she saw me, there was a perplexed look on her face, as if she was trying to place where she knew me from. I meandered around the shop while she was busy. I saw the price tags and did a low whistle. When the customer finally left, Dana approached me.

"You're the private investigator I spoke with a few days ago. How can I help you?"

I was pretty sure Howie had filled her in on our conversation. She was biting her lower lip, which told me she was nervous. I wondered what she had to be nervous about.

"When we last spoke, you told me that the only contact you had with Claire's husband was to say hello when he came to pick up Claire. Now I find out that you were sitting at a bar having a drink with him. Why is that?"

"I'm sorry I lied to you. I didn't know if Howie wanted me to say anything since he was asking me about his wife."

I thought it was interesting that she called him Howie as opposed to Mr. Stevenson, since they really didn't know each other.

"I'm expecting my boss any moment. Are we finished?"

I was pretty sure she was lying. If I pushed hard enough, I bet she would have told me the truth, but I decided to let it go for now. It was better that Dana didn't know I suspected her of having an affair with Howie.

"Yes, thank you for your time."

Just as I was leaving, a very smartly dressed woman, probably in her fifties, walked into the shop. I was hoping this was Linda Crawford.

"Ms. Crawford?"

"Yes."

"My name's Maddie Landon. I'm looking into the death of Claire Stevenson. Do you think I can have a moment of your time?"

"We can talk in my office. Follow me."

"Are you with the police?" she said as she motioned me to sit.

"No. I was hired by Mr. Stevenson's attorney."

"Oh, was he arrested?"

"No, but he does have counsel."

"I see." Though I'm not sure she did. "What can I do for you?"

"Can you tell me what you know about Claire?"

"She was a lovely person and was very good at her job. To tell you the truth, we didn't talk about personal matters."

"She never talked about herself at all?"

"We basically kept our conversations on a business level. I'm a very private person and I got the feeling that Claire was, too. If something was going on with her, she didn't confide in me."

"When you were with her prior to her death, did she seem preoccupied?"

"Again, I didn't notice anything. I'm sorry. I wish I could be of more help, though I did happen to see her in town one day. She was getting out of a car. I think there was a man in the driver's seat, but I didn't pay any attention to him."

"Could it have been her husband?"

"I guess."

"Do you remember anything about the car?"

"Only that it was old. I mean a car that you don't see around anymore."

"Maybe a classic?"

"Sorry, I'm not a car person."

"Do you remember the color?"

"Could have been silver but I can't say for sure. It was a while ago."

I was pretty certain Howie did not have an old car.

"Thank you for your time. Here's my card in case something else comes to mind."

As I walked out, I thought about what Ms. Crawford told me. I'm not sure it was anything. It could have been someone just dropping her off. But all was not lost. I was now pretty sure Dana and Howie were having an affair.

CHAPTER 17

As soon as I got into the office, I checked my emails. I was happy to see that my source sent me Howie's phone records. I quickly printed them out and started going through them. Most of the telephone numbers I didn't recognize, but what caught my attention was one number that showed up several times in the late evening. I remember speaking to one of Claire's friends who mentioned Howie was getting some late-night calls that he seemed upset about.

I tried to find out who that number belonged to, but I wasn't having any success. It could have been from a burner phone.

I picked up the phone and called Howie. He answered right away.

"Are you calling to harass me again?"

I ignored his remark. "I need to know who 917-300-2197 belongs to."

"How did you get that number?"

Howie sounded scared. "Does it matter? Who does it belong to? Is it to the guy you owe money to?"

"Look, you're asking for trouble. These guys are dangerous."

"That's my problem. I have to find out if they had anything to do with Claire's death."

"His name is Pete but he's just the person who collects the money."

"How much did you owe them?"

"Hundred and fifty thousand," he answered sheepishly.

"Did you pay any of it back yet?"

"I paid back seventy-five thousand."

"Where did you get the money?"

"I took out a loan against the house."

"How did you manage that without Claire knowing?"

Howie's silence told me he forged his wife's signature.

"Did Claire know what was going on?"

"No. I didn't want to get her involved."

"Well, you may have." I wanted to choke him. "What was the interest rate?"

"Twenty percent for every week it wasn't paid off. These guys mean business."

"You should have realized that before you got involved with them."

I hung up and thought about what Howie said. Though I've been in dangerous situations before, mostly when I was on the police force, I didn't see any alternative if I wanted to find out if these guys had any connection to Claire's death.

I called the number that was in front of me.

"Who is this?" a man's voice answered.

"Can we meet?" I said.

"I don't meet with people I don't know."

"I'm helping out a friend. My name's Maddie."

"What's this about?"

"Can we discuss it in person? I'll make it worth your while."

"You better not be pulling my leg."

"Never."

"Be at Jimmy's Corner in half an hour."

"I'll be there."

Before leaving, I holstered my gun and checked to see if I had enough cash on me.

I hailed a cab down to West Forty-fourth Street. The place was a dive but it had character. The theme was about the sport of boxing. The walls were lined with photographs of heavyweight boxers and posters advertising high-ranking boxing contenders. There was a life-size cutout of Joe Louis nailed to the wall. You get the drift.

I went up to the bartender and told him Pete was expecting me. He pointed in the direction of the far end of the bar.

"Pete, I'm Maddie. Can I buy you a drink?"

Pete was skinny, scruffy-looking, about forty years old, with mousy brown hair.

"I'll have a scotch and soda," he said to the bartender.

"And I'll have a glass of Merlot."

I took a seat next to him.

"You got something for me?"

I was hoping a hundred bucks was enough as I placed it on the bar.

"Let's dispense with the chitchat. What do you want?"

"I heard that Howie Stevenson owes your boss money."

"Who did you hear that from?"

"Mr. Stevenson. I'm helping him out. You heard his wife was murdered?"

"That's what I've been told."

"I was hired to find out who killed her."

"Don't you know it's always the husband?"

"Let's say it isn't. Any guesses who it might be?"

"Lady, I don't know what your angle is but you're barking up the wrong tree."

"Look, I know you're just the messenger. I'd like to meet with your boss and let him tell me that to my face."

"Hey, if I were you, I'd drop it. You're just looking for trouble, but it's your funeral. I'll pass the word on. Where can I get a hold of you?"

I gave him my card.

"Thanks for your time, Pete."

"Don't mention it."

I paid for the drinks and left.

Walking out of the place, I questioned what I was getting myself into. Was I scared, hell yes, but I needed to find out what was going on. When I was a cop, I had my partner to back me up. Now it was just me.

CHAPTER 18

I took a cab back to the office and slid my gun back into my desk drawer. I was contemplating my next move. I picked up the phone and called Sarah James.

"Sarah, this is Maddie Landon. How are you?"

"Has something come up?"

"No, but I had a question. You mentioned that Claire's parents died in a plane crash. Did she have any other relatives?"

"She had an aunt, her father's sister. Her mother was an only child."

"Do you know why her aunt didn't take Claire to live with her?"

"I don't. And I doubt Claire knew at the time since she was only seven. If she did find out, she never told me."

"Did this aunt stay in contact with Claire?"

"I know she sent her presents from time to time at the foster home."

This is the second time I got the feeling Sarah was jealous of Claire. What was that about?

"Do you think Claire may have been in touch with her after she left foster care?"

"Though Claire and I were very close, there was a side to her that I could never figure out."

"What do you mean?"

"I got the feeling there were things Claire kept to herself. She never mentioned being in contact with her aunt but that doesn't mean she wasn't."

"Do you know her aunt's name?"

"The name Grace comes to mind, but I can't be positive."

"What was Claire's maiden name?"

"It was Matthew. I knew most of the people that attended Claire's funeral and I'm pretty sure her aunt wasn't there."

"Well, if no one knew they were in touch, perhaps her aunt didn't know that Claire had died. Do you know if she lived in New York?"

"I'm pretty sure she lived in Manhattan, but that was when Claire was in foster care. I have no idea where she is now."

"Thank you, Sarah. You've been a big help."

"Please let me know if you find out anything."

I sipped my coffee and ate my sandwich slowly. I should check with Howie if he knew Claire had any contact with her aunt. Searching on my computer under the name Grace Matthew in Manhattan with an age range of fifty-five to sixty-five, there were two possibilities. The first report listed a Grace Matthew, but it appeared that Matthew was her married name. The second report listed a Grace Matthew living in the seventies on the East Side. She was fifty-seven years old. There was no information on her relatives, but there was a cell phone number listed for Ms. Matthew.

I picked up the phone and called Howie. He answered right away.

"Howie, it's Maddie. I have a question. I was told that Claire had an aunt on her father's side. Did Claire ever mention an aunt?"

"She did, but as far as I knew, they weren't in contact."

"When Claire died, did you try to locate this person?"

"No. Even if I wanted to, I didn't know her name or where she lived. Do you think they were in touch?"

"I have no idea." I decided not to mention that I was going to try and contact Grace Matthew.

"Wait, still no word on who Claire was having an affair with?"

"Not yet. I'm working on it."

I hung up and thought about what both Sarah James and Paula Frankel said about Claire. Each, in their own way, thought Claire had trust issues. I know very well what it's like to be abandoned and not to trust people. I was sort of getting a clearer picture of Claire and what she must have gone through. It couldn't have been easy for her.

Instead of calling Ms. Matthew, I thought it would be better if I paid her an in-person visit. For all I knew, she may not be aware her niece died.

I was curious about my own aunt, the one I never met, yet I was still hesitant about whether I wanted to contact her. I did wonder if she knew who my father was. Unless I go to Philadelphia and see this woman, all of my questions will remain unanswered.

CHAPTER 19

In the morning, after showering and having breakfast, I went to see Grace Matthew. What were the chances Claire had any sort of relationship with her aunt, someone who left Claire at the foster home when Claire had no one else to count on?

I arrived at Ms. Matthew's townhouse and was lucky to find a parking spot right in front. The door was answered by a very handsome woman, still beautiful at her age. There was a definite resemblance to her niece. They both had the same large dark brown eyes and beautiful full lips. She was dressed in business attire, a blue jacket and matching skirt with a white silk blouse.

"Ms. Matthew, my name is Maddie Landon. I'm a private investigator. Do you know a Claire Stevenson?" She had a surprised look on her face.

"Why are you asking?"

"May I come in and speak with you?"

"I'm on my way to work. What is this about?" she said in a hurried manner.

"Did you know Claire died?"

"Yes."

"I'm sorry to bother you, but do you think we can have this conversation inside?"

Ms. Matthew brought me into a sitting room off the kitchen. It led to a patio that was large enough to entertain guests. I was jealous. The white lacquered chairs were upholstered in a yellow and black print. The floor was done with terracotta-colored stone tiles.

"How did you find me?"

"Sarah James, the woman who grew up with your niece at the foster home, remembered your first name. I suppose Claire may have mentioned you at one time. Ms. James didn't know if you had a relationship with Claire but she remembered the presents you sent her."

"That was such a long time ago," she said, more to herself than to me. "I didn't learn about Claire's death till after the funeral. We had been in touch, and when I hadn't heard from her in a while, I didn't know what to think. The last time I called, her phone was disconnected. That worried me, so I finally got in touch with her husband, though I just said I was a friend. That's when he told me she had died. I was so stunned I didn't ask him any questions. I hung up quickly. I checked the newspapers in the town Claire lived and found out that she died under suspicious circumstances. Did someone hire you?"

"Her husband's attorney hired me to look into her death."

"Does that mean Claire's husband was arrested?"

"Not as yet, though he may be a suspect. Can you tell me about your relationship with Claire?"

"You probably know that I was her only living relative. I will always regret that I didn't take her in."

"Why didn't you?"

"I was fairly young myself and my career was taking off. The company had me traveling a lot. To tell you the truth, I was scared. I didn't know how I could manage with a young child. Unfortunately, I realized too late that I never should have left her at the home. I tried to make it up to her. When she left foster care at age eighteen, I paid for her college tuition and we began keeping in touch." There were tears trickling down Ms. Matthew's face.

"I'm not sure why, but Claire wanted to keep our communications secret. We met about once a month, usually for dinner."

"Did you ever marry or have children of your own?"

"I was engaged once. We were very much in love, but he died very young of cancer."

"I'm so sorry."

"This may sound morbid but I thought in some way it was my punishment for leaving Claire in foster care."

I didn't know what to say so I said nothing. It's hard for me to be sympathetic, maybe because I know how it feels to lose the most important people in your life.

"Can you tell me what you talked about?"

"First of all, I don't believe my niece killed herself. Any number of people knew about her heart condition."

"I'm sorry to have to tell you this but Claire was poisoned. Whether her heart condition contributed to her death has not yet been determined."

"Oh my god! I can't believe it," she said. "Who would do such a horrible thing? My poor niece." Ms. Matthew was sobbing.

"We don't know," I said softly. I waited till she gained her composure.

"Did she talk about her marriage?"

"I was encouraging her to leave Howie, not because he was a bad person, but because he was going to drive them into financial ruin. He couldn't stop gambling. Claire was a little naïve. She wanted to believe him when he said he would quit."

"Do you know if she told Howie she was going to divorce him?"

"She said she planned on it, but I don't think she actually started divorce proceedings before her death."

"Did you know she was pregnant?"

"Yes, we talked about it the last time I saw her. She wasn't sure who the father was."

"Do you know if she was planning on keeping the baby?"

"She was. I told her I would help her financially in case she decided to leave Howie."

"Did she tell you who she was having an affair with?"

"No, just that it was someone she had known for a while."

"Do you think her husband might have killed her?"

"I can't answer that. I only know Howie through Claire, and I don't pretend to know what people are capable of."

"Did she say why she was having an affair?"

"I think she chose Howie because he made her feel safe. She loved Howie, but I'm not sure she was passionately in love with him."

"What do you mean by that?"

"Losing her parents was very traumatic for Claire. And unfortunately, her foster parents were not able to give Claire the love and stability she needed."

I thought what Ms. Matthew said was very telling.

"Can you think of anything at all that Claire might have said that can lead me to the person who killed your niece? It could be a passing remark that at the time seemed insignificant or unimportant."

"If I do, I'll contact you. Please find out who killed my niece. She was all I had in the world."

"I'll do my best." I gave her my card before leaving.

Why did Claire want to keep her relationship with her aunt a secret? What other secrets did Claire keep?

CHAPTER 20

I drove to my office and found a spot on a side street.

As soon as I opened my car door, someone grabbed me from behind, threw a hood over my head, and shoved me into a vehicle.

"What, what do you want? I can't breathe." I was twisting all around.

"Just shut up."

"Please... I can't breathe."

"If you open up your mouth one more time, it'll be the last time you take a breath."

I had no idea what was going on. The hood was suffocating me. I was trying to regulate my breathing since I didn't want to pass out. I couldn't tell how many people were in the car. No one spoke. All these thoughts were running through my head, none of them good. About fifteen minutes later, the car stopped. Someone grabbed me and pulled me out of the car. The next thing I knew, I was being dragged and then I heard a door open. I was pushed down in a chair and my hands were tied behind my back.

"I'm going to take the hood off and put a blindfold on you. Look straight ahead. If you try to turn around, I'll kill you."

I did as he said. Before the blindfold was on me, I could see I was in a room, maybe a basement. It appeared to be completely empty. I could feel the presence of another person.

"Why were you asking about us?" the man said in a harsh tone. He had an accent I couldn't identify.

At first I didn't know what he was talking about, so I hesitated. The next thing I knew I was punched in the stomach so hard I cried out in excruciating pain.

"I'm not going to ask you again."

"I'm trying to find out who murdered Claire Stevenson," I said, trying to catch my breath.

"And you think we had something to do with it?"

I wasn't sure who he meant by "we" but I didn't care. I just answered quickly.

"No," I lied. "I just wanted to find out if what Howie told me was the truth. He said half of the loan was repaid."

"Listen, little girl. I'm not interested in you getting up in our business or demanding that you speak to us. Do you understand?"

"Yes."

"Do you think we should teach her a lesson? My partner here likes pretty girls."

I felt someone breathing on me. His breath was sour. I was shaking. His hand was on my face and then lightly brushed across my breast. Panic was starting to set in.

"That wasn't part of the deal. Let's just go."

"Are you sure? Who's going to know?"

"The boss isn't going to like it. Now let's get out of here."

"Maybe we should leave her here. That will teach her not to meddle where she doesn't belong."

If they leave me here, I'll die. Who's going to find me? I started to hyperventilate, sweat pouring out of me.

"Don't be stupid. We can't leave her here. Let's go."

The next thing I knew, the hood was back on, my hands were untied, and I was being dragged back into a car. I was shaken up as we rode in silence for a while. Then the car stopped.

"If you interfere any further, you won't be so lucky the next time. And tell Howie we'll be paying him a visit soon."

The next thing I knew, the door opened and I was shoved onto a cement pavement, my backpack thrown on top of me. I quickly took the hood and blindfold off. I didn't know where I was. I appeared to be in a deserted lot somewhere. My hands were shaking as I reached into my backpack for my phone to call Annie.

"Maddie, I can hardly hear you."

"I'm not sure where they dropped me."

"What are you talking about?"

"I'll explain later. I need you to pick me up."

"Where are you?"

"I'm in a deserted lot. It looks like there once was an ironworks factory here, but now it's abandoned. There are no street signs. They grabbed me a few blocks from my office and then drove about fifteen minutes."

"Okay, hold on. I'm checking if there's an old ironworks factory in Manhattan or the Bronx. Wait a second. I think I might know where you are. Hopefully, if I have the right location, I should be there in about twenty minutes. I'm keeping my phone on. Are you hurt?"

"I think my ribs are cracked. Out of nowhere, a guy grabbed me, placed a hood over my head, and shoved me into a car. There was another guy with him."

"Do you know why?"

"I didn't at first. Then I realized it was the loan sharks Howie owes money to."

"How did they know you were looking into them?"

"It's a little bit of a story I'll tell you another time. I feel nauseous. I think I'm going to be sick."

"I'm on my way. Talk to me."

"Oh no!"

"What's the matter?"

"When they threw me out of the car, my jeans ripped."

"Jesus! You're worried about your jeans?"

"I'm just saying. There was a moment when I thought one of the guys was going to rape me. I don't think I've ever felt so vulnerable."

"Did you see their faces? Anything that could identify either guy?"

"No. I was completely in the dark the whole time. My insides feel like they're on fire."

"Just so you know, Doug was ecstatic when I told him where we'll be sitting at the game on Sunday."

"Are you trying to distract me?"

"Nothing gets past you."

When I finally saw Annie's car from a distance, I slowly picked myself up off the ground and tried to wave. Though it couldn't have been more than thirty minutes since I called Annie, it seemed like I had been waiting for hours.

"I see you, though I'll have to give most of the credit to Google," Annie said.

Annie opened her car door and helped me in.

"I'm taking you straight to the emergency room."

"I'll go home and take some aspirin. I'll be alright."

"Sorry, but we're going to the hospital. You can hardly walk. I'll wait with you."

I didn't have the energy to argue. I closed my eyes.

"We're here," Annie said twenty-five minutes later. I must have nodded off.

Annie helped me out of the car and we went into the emergency room.

"I'm going to park. I'll be right back."

Thankfully, the emergency room wasn't busy. I had to register at the desk and then wait till I was called.

"I just remembered my car is a few blocks from my office. I can't leave it there," I said to Annie when she got back.

"We'll figure it out later. Does it hurt when you breathe?"

"Yes."

"Hopefully nothing's broken. Do you think you should call the police?"

"No. I have no idea who these people are, and I don't want to get the police involved in my investigation."

"Okay. I'm just glad they didn't kill you."

"I really don't think that was their intention. I think they just wanted to scare me."

"I think they made their point," Annie said.

Twenty minutes later, I got called into a large room with beds set up for patients.

"So what happened to you, young lady?" the doctor said.

"A very mean man punched me in the stomach."

"Is that a joke?"

"Yeah! Just kidding." I didn't want the doctor getting the police involved.

"I'm pretty confident it's just a bruised rib but we'll take an x-ray to be sure."

An hour later, the doctor gave me the news that two ribs were bruised but not broken. Except for taking painkillers and rest, there wasn't much they could do for me. He said if my breathing became a problem, not to neglect it since it could lead to other serious issues.

"I guess from the look on your face you're going to live," Annie said as I hobbled toward her.

"Don't make me laugh; it hurts too much. I have to pick up the painkillers the doctor prescribed at the pharmacy here."

"Aren't you lucky. That should take away all your anxiety for a while."

"Very funny."

When we got back to my car, Annie insisted on following me to my apartment.

"Listen, please don't tell Doug I was almost raped. I have no intention of telling Jesse."

"Your secret is safe with me, though you might think about talking to Dr. Goldberg about it."

"I can always count on you for unsolicited advice."

"I'm here to protect and serve," Annie said, saluting me.

Annie followed me back to my garage and then insisted on taking the elevator with me up to my apartment.

"I'll be alright. Don't you have a matrimonial practice to run?"

"I'm out of here. Call me if you need anything."

"Love you."

As soon as Annie left, I took two painkillers and was fast asleep in five minutes. When I woke up, it was dark and I was slightly disoriented. My side hurt. I slowly got out of bed, wincing as I moved. It was after 9:00 p.m.

I wanted to get back in bed, but thought it was probably wise to try and eat something. I found my phone in my backpack. There were three messages: Greg, asking me to call him back, and Jesse and Annie.

I really didn't feel like talking to anyone, but I knew Jesse and Annie would worry.

I called Annie first and told her I slept for a few hours, but intended to go back to sleep as soon as I had some toast.

Next call was to Jesse.

"Hey, I'm sorry I missed your call," I said when he answered.

"Were you sleeping? You sound groggy."

I went on to explain my conversation with Howie and what followed, leaving out some details.

"What the hell were you thinking when you contacted this guy?"

"I was doing my job, just like you would do," I said a little too sharply.

"I just feel helpless. I don't want anything to happen to you."

"Neither do I. Thank heavens for painkillers. From what I told you, do you think these guys were involved in Claire's murder?"

"Obviously I can't be sure, but I doubt it. For one thing, you would probably be dead now. Also, I doubt if poison would be their method of murder."

"Both valid points, though I can't rule them out completely."

"Don't forget about Howie. He had plenty of motive."

"What about his alibi?"

"I wouldn't put too much stock in what his partner said."

"Maybe. I'm fading quickly. I'll talk to you tomorrow."

"Sleep tight. Call me any time, day or night. I know you're tough but I worry."

Now I'm really glad I didn't mention that I was almost raped.

Besides not having the energy to eat, just the thought of toast made me nauseous. Instead, I decided to take another painkiller and go back to sleep.

My phone was buzzing just as I was nodding off. It was Greg again.

"Where have you been? Didn't you get my call?"

"For your information, I was abducted and wound up with two bruised ribs."

"What? What happened?"

"I just took a painkiller. Let's talk in the morning," I said and hung up. I realized I didn't ask Greg what transpired when Howie was questioned again by the police. It would have to wait till the morning.

CHAPTER 21

I must have slept like a rock since it was 8:00 a.m. the next time I looked at the clock. I slowly got out of bed. My side was still hurting. I walked into the bathroom, deciding if I was up to taking a shower. I was dreading the task but thought I would probably feel better if I did.

The steamy hot water felt luxurious against my skin. My body shivered when I thought of that man touching my face and brushing his hand against my breast. I wanted to kill him. Even when I was a police officer, I never came close to being raped or murdered.

I dried myself off, slipped on a pair of boxer shorts, and carefully pulled a T-shirt over my head.

I called Greg while I was pouring some Cheerios into a bowl.

"Tell me what happened?" he asked when he picked up.

"First, let me know what transpired at the station?"

"They had a million questions, but at the end of the day, they still had no concrete proof. They made it pretty clear that Howie was their main suspect. I tried to point them in another direction. I told them I thought Claire had a lover. I'm pretty sure they didn't appreciate my input. Now tell me what's going on."

I explained what happened from the time I spoke to this guy Pete and the guys that took me.

"The doctor said my ribs are bruised. Nothing broken. I'll just be in slow motion for a little while."

"Do you think you should call the cops?"

"Absolutely not. I don't want them involved."

"What about Claire's lover. Do you think you'll have any luck finding this person?"

"I don't know. My concern right now is that Howie might be having an affair. If he is, I hope the police don't find out."

"Maybe we should get together tomorrow and brainstorm. I can come to your place."

"Too early for that. I'll talk to you later."

Brainstorm my ass. Maybe he thinks if we spend more time together, I'll cave and sleep with him. At one time, I would have done almost anything to sleep with Greg. What Annie said about Greg taking advantage of me, I thought she was wrong at the time, but now I'm not so sure. When we were on the police force, he was technically my boss even though we were partners. I was excited when I was partnered with Greg. I didn't realize at the time that I wanted to please him. Greg probably knew that and used it to his advantage.

The phone startled me.

"Hey, Annie."

"You sound better."

"I slept like the dead. Though I'm still sore, at least I can get around with a minimal amount of pain. Not to worry, since I plan on staying in one more day."

"I need you to be in tip-top shape for the game on Sunday. I'm looking forward to those stadium hot dogs and beer."

I smiled. "And I'm looking forward to the Mets crushing the Dodgers."

"You are so competitive."

"I know and I love it. By the way, I should have that asset search for your client within the next few days."

"I hope we'll have some good news. Talk later."

I got back in bed and turned on the TV. I was flipping through the channels when I came across a Law and Order episode. Wow, I was surprised reruns were on during the day. I watched as Lennie Briscoe and Mike Logan, the main detectives on the show, were following someone hoping that person would lead them to the killer.

Though I was watching, my mind was on the case. If someone poisoned Claire, how did they do it? It would have to be someone who knew her fairly well.

I grabbed a pad and pen from my nightstand and thought about all the people who were close to Claire. There were Sarah James and Paula Frankel, her two friends. I thought I could eliminate them. Howie was still high on my list. Howie's partner, Gavin Stone, probably didn't know her well enough, and what would his motive be? Who else was in Claire's life? What about Dana Thomas, the young woman Claire worked with at the boutique? Again, I couldn't see what possible motive she would have.

I had to keep an open mind, but finding out the name of Claire's lover was my top priority. That, and confirming Howie was having an affair. If he was, it wouldn't help his case, but at least we wouldn't be blindsided if the police found out and we were in the dark.

I must have fallen asleep. I heard this buzzing sound and couldn't imagine who was at my door, when I finally realized it was my phone.

"Hello," I said in a groggy voice.

"You sound half asleep."

"I took half a painkiller and must have fallen back to sleep."

"Are you feeling any better?" Jesse asked.

"I'm still pretty sore but the good news is I'm not in as much pain."

"I thought I would come over tomorrow evening instead of Saturday morning."

"I'd like that. But don't expect a home-cooked dinner in my condition."

"Was that intended to be a joke?"

"How about we bring in Chinese?"

"Why don't I come with groceries and cook us dinner."

"I like your plan better."

"I bet you do."

"You know you have to be exceptionally nice to me in my condition."

"I'll keep that in mind. I'll see you around 7:00 p.m. Stay out of trouble until then."

"Will do."

Why couldn't I tell Jesse what that guy did to me? If his buddy hadn't stopped him, he would have raped me. I pulled the covers tightly around my neck, my body shivering just thinking about what could have happened.

CHAPTER 22

Jesse came the next evening with two bags full of groceries. I don't think I've ever bought that many groceries at one time in my entire life.

"How are you feeling?" he said, as he gently kissed me on the lips.

"Still sore, but I'll live."

I poured each of us a glass of wine as Jesse was preparing dinner. I did my part and watched.

"Are you sure you can mix wine with painkillers?" Jesse asked.

"I haven't taken one since this morning. I'll be okay."

"Annie would be very disappointed if we missed the game on Sunday. I know she's looking forward to those stadium hot dogs," Jesse said, grinning.

"One glass, I promise. You know I think you would have made a wonderful chef," I said. "Did you ever entertain it as a career?"

"No, cooking for me is kind of therapeutic, but I never wanted to be a chef. Most of the time growing up, it was just me and my mother. When she was cooking, she put me to work. I had to wash and chop the vegetables. I saw how she combined different ingredients, and I guess I picked up my cooking skills from her."

"I can't say my mother was a great cook, not even a good cook. She made simple meals. It was my father that did most of the cooking. When Aunt Jenny came to live with me, she rarely cooked. She worked odd shifts at the hospital, so I usually brought something in or ate at Annie's house."

"I can teach you."

"No thanks. I think I'll pass." Jesse tried to suppress a smile.

Jesse made a delicious meal of shrimp with grilled vegetables in a light garlic and wine sauce.

"I met with Claire's only living relative, her Aunt Grace, her father's sister," I said, as we sat down to eat.

"Did she say why she didn't want to raise Claire?"

"She was young and her career was just taking off. She was traveling a lot and didn't think she could take care of Claire. I got the impression she regrets her decision. From what her aunt said, Claire wanted to keep their relationship a secret. She did say something interesting. She thought Claire married Howie because she would feel safe with him, not because she was deeply in love with him."

"Claire's foundation sounds pretty rocky. I can see how she might feel that way after losing her parents at such a young age and then having to grow up in foster care. She probably needed to be with someone who would take care of her and make her feel protected."

"I guess I can't compare myself to Claire. She lost her parents at seven and then she had to go into foster care. I was fortunate to be adopted at birth and have parents who loved me."

"That's true, but I can't imagine what it was like for you at only twelve to lose your parents in an automobile accident while you were in the backseat when it happened."

"I'm grateful I have little memory of that night, though I could never understand how cruel life could be, taking them away from me."

"We know life isn't always fair. I wish it were," Jesse said, lightly touching my hand.

"Let's get back to the aunt," I said, feeling a little uncomfortable focusing on my past. "She advised Claire to divorce Howie because she felt he would put them in financial ruin because of his gambling problems. She didn't know if Claire confronted him before she died."

"Does she have an opinion on whether Howie could have killed Claire?"

"She doesn't, though she did say she thought Howie wasn't a bad guy for whatever that's worth. I think the person who poisoned Claire was someone she knew, since there was no forced entry, according to the police report."

"Unfortunately, that doesn't narrow it down. There does seem to be quite a bit of circumstantial evidence against Howie," Jesse said.

"But if he didn't know about the baby, why would he kill her? There could be someone out there who may have felt threatened and wanted Claire dead. Unfortunately, I'm no closer to knowing who that person is than when I started."

"You only have Howie's word that he didn't know about the baby. You'll figure it out."

I winced as I felt a pain when I moved.

"Are you okay?"

"Yeah, just a slight twinge."

"Do you want to talk about it?"

"I've told you everything. There's no point in going over it again."

"Well, I'm here if you want to talk."

"Thank you," I said, kissing Jesse on the lips.

***

On Saturday, we stayed in and played chess. Jesse is slightly better than me and with my competitive nature, it drives me crazy. For dinner, we brought in Italian food from a neighborhood restaurant.

At the Mets game on Sunday, I came prepared with my baseball mitt. I noticed Jesse grinning when he saw me bringing it with me, though he didn't say a word. I hadn't been to a ball game in a very long time. Unfortunately, baseball games don't have the same allure as they once had when my father and I went together.

I was still enthusiastic, yelling at the umpire when I thought he made a lousy call or cheering when the Mets got on base. Annie kept shouting to the guy who was selling the hot dogs: "Hot dog man, over here." Both Jesse and Doug thought all of this was very amusing. I had a good time. The field was as beautiful as I remembered it. I was happy that the Mets won a close game—the only thing missing was my father whispering in my ear the players' names as they were coming up to bat.

CHAPTER 23

I walked Jesse to his car on Monday morning. As we said goodbye, I held Jesse tightly for a few moments and then watched him drive away. I still wasn't sure if Jesse was okay that I was working with Greg, but I was thankful he didn't bring it up again, at least for the time being.

I went back upstairs to shower. I was feeling a lot better, though when I moved in a certain way, I would grimace in pain. It only reminded me of how close I was to being raped.

As I was pouring my second cup of coffee, I tried to concentrate on what was ahead of me. My plan was to follow Howie. If he was having an affair, I wanted to know. I didn't want to alert his receptionist I was looking for him, so I thought I would take my chances and drive to his office before he left for the day.

I found a spot near Howie's real estate office where I wouldn't be seen when Howie came out, but where I had a clear view of the front door. At 7:12 p.m., both Howie and his partner Gavin exited their building. They spoke for a few minutes, then Howie got into his car.

Since I'm not that familiar with the roads in this area, I wasn't sure where we were headed. At some point, I realized Howie was not going in the direction of his house. We were taking backroads, which made it more difficult to follow him. I didn't want to get too close, but I didn't want to lose him either.

I watched as Howie finally stopped in front of a six-story apartment building. I parked down the street and noted the address of the building. While I was figuring out what to do next, I stayed in my car.

I finally got out and stretched. Slowly walking up to the building, I was hoping I wasn't going to bump into Howie coming out. I waited till I saw an elderly man open the front door and quickly slipped in behind him. As I was looking through all the names on the lobby directory, one name popped out: Thomas. There was no first name listed. Thomas was a pretty common last name. Was I right? Could it be the Dana Thomas from the boutique store that he was seeing? If it was her and the police found out, I had no doubt they would arrest Howie with everything else they had on him. I left and headed home.

I parked my car in my building garage. Normally, I don't think twice about walking to the garage elevator, but I was a little uneasy since I was abducted. I quickly looked all around, making sure nobody was about to jump out and attack me.

When I got upstairs, I opened up my computer and did a search on Dana Thomas. There was one listing that came up with an address in Ardsley, New York, the same address I was just at.

I dialed Howie's cell phone number and was surprised he picked up.

"What the hell do you think you're doing?" I said before he had a chance to answer. "Do you realize the police might have you under surveillance? If they find out you're having an affair they'll arrest you."

"What the hell. Were you following me? And it's not what it seems."

"Stop bullshitting me. I don't believe you and neither will the police. We need to talk tomorrow," I said and hung up.

Why are people so stupid? Why would he carry on with Dana now when he was the main suspect in his wife's murder? Obviously, he wasn't thinking with his brain.

***

The following morning, I was out the door by 7:30 a.m. I went over to Howie's place to read him the riot act. My job was to do whatever I could to prove Howie was innocent. Whether I had my doubts didn't matter.

The look on Howie's face when he opened the door was anything but welcoming.

"Tell me what's going on?" I said as we were standing in his hallway.

"When I asked Dana to meet me at the restaurant to see if Claire had said anything to her, that was true. There was nothing going on with Dana before that. I wasn't having an affair with her. She was very sympathetic and a good listener."

"None of that matters. You know what, Howie, for now you're going to have to stop seeing her. As I mentioned, if the police get wind of your relationship, they won't care whether you started seeing Dana before or after Claire died. Can you understand that? I suggest you stop calling her too. The police can track your calls. I'm not kidding with you, Howie. This is serious. If you're a suspect and they find out you've been having an affair, they won't be so nice and ask you any more questions. They'll just arrest you. When this is over, you can do what the hell you want. Do we understand each other?"

I could tell Howie was not happy with me. Did I care? I didn't want my investigation screwed up.

"You're a big boy, Howie. You'll live. I think you realize the consequences if you keep seeing Dana. By the way, I spoke with Claire's aunt. Apparently, they were in communication with each other, but for some reason Claire wanted to keep their relationship a secret."

"I didn't know," Howie said with a chilly attitude.

"Her aunt told me she had encouraged Claire to leave you because of your gambling problems."

His eyebrows shot up.

"Did she ask you for a divorce?"

"No. We fought about my gambling situation but that was it."

"That's a pretty mild interpretation of what was going on. Do you have any clue how these people could screw with you and make your life a living hell?" Howie didn't answer. "I suggest you seek help."

I left Howie wondering if he was going to heed my advice. While driving back to the city, I called Greg.

"I found out that Howie has been having an affair with this woman Dana who worked at the boutique shop with Claire," I said, when Greg answered.

"Oh great! I got more bad news. I just heard from my source in the police department. The DNA sample taken from the fetus revealed that Howie is not the father of Claire's baby."

"Shit! What now?"

"We'll have to wait and see. The police might want to gather more evidence before they bring him in again."

"I think you should be the bearer of this news," I said.

"Yeah, I'll tell him. Did you mention to Howie you found out about his affair?"

"I read him the riot act and told him to put an end to it. In the meantime, we need to find out who Claire was having an affair with. If it comes to a trial, this person would be a viable suspect as an alternative to Howie. But right now, I'm at a loss on how we can find out who this person is," I said.

When I got into my office, the first thing I did was check my emails. I noticed an email from my source that does my asset searches. I opened it up and downloaded the report. Annie was going to be very happy when she saw the results of the search. Her client's husband had been a naughty boy, stashing money away in several different banks. *This guy's probably thinking he got away with hiding money from his wife. He's in for a big surprise.*

I sent an email to Annie attaching the report and wrote to her that Christmas had come very early for her client.

As I sent it off, my phone buzzed.

"Is this Maddie Landon, the private investigator?"

"Yes, can I help you?"

"I have some information that I think you would be interested in."

"Okay, I'm listening."

"No, not over the phone. You never know who's listening."

I thought this person might be both paranoid and a kook.

"Can I at least know your name before I agree to meet you?"

"It's Toni with an 'i'. My last name is Jones."

I didn't actually believe that was her real name. "Where would you like to meet?"

"Bryant Park. I'll be sitting at a table closest to the entrance by Sixth Avenue and Forty-second Street. I'll be wearing a Yankee's baseball cap turned backward. Be there in an hour."

"I'll see you then." Besides the fact I hated all the cloak and dagger, she might be a Yankee fan.

I headed out and took a cab to Bryant Park. The eastern half of the park is occupied by the main branch of the New York Public Library. The western half contains a lawn, shaded walkways, meeting tables, snack bars, and restaurants.

I got there early since I wanted to spot her as she was coming into the park. Fifteen minutes later, a woman with a Yankees cap turned backward sat down. She looked harmless, but for all I knew, she could have a gun stashed in her handbag. Now who was being paranoid?

I approached her slowly. She must have sensed me coming, since she looked up as I was nearing her table.

"Toni Jones?"

"Please sit. I want to thank you for coming. I'm sorry for all the secrecy but you can't be too careful."

"Why am I here?"

"I know who you are, and I know you're investigating the murder of Claire Stevenson."

"How do you know that?"

"Let's just say, a friend of a friend."

For the sake of finding out what she had to say, I didn't push any further.

"Go on."

"About a year ago, I bought a house from Howie Stevenson. Well, actually from his partner, Gavin Stone. Not too long after I moved in, I had a call from Mr. Stone. He wanted to know if everything was okay with the house, and as a thank you, he wanted to buy me a drink. I thought it was a little odd but what the heck.

"At first everything was going well. We had drinks and some appetizers at a local restaurant near me. Since he seemed like a gentleman, I invited him back to my house for a glass of wine. We were having a nice time. Then he kissed me but I didn't want it to go any further. He kissed me again, this time harder. I pushed him away and told him we should call it a night. He wasn't taking no for an answer. I finally threatened to call the cops and that's when he backed down. He left and that was the end of it."

"Why are you telling me this?"

"I just thought you should know."

It sounded more like a warning.

"Well, I appreciate you coming forward."

"Good luck with your investigation." And with that, she got up and left.

That was weird. I didn't know what to infer from her story. She could have been making it up if she had some sort of grievance against Gavin Stone. Did I believe her? I wasn't sure. Even if I did, what did this have to do with Claire's death? I didn't see the connection.

CHAPTER 24

Whether I believed Toni Jones or not, I wanted to confront Gavin Stone.

"Mr. Stone, it's Maddie Landon," I said when he answered. "Would you happen to have a few minutes to speak with me sometime today?"

"I guess. What is this about?"

"Just some follow-up questions."

"I have some free time about 2:00 p.m. Actually, I'll be in the city so I can swing by your office."

"You have the address?"

"Yes. It's on your business card."

"Right. I'll see you later."

Gavin Stone walked into my office a little after two o'clock, casually dressed in khakis and a black cotton T-shirt.

"Thank you for coming in. Please sit. Will you join me in a cup of coffee?"

"Yes, black, no sugar."

I was debating how to pursue my line of questioning without him feeling ambushed. I'm not sure I had enough subtlety to pull it off.

"How is your investigation going?" he asked.

"Howie's lucky you gave him an alibi or else he would be in jail right now."

I noticed him shift slightly in his seat.

"I had this weird conversation with a woman named Toni Jones. Does the name sound familiar?"

"I never heard of her."

"Are you sure? She said she purchased a house from your real estate firm about a year ago. You sold it to her."

"I sold a house to someone named Toni James, not Jones."

I wonder why she lied about her last name?

"She said you took her out for a thank you drink, and then went back to her house, where things got out of hand."

"What did she say?"

"That you got aggressive and wouldn't leave until she threatened to call the police."

"That's not the way I remember it. And what has that got to do with Howie or Claire for that matter?"

"I was curious why this woman contacted me."

"Look, I don't know exactly what she said but she came on to me. I left as soon as I realized she wasn't playing with a full deck. I didn't need some wacko calling the police and telling them I tried to rape her."

"So she was making all this up?"

"I don't know what to tell you. Is this why you wanted to speak with me?"

"That's one of the reasons. The last time we spoke, you told me that Howie had never mentioned to you that his wife was having an affair. It seems a little odd that being partners he didn't confide in you."

"Maybe he was embarrassed that his wife was cheating on him."

"That must be it. Well, thank you for coming in. I'm sorry about the situation with this woman Toni. Clearly she wanted to make trouble for you." Did I believe what I said to Gavin Stone? No, but he didn't have to know that.

"I hope you find out who killed Claire," he said as he was walking out the door.

"One last question. What time did you say Howie left the bar the day Claire died?"

"I think it was a little before 9:00 p.m.," he said, though he didn't sound very confident.

"Well, thank you again."

There was definitely something going on with Mr. Stone. He was lying about something. I just wasn't sure what.

At 4:30 p.m. I headed to the boutique shop in Scarsdale. I wanted to take another run at Dana Thomas now that I knew she and Howie had been seeing each other.

I waited outside the store until I saw Ms. Thomas closing up for the night. She saw me and looked the other way.

"Ms. Thomas, can I have a word please?"

"What do you want?" she said in an irritated manner.

"I noticed there's a Starbucks right by the train station. Can I buy you a cup of coffee? I know you might be angry with me because I told Howie not to see you for now. I understand that might be upsetting, but it's better than him winding up in jail if the police found out. Don't you agree?"

She seemed to relax a little. We walked toward Starbucks. We each got a cup of coffee and sat down outside on their back deck.

"So when did you and Howie start seeing each other?"

There was a slight hesitation before she answered.

"Not too long after his wife died."

"So it's a fairly new relationship?"

"I guess."

"He was with you the day Claire died, not with his partner. Isn't that right?"

"What are you talking about?"

"I'm talking about the fact that you were having an affair with Howie before Claire died." I took a gamble that I was right.

"Howie wouldn't have cheated on his wife if she wasn't cheating on him. He knew about the affair, so what was the harm?"

"Howie lied to the police and so did his partner."

"He was afraid how it would look if the police knew he was having an affair. You can understand," she said with a defiant look.

"Yes I can, but if the police find out, how do you think it will look to them?"

"We just didn't know what to do. I'm sorry."

"Does Howie have any idea who Claire was having an affair with?"

"No. I'm positive."

As we walked out, I turned to Ms. Thomas. "I meant what I said to both you and Howie. Stay away from each other or I'll go to the police myself."

I picked up the phone to update Greg on the situation.

"Maddie, any good news?" Greg said, as soon as he answered.

"Actually, it gets worse. I found out that Howie was with Dana Thomas the day Claire died."

"So he lied to us when he said he didn't start seeing her till after Claire died."

"That about sums it up, plus both he and Gavin Stone lied to the police about Howie's alibi." I needed to speak with Howie at some point. Was it possible Claire found out about his affair and demanded a divorce?

"Okay. Let's keep this to ourselves for now. Anything more about Claire's lover? That would really help Howie."

"None of the people I spoke with could give me a name. I can't believe there isn't someone who knows."

"Did you canvass everyone in the area where they live?"

"I spoke to two neighbors."

"Go back and speak with the other neighbors. Maybe somebody saw something."

"I got nothing else going on at the moment. I might as well."

By the time I got home, I was tired and frustrated. I looked in my refrigerator and saw I had some tuna fish salad. I made a sandwich and added some potato chips to my plate.

I turned on the TV and watched the news. They were interviewing a family whose son was taken a few years ago and was recently found dead. I cringed listening to it. It brought me back to my parents and what they wanted for me, to locate my biological parents.

Though I now knew my biological mother died, I had no idea who my father was and if he was still living. I needed to find out. I wanted to take a break from the case, so I decided I would drive down to Philadelphia in the morning and introduce myself to an aunt I'd never known. The thought sent chills through my body.

CHAPTER 25

I left early the next morning. Lucy Grainger lived in Chestnut Hill, an affluent area in Philadelphia. I set my GPS to Ms. Grainger's address. The drive took about an hour and forty-five minutes. Fortunately, traffic was going in the other direction.

The street she lived on was lined with beautiful oak trees and brownstones. I parked on the opposite side of her street and turned off the engine. Now that I had come all this way, my legs wouldn't move and my stomach was doing flip-flops. I could sit here and wait until she came out, but then what? Maybe she wasn't home. For all I knew, she could be in the south of France. *Okay, Landon, quit stalling. Only one way to find out.*

I slowly got out of the car and walked across the street. I stared at her front door for what seemed like an eternity. Then I walked up the five steps, and with my finger shaking, I rang the doorbell.

The brown wooden door opened, and I saw the look on this woman's face. For a moment, she just stared at me.

"OH MY GOD! You are beautiful! I was hoping this day would come."

I wasn't sure how to respond.

"I didn't mean to overwhelm you. Please come in," she said. "I don't even know your name."

"It's Maddie, Maddie Landon." Lucy Grainger had my green eyes. She looked at least ten years younger than her sixty years. My right leg was shaking.

"That's a pretty name. When you were born, my sister, your mother, named you Emma, but Maddie suits you. You must have a million questions. Please sit down."

My mouth was dry. "Do you think I can have a glass of water?"

"Of course."

The living room was warm and inviting, done in soft colors of beige and light blue. While she went into the kitchen, I picked up a photo that was on a table behind the couch. I knew as soon as I looked at it that I was staring at my mother. Chills went right through me. Those green eyes were my eyes.

"You look just like her," she said, startling me as she handed me a glass of water.

"How did she die?"

"It was very sad. Her appendix ruptured and she died of sepsis."

And then I just blurted out: "Why did she abandon me?"

"Lydia was only sixteen when she got pregnant. Our parents were very religious and the scandal would have been too much for them. They didn't want to raise the baby. Your mother was heartbroken. They sent Lydia to live with an aunt in South Carolina until you were born. When Lydia finally married, she was ashamed to tell her husband that she had a baby out of wedlock. That's why she never looked for you. She was always so conflicted. The adoption attorney told Lydia that her baby was going to a wonderful couple, both teachers that could provide for you."

"What about my father? I was told he wasn't listed on the original birth certificate."

"She never told us who he was. We thought that maybe he was into drugs or in a gang."

"I see." I was having trouble digesting what my aunt was telling me.

"When my sister died, I contacted Mr. Logan's office and told his receptionist. I wanted him to know in case you ever decided to look for her. He must have shared that information with you."

"He did. When you called the attorney's office, why didn't you leave your name?"

"I was stupid. I got cold feet. I'm sorry."

Was there something she wasn't telling me?

"So her husband never knew I existed?"

"Right before Lydia died, she told her husband she had a baby. It's a shame she couldn't bring herself to tell him years ago. I only hope you can forgive her."

"How come she never had any other children?"

"I don't know. We never discussed it, but maybe her husband can provide that answer."

"I'd like to try and find my father. Do you remember any of Lydia's friends from childhood that I could get in contact with?"

"There was someone she was very close to. Give me a day or so."

"Thank you."

"Have you had breakfast? I thought if you could stay a little while, we could get something to eat."

"I'm okay with that."

We drove to a cute coffee house a few miles from Lucy's place. When I looked at the menu, they basically served breakfast and lunch. The waitress came and we ordered.

"Without prying too much, can you tell me a little bit about yourself?" Lucy said.

"Well, I'm a private investigator." I didn't want to get into the fact that I was a former police officer and why I left the police force. "I live in Manhattan on the Upper West Side." I wasn't sure what else to say.

"What about family?"

"My parents died when I was twelve in an automobile accident. My mother's sister came to live with me." I could see tears in Lucy's eyes.

"I'm so sorry. I wish I could have been there for you. I can't imagine what you must have gone through."

I remained quiet.

"What were your parents like?"

"They were both teachers, which you already knew. They were wonderful parents. I was very fortunate."

"Do you have any other family?"

"I have a first cousin who's been like a big brother to me. He's married with a young son, Noah. They're my family. Unfortunately, my aunt died when I was nineteen."

"I can understand why you might want to find out what happened to your birth father. Are you married?"

"No. I have a boyfriend, Jesse, who's also a private investigator. Are you married?"

"I've been divorced for several years now. I date, but right now no one I can see for the long distance."

"What kind of work do you do?"

"I'm an analyst at a brokerage firm."

"I like to know my money is safe in the bank."

"At your age, you should invest in some good growth stocks. If you're interested, I could make some suggestions."

"Maybe. I'll have to think about it." I knew that wasn't going to happen.

"You know your mother became a teacher because of you. I think it had something to do with the fact your parents were teachers. It breaks my heart she'll never know you. I'm really happy you came to see me. I'm hoping we can get to know each other a little better."

I was at a loss for words.

"Do you think Lydia's husband would mind if I went to see him? I'd like to ask him a few questions."

"I think he'd be happy to meet you."

"I'd like to talk to him before I go back today. Where can I reach him?"

"He's probably at work. He's an accountant at a small firm about twenty minutes from here. I can't imagine he won't make time to see you."

We drove back to Lucy's house and said goodbye outside. I could tell she wanted to say more but something stopped her. There were tears running down her cheeks. "I'm so sorry." She hugged me and told me she'd be in touch.

As I drove away, she waved. After all these years, I wasn't sure how I should feel. Maybe I was expecting too much from myself.

I stopped to get gas and called Scott Reed.

"Mr. Reed," I said when he answered. "My name's Maddie Landon."

"Yes, Maddie. Lucy said you might call."

"I'm in Philadelphia and I was wondering if I could see you?"

"Of course. Where are you now?"

"I'm somewhere in Chestnut Hill."

"Why don't I come to you? There's a park not far from where you are where we could sit and talk. They also have vendors that sell food if you're hungry."

He gave me directions to the main entrance of the park. He said he could be there in thirty minutes. I found a parking spot and waited in the car for a while and then walked to the main entrance of the park. About fifteen minutes later, I saw a man in a suit walking toward me.

"Maddie, hi."

Scott Reed was probably in his early sixties. He looked like the actor Tom Hanks.

"If I'm staring, I'm sorry. It's just that you look so much like Lydia. Before we sit, would you like anything to eat?"

"How about one of those large soft pretzels and a coffee."

"Can I talk you into mustard on that pretzel?" he said.

"Why not?"

He smiled.

After Mr. Reed got us each a pretzel and coffee, we parked ourselves on a bench.

"I hope Lucy didn't bombard you with a lot of questions."

"No, she was fine. I asked her why Lydia gave me up for adoption. What did Lydia tell you?"

"That she was young, and her parents, because they were very religious, forced Lydia into giving you away. She told me her parents sent her to live with a relative because of the shame they felt. I want you to know I wish she had told me from the beginning; then maybe you would have been in our lives."

"How come you never had children?"

"I have a problem. I have little to no sperm count. Lydia didn't want to adopt. It wasn't till after she told me what happened that I realized why she never wanted to adopt."

"Why?

"She felt she didn't deserve to have a baby. If only she would have told me during our marriage, everything would have been different." I could see the pain in his eyes.

"She didn't by any chance confide in you who the father was?"

"No, she never did. Do you plan on looking for him?"

"I think so. Ms. Grainger said she would get me the name of Lydia's childhood friend. Maybe this person might know something."

"Perhaps. She did have a good friend from when she was teaching, but I don't know if Lydia would have confided in her. I'll be glad to give you her name."

"Thank you."

"Are there any questions you would like to ask me about your mother?"

"Would it be possible to have this conversation at another time?" I was feeling a little overwhelmed.

"Of course. Can I ask you something?" Scott Reed said.

"Sure," I said slowly.

"Do you have people in your life who love you?"

"Yes."

"Lydia would be happy. I know I'm not your father but you can always count on me if you need anything or you just want to talk."

"Thank you." I was holding back tears.

We chatted about Philadelphia. He told me that he and Lydia used to love to come to New York to see the Broadway shows. They'd make a weekend of it and stay in a hotel. Looking back, he said, he wondered if Lydia had stared at every young woman in the hopes of seeing her daughter.

Scott Reed walked me to my car. He gave me the name of the woman who was friends with Lydia and we said goodbye.

I sat in my car for a few minutes. I couldn't help but feel moved by what Mr. Reed told me. Then a thought occurred to me. If Lydia never told her husband that I existed, maybe she never told my biological father either. Is it possible he never knew about me?

CHAPTER 26

I suddenly had the need to see where Lydia lived growing up. House number 35 was a small wooden-framed home with a red door and a front porch in West Philadelphia. The neighborhood seemed lower middle class. Of course it could have been different more than thirty-something years ago.

I parked, walked up the three steps, and rang the bell. A woman with a young girl hanging from her mother's leg opened the door.

"I'm sorry to bother you. My grandparents lived here many years ago. I was in the area and I remembered all the good times I spent with them. I guess I got nostalgic." I knew I was being deceptive. A professional habit.

"I'm really in a hurry and I have to get ready to leave."

"Would you happen to know anyone on the block who has been living here for quite a long time?"

"To tell you the truth, I really don't know many people in the area. We just moved here about eight months ago." I got the feeling she wanted to get rid of me.

"Well, thank you."

As I approached my car, I noticed an elderly woman with a slight hunchback walking with a cane.

"Hello," I said.

"Oh, hello, dear. I didn't see you. Do you live around here? You don't look familiar."

"No, ma'am. I live in New York City."

"Ah, the Big Apple. What are you doing here?"

"There was a family that lived on this block many years ago, in #35. James and Martha Peterson."

"Oh yes, a lovely couple. They had two pretty girls. I think Mrs. Peterson died about ten years ago, but I can't be sure since my memory is terrible these days. Don't get old, young lady." I smiled. "I think their children moved away a long time ago."

"Were you friendly with the Petersons?"

"Back then, everyone knew each other. Our doors were never locked. We had block parties in the summer. Each of us would make a dish and we'd set it up outside on a few tables. We had so much fun. Now everything has changed. I barely know my next-door neighbor and I always lock my door. The neighborhood has changed. It's such a shame."

"Do you live by yourself?"

"I have someone who comes in and helps me with the cleaning and the groceries. My legs are not so good anymore. My husband, Frank, died three years ago. He was such a dear."

"What can you remember about the Petersons?"

"You ask so many questions. Are you a reporter?"

"Oh no. I promised a friend if I was ever in the neighborhood I'd inquire about them." After I said it, it sounded pretty lame. I thought it better not to mention they were my grandparents. I didn't want to have to explain anything.

"They were church-going people. We went to the same church back then. They raised their children to be good Catholics. The mother was very strict with the girls.

You never know what goes on behind closed doors. I really can't remember too much else."

That was strange. What did she mean by that?

"Well, I appreciate your time. Can I help you with anything?"

"That's very sweet but I'm just getting some exercise."

"It was very nice meeting you. Take care."

On the ride back to the city, I mulled over everything I learned from both Lucy Grainger and Scott Reed. It seems as though my grandparents were very strict Catholics, and the humiliation of having a pregnant daughter was something they couldn't live with. All these years I imagined horrible thoughts about my birth mother. But the reality was she was pregnant at sixteen and wanted to keep me. Instead, her parents sent her away to have her baby. Living with that kind of secret because she was made to feel shame must have been so painful for my mother.

By the time I got home, it was late and I was exhausted. At least I went to sleep with the comfort of knowing that my birth mother wanted me.

***

In the morning, I called Patty Gray, my birth mother's friend from when she taught school.

"Ms. Gray, my name is Maddie Landon. I got your name from Scott Reed, Lydia Reed's husband."

"Oh yes, how is Scott?"

"He's fine. Is this a good time to speak?"

"I'm in the teacher's lounge in between classes. What can I do for you?"

I debated whether I should tell her what my relationship to Lydia was. I didn't want to divulge Lydia's secret if she didn't want anyone to know. I just couldn't think of any other way to ask her what I needed to.

"Before Lydia passed away, she told her husband that she had a baby when she was very young, that her parents forced her to give up for adoption."

"I don't know what to say. Poor Lydia. I always felt she was hiding something."

"How so?"

"Whenever the past was brought up, there was a look that would come over her face. It's hard to describe. It was as if there were dark secrets that she wanted to keep hidden."

"Did she, by any chance, mention a boyfriend she had when she was a teenager, or maybe not necessarily a boyfriend, just a friend?"

"She mentioned a boy she knew from school but never told me his name."

"Was there anything she said about him that you can remember? Did she say if they went to the same school or were in the same grade?"

"Why are you asking all these questions?"

"It's complicated."

"You're Lydia's daughter?"

I wasn't sure what to say. I hope my silence would be enough.

"I got the feeling she didn't want to talk about it, so I didn't push her. It wasn't my place."

"So she never said anything about him?"

"I don't think so. I'm sorry."

"Look, if you remember anything else, will you please contact me?"

"Of course."

I gave Patty Gray my number before we hung up.

My phone rang as I disconnected. I didn't recognize the number.

"Hello."

"Maddie, it's Lucy Grainger."

"Oh, hi." I was surprised to hear from her so soon.

"I couldn't stop thinking about you after you left. I felt bad that I never got to show you more photos of your mother. Anyway, I did find the name of Lydia's childhood friend. Her name was Janie Berg. Unfortunately, I don't know what happened to her, but she lived on the same block as we did. Hopefully that helps."

"It does. By the way, can you tell me what high school Lydia went to?"

"Yes. It was Halsey High School. Why?"

"I was just curious." I didn't want to mention my conversation with Patty Gray.

"Every once in a while, I get up to New York for both business and pleasure. Maybe we can have dinner together some time."

"Yes, that would be nice," was all I could think of saying.

At the moment, I didn't know how I felt about any of this. It was almost as if I didn't feel anything at all.

CHAPTER 27

My phone rang again. It was Greg.

"Maddie, anything to report?"

"Not yet. I need to have another chat with Howie's partner. I'm interested in why he lied for Howie about his alibi. Also, I plan on knocking on some doors later to see if any of Howie's neighbors saw anything. Maybe we'll get lucky. By the way, how did Howie take it when you told him it wasn't his baby?"

"He was devastated."

"Do you believe him when he said he didn't know Claire was pregnant?"

"I want to believe him. Keep me in the loop," he said and hung up.

Greg seemed all business. I wonder if he was backing off. Isn't that what I wanted?

Before going up to Scarsdale to canvass neighbors, I wanted to locate my mother's childhood friend Janie Berg. She might be able to provide more information about this boy that Lucy Grainger mentioned. Now that I knew they went to the same high school, it gave me more to go on, even though it might be a shot in the dark. Still, too many unknowns.

I went into my databases and entered the name Janie Berg along with the street she had lived on many years ago. The report I pulled up listed a Janie Miller in Wilmington, Delaware. I was able to obtain her cell phone number, but I thought it would be best to speak to Janie Miller in person.

I headed up to Scarsdale around 2:00 p.m. I was interested in talking with the next-door neighbor who was interviewed by the police. I heard my phone ringing just as I was about to get out of the car.

"Hey," I said to Annie when I answered. "I'm sorry I didn't call yesterday. I was exhausted by the time I got home. Why don't we catch up and get a drink later."

"I'll meet you at The Dead Poet, say at 6:00 p.m."

"Okay."

As I was closing my car door, I noticed Janice Levy peeking through her living room window. I did a quick wave and knocked on Margo Beck's door. The woman who answered was exotic-looking, with full lips, dark wavy hair, large blue eyes, and a willowy figure.

"Yes, can I help you?"

"My name's Maddie Landon and I'm investigating the death of your neighbor, Claire Stevenson."

"I already spoke to the police."

"I'm not with the police. I'm a private investigator."

"Oh! Did Howie hire you?"

"His attorney did. Can I come in? I'd like to ask you a few questions."

"Please. I can't imagine Howie killed his wife. He loved Claire."

We were sitting in her kitchen. It looked recently remodeled with stainless steel appliances, including a stove that could have come right out of Julia Child's kitchen. I liked the combination of the white wood and glass cabinets.

"Can I get you a cup of coffee?"

Mrs. Beck seemed very self-assured and comfortable in her own skin.

"Yes, thank you, black, no sugar. Why do you think Howie had nothing to do with his wife's death?"

"Just a feeling."

I didn't agree. I thought most people, if they're pushed far enough, were capable of murder. Maybe it's the cop in me talking.

"How long have you known the Stevensons?"

"Since we moved here about six years ago."

"You told the officer who interviewed you that you socialized with the Stevensons."

"Yes, not often, maybe three or four times a year. I never saw anything between them that made me feel uncomfortable. I'm not saying they never disagreed or argued, but what couples don't?"

"Did you ever spend any time with Claire alone?"

"Yes, of course."

"Did you know Claire was having an affair?" I didn't want to mention Howie's affair since as far as I knew, the police hadn't found out yet.

"No, I didn't, but I'm not saying it surprises me."

"What do you mean?"

"There's nothing specific. Claire struck me as someone who kept things to herself. I never quite got the feeling she was completely present when we were together."

I thought that was an interesting observation and not that different from what other people had said about Claire.

"Did you notice anyone besides her husband at the house during the days leading up to her death?"

"I'm sorry, I don't remember."

"Thank you anyway. Here's my card in case you think of something."

As I was on my way to the next house, I saw Janice Levy crossing the street, coming in my direction.

"Hello, Mrs. Levy."

"Please, call me Janice. Did you find out anything more about the mysterious woman at the bar with Mr. Stevenson?"

"I'm sorry I can't talk about an ongoing investigation, but I certainly appreciate your information." I didn't want to alienate her, since a nosy neighbor can have its advantages in an investigation. "But I do have a question." I could see she was eager to hear it. "Did you ever see Mrs. Stevenson with anyone besides her husband?"

"Well of course there's the gardener, but I guess that doesn't count."

"Did you ever see someone in an old car, possibly a classic that may have been parked in front of their house?"

I could tell she was thinking real hard.

"I can't be sure, but if I remember anything, I'll be certain to call you."

"That'll be great." I hope she didn't pick up on my sarcasm.

I knocked on five more doors. Someone was home in two of the houses but had no new information to share about the Stevensons. Well, this was a waste of time. Whoever Claire was involved with, they were very discreet.

CHAPTER 28

I was fortunate to find a parking spot not too far from The Dead Poet. Annie hadn't arrived yet, but the hostess seated me anyway. I ordered a glass of wine while I waited.

"Hi, sweetie," I said as Annie leaned in to kiss my cheek.

"Did you start without me?"

"I just ordered my first glass. I'm starving since I haven't eaten all day."

"Well then, let's get some food in you. I can't have you falling apart on me," Annie said.

When the waitress came over with my wine, Annie ordered a Cosmo and I ordered a few different appetizers.

"Start talking. I want to know everything you found out in the land of brotherly love."

"Well, I met my aunt. She's an analyst for a brokerage firm."

"It appears you come from good stock so far."

I laughed. Always the optimist.

"She told me that my mother was sixteen when she got pregnant. She wanted to raise me but her parents were very religious. The scandal would have been too much on the family if Lydia kept the baby. They actually sent her to live with an aunt in South Carolina until I was born."

"Wow, that poor girl."

"It gets even worse. Because of the shame her parents made her feel, she never told her husband about the baby until she was dying."

"That's awful. Did you meet her husband?"

"I did. I really liked him. He seemed like a lovely man and was genuinely happy to meet me."

"I can tell that something's bothering you."

"I'm just not sure how I feel about having a relationship with my aunt. I mean, I liked her, and she was so thrilled that I came to see her. But I don't feel any connection to my aunt. Isn't that weird. Shouldn't I feel something?"

"You just met the woman. I think you expect too much from yourself. The good news is you don't have to decide now. Don't stress about it."

"You're right. Also, I might have a slim lead on who my father might be. From a coworker when my mother was a teacher, I was told there was a boy in the picture at that time. Apparently, they went to the same high school. I tracked down a childhood girlfriend of my birth mother who now lives in Delaware. I want to go down there and talk to her. Maybe she knows more. Also, I was thinking if I could get a hold of Lydia's high school yearbook, maybe someone could identify him. It's a long shot since he may not even be my father, but that's the best I got at the moment."

"When do you plan on going?"

"I was thinking that I'd rope Jesse into going with me this weekend."

"I still can't believe what Lydia's parents did to her. She must have been heartbroken."

"Maybe it was meant to work out the way it did," I said.

"Is that your way of protecting yourself from getting hurt?"

"Maybe you're in the wrong profession. Instead of a lawyer, you should have been a therapist."

"I'm positive Dr. Goldberg would tell you exactly what I said."

"I'll let you know when I see her on Monday. How's everything at the Law Offices of Greene and Berger?"

"Business is slowly building. I actually feel less stress than when I was working for my boss. I always felt pressure that I had to bring in new clients, otherwise my boss wasn't happy with me."

"Oh, I almost forgot. Greg found out that Howie is not the father of Claire's baby."

"Wow. This just gets better and better."

After we each had another drink and finished our appetizers, we shared an Uber home. As soon as I got in, I called Jesse.

"Hey, pretty boy."

"Is that your idea of foreplay?"

"If that works for you. How would you like to spend an all-inclusive paid weekend in Wilmington, Delaware?"

"I do like the sound of all-inclusive."

"I thought you would."

"What's going on?"

I recounted everything that I found out in Philadelphia.

"Please don't say you're sorry and all that other crap," I said to Jesse.

"I wasn't going to."

"Good. Are you game for this weekend?"

"Count me in. I'll be there bright and early on Saturday."

"I've had two glasses of wine, so I apologize in advance if I say anything crazy."

"I kind of like you when you've had a bit too much."

"Oh yeah! I'll remember those words. How are things in your neck of the woods?"

"Kind of boring without you."

"You do know how to charm a girl. I won't book a hotel room since I'm not sure where we'll wind up. I'm guessing getting a room won't be a problem."

"You're in charge. I'm just in it for the free food and whatever else this weekend includes." I laughed. "I'll see you Saturday. Love you."

"Right back at you."

***

I was up very early the next day and went for a run. By mile two, my side was hurting. I didn't want to push it since I hadn't run since my encounter with my kidnappers. It still rattles me just thinking about it. On my way back, the sun was peeking through.

"Ms. Maddie, you're up early."

"Hi, Louis. I wanted to get a run in before I started my day. How's the world treating you?"

"I got up, put my pants on one leg at a time, then slipped on my shoes; then I got to see you. So, I say things are pretty good."

"Well, I'm off to fight crime. Have a good weekend."

"Be careful out there."

I quickly showered, had breakfast, and was out the door. I was in front of Gavin Stone's house by 8:30. Stone lives in Rye, New York, which is situated on the Long Island Sound in Westchester County, about thirty-five miles north of the city. There was a black Audi in the driveway. On my tippy toes, I peeked into the window of his two-car garage and saw another car.

I rang the doorbell twice before the door opened.

"I'm just on my way out. What are you doing here?" he said with a surprised look on his face.

"I need a minute of your time."

"What's going on?" he said as he barely opened the door to let me in.

"You could be in serious trouble. You lied to the police about Howie's alibi. Why did you do it?"

"What are you talking about?"

"Stop playing games. His girlfriend gave him up."

"Are you going to report me?"

"First, answer my question."

"Howie asked me to. He knew it would look bad if the police found out he was having an affair."

"So you knew about the affair?"

"I'm sorry I couldn't tell you. Howie asked me not to."

"You believed Howie when he told you he was with Dana?"

"Why wouldn't I?"

"You got to be kidding me. You really have no clue?"

"No, I believed him," Gavin said with a concerned look on his face. "You think he killed Claire?"

"It never crossed your mind?" I asked.

Gavin didn't answer me.

"Are you going to tell the police?"

"I'll think about it."

Maybe he'll have some sleepless nights. He deserves to worry.

"Aren't you supposed to be on Howie's side?"

"I am on Howie's side, but I still need to know the truth."

"I have a client that I'm showing a house to in forty-five minutes. I have to get going. Again, I'm sorry I lied to you."

As he was about to drive off, I stopped him.

"I noticed you have a second car."

"Oh yeah. I usually drive it on the weekends."

"What kind of car is it?"

"It's an old model Mercedes. Look, I gotta go," he said, driving off.

CHAPTER 29

Before heading to my office, I tried taking another look into the garage, but it was too dark inside and I could barely reach the narrow window to see anything.

My phone rang as I was getting into my car.

"Hello."

"Ms. Landon, this is Paula Frankel, Claire's friend."

"Yes. How are you?"

"I'm okay. I was calling because I thought more about our recent conversation. You said I should contact you if I recalled anything."

"I'm listening."

"Claire was worried about something. It didn't have anything to do with Howie's gambling debts. It was something else."

"She could have been worried that she was pregnant," I said.

"Actually, it was more like she was afraid of someone."

"Why do you say that?"

"It was something she had mentioned a while ago. She told me she had made a mistake and gotten involved with someone she realized could be dangerous. She only saw him a few times, but he wasn't very happy when she told him it was over."

"Was she afraid he was going to hurt her?"

"That I don't know. I only know he had called her in the past few months."

"Did Claire happen to say if he left any threatening messages?"

"If he did, she didn't mention it to me."

"Is there anything else you can remember?"

"I don't think so. If only she would have confided in me. She seemed so lost. I wish I could have helped her."

"Sometimes it's hard to admit to someone we're close to how things really are. Thank you for contacting me."

"Please let me know what you find out."

What if the person she was afraid of killed Claire and the father of her unborn baby was someone else? Why so many secrets?

***

Saturday morning Jesse was at my apartment by 8:30.

"Well, you are a man of your word. You did say you'd be here early," I said, kissing Jesse as he came in.

"I didn't have a chance to eat. I'm starving."

"I thought we'd pick up some breakfast at the deli down the street and take it with us. It'll save some time."

"I'm okay with that."

We picked up egg sandwiches on hard rolls and coffee and headed to Delaware in Jesse's black Honda.

"So how are things going with your ex-partner?" Jesse said.

"We've only seen each other once and that was to go over the reports Greg was able to obtain from someone inside the police department."

"Where's his office?"

Why did he have to ask me that?

"He doesn't have an office as yet. I had to look through the reports at his apartment. It was strictly business," I said, rubbing Jesse's leg.

"I trust you. It's him I don't trust."

"I can handle myself. I'm a big girl."

"Yes, you are. And stop rubbing my leg if you don't want us to get into an accident."

"Aye, aye, sir. By the way, I found out that both Howie and his partner Gavin Stone lied to the police about Howie's alibi. It turns out Howie was allegedly with his girlfriend at the approximate time his wife was dying. Howie told his partner to lie for him because he didn't want the police to know he was having an affair. I'm just hoping the police don't find out."

"What, that he lied about his alibi or the affair?"

"Obviously both. They'll definitely arrest him if they do. And another tidbit, Howie is not the baby's father."

"What's your take? Do you think Howie killed his wife?"

"I go back and forth. It seems Claire had ended an affair she was having a while ago and from what I was told, this guy, whoever he is, may have been harassing her."

"She did get around."

"Yeah. You're right about that. I really don't think she was promiscuous. I think she was troubled."

"That's another take on it."

We arrived in front of Janie Miller's house by 11:45 a.m. It was a brick ranch home on about a half-acre of land. We walked up the paved walkway and knocked on the door. A man answered.

"Can I help you?"

"I was looking for Janie Miller. I was told she was a childhood friend of Lydia Reed."

"That's true, but who are you?" The man I was looking at appeared to be in his fifties, tall, good-looking, with high cheekbones and a dimple in his chin.

"Lydia was my mother."

He looked as if he had just seen a ghost.

"Come in. My name's Paul, Janie's husband. Janie," he shouted, "we have company."

Janie walked into the room and looked straight at me as if she was trying to decide if she knew me from somewhere.

"Honey, this is Lydia's daughter."

"Oh my god! I can't believe it. You look so much like her. It's uncanny."

Janie had an athletic body. Maybe a runner. She had a wholesome, outdoorsy look.

"This is my boyfriend, Jesse." Jesse and Paul shook hands.

"Where did you guys drive from?" Paul said.

"New York," Jesse said. Janie kept staring at me.

"I can't believe you're here," Janie said. "You spoke to Lucy?"

"Yes. She's the one who told me that you and Lydia were childhood friends. Were you in contact with Lydia?"

"Yes. We didn't see each other often but we spoke on the phone all the time. Besides her parents and her sister, I was the only other person who knew about the baby. It bonded us forever. I know you must have questions, but I have questions too."

"Look," Paul said, "it's lunchtime. Would you like to stay? We can grill hamburgers and hot dogs and sit outside on the patio."

"We would love for you to stay for a while," Janie chimed in.

Jesse and I looked at each other. "If you're sure, we'll take you up on your offer."

"Great. Why don't we move this outside on the patio," Paul said. "How about some wine, if it's not too early for you guys."

"No," Jesse and I said in unison.

While the hamburgers and hot dogs were being grilled, we chatted. Well, mostly they chatted about how they wound up in Wilmington. We finally sat down to eat. The back of the house was surrounded by woods. It was quiet, with no other houses close by.

"How did you find out that Lydia was your birth mother?" Janie asked.

"It's sort of a long story. The very short version is through the adoption attorney. My adoptive parents provided me with the attorney's name." That seemed to satisfy her.

"I really don't mean to be nosy, but can I ask why you waited all these years to look for Lydia?"

"I had my reasons, which I'd rather not get into now."

"I'm sorry if I made you uncomfortable. Please forgive me."

"No need to apologize. I heard there was a boy who Lydia liked in high school. Would you happen to remember his name?"

"Brian Gates," she said, without hesitating. "Wow, that brings back so many memories."

"What do you remember about him?"

"He was very cute. Lydia was shy around boys, but boys liked her. She was so pretty. I have photos to show you. Brian lived two blocks away, so we all knew each other and went to the same schools. I knew he liked Lydia. I could tell since he would make a point of walking by when we were sitting outside in front of Lydia's house."

"Do you think this boy Brian got her pregnant?"

"She never told me who it was."

"Would you happen to have a yearbook from when you graduated high school? I'd like to see what this boy Brian looked like."

"I think it's in the family room. Hold on a second and I'll get it."

A few minutes later, Janie came back with her yearbook.

"This is your mother."

It looked similar to the photo I saw at my aunt's house. It was almost painful to look at. Jesse leaned over to look at my mother's photo.

"She was very pretty," Jesse said.

"This is Brian Gates, the boy I mentioned."

I was trying to see if we had any of the same features, but I couldn't be sure from the small photo. He wore glasses so it was hard to see the color or shape of his eyes. His sandy-colored wavy hair was parted off to the side. Unfortunately, I had no clue whether this boy was my father. I handed the book back to Janie.

"What I'm trying to figure out is what people thought happened to Lydia when she was gone for all those months."

"There's something I have to tell you. Something no one else besides Lydia and I knew."

CHAPTER 30

"First, I have to tell you about Lydia's parents. They were very strict Catholics. The girls weren't allowed to date or wear makeup. When Lydia found out she was pregnant, she told her parents she was raped."

"WHAT! Why?"

"She was afraid. She didn't know how her parents would react. It's hard to understand if you don't come from a family with god-fearing parents. She thought if she told them she was raped they couldn't blame her. Don't forget, she was only sixteen and she was so scared."

"But didn't she think her parents would go to the police?"

"No. She believed her parents would be too ashamed for them and Lydia. She was right. They never reported it. Lydia had told her parents she never saw the person's face and didn't want to go to the police. No one knew except me and Lydia that she wasn't raped. I kept that secret until now."

"Still, people must have wondered what happened to her."

"Her parents told everyone that Lydia was having behavioral problems, so they had to send her to live with her aunt in South Carolina to straighten her out. No one knew about her pregnancy, and she never told anyone as far as I know."

I didn't know what to say or think. All the shame and lies Lydia had to live with.

"I'm sorry you had to find out. I can tell you this much. She never wanted to give you up. It broke her heart."

I was forcing myself to hold back the tears.

"What happened when she got back from South Carolina?"

"She went on with her life as if nothing happened. It wasn't until she finally moved out and went to college that she got her life back. She started seeing a therapist during that time. But even though she was in a better place, you always weighed on her mind."

I didn't want to cry but I could feel my eyes misting. Jesse put his hand on my knee.

"When Lydia was dying, she told her husband everything. He said he wished Lydia would have told him sooner and then they could have looked for you. I think he was hurt that she never confided in him until the end, though I'm glad she finally unburdened herself," Janie said. "It's a shame she never got to meet you. I could see her face now. She would have been over the moon."

At this point, I was emotionally drained and didn't want to talk about family anymore. I think her husband Paul saw that in my face. He changed the subject and asked us about New York.

After lunch, I was anxious to leave. I was thankful that Janie didn't bring out any other photos of my mother, though she did give me one photo of Lydia as we were leaving. I quickly put it in my bag since I didn't want to look at it right at that moment.

We got in the car and Jesse still hadn't said anything, for which I was thankful. When he finally spoke, he asked me what I wanted to do for the rest of the weekend.

"Why don't we explore the area? It's so nice out and I've never been here before." I was trying to cheer myself up, though I'm sure Jesse saw right through me.

Jesse pulled over so we could check out what was nearby that would be of interest. We decided to take a ride over to the Nemours Estate, home of the late industrialist and philanthropist Alfred I. duPont. On the grounds was the estate mansion and the largest French-style formal gardens in North America.

When we arrived at the estate, we didn't realize how much there was to see. We never went inside the mansion, but just explored the beautiful gardens. Jesse was in charge of taking photos. After two hours, we were both exhausted and decided to find a place to stay for the night and have dinner.

I didn't have to go any further when I saw the Inn at Montchanin. It looked heavenly. I called immediately and I was fortunate they had one room left. When we got there, it was almost seven. We showered, dressed, and went down to the dining room, where we were seated by a window. The chairs had cushions with a leopard-looking design. One night at the Inn was going to cost a fortune, but I didn't care.

"You certainly know how to wine and dine a guy."

"I do, don't I," I replied, grinning at Jesse.

The waiter came over and we both ordered a glass of Cabernet Sauvignon. When the waiter left, Jesse said, "Do you want to talk about the elephant in the room?"

"I don't see any elephants roaming around."

Jesse smiled and put his hands over mine.

The waiter came with our drinks and we ordered. We each had the Crab Bisque soup. Jesse ordered the seared scallops and I had the pan-seared duck.

"Right now I'm feeling overwhelmed and I want to wait a little while before I start looking for my father."

Janie had told me that she hadn't seen or heard from Brian Gates since she moved from their neighborhood when she was eighteen.

"I just want you to know you can tell me anything. You're not alone in this."

"I appreciate it, but it's not always that simple," I said, and we left it at that.

Dinner was fabulous and so was our night at the Inn. I had so many thoughts swirling around in my head I thought it was going to explode.

"I can tell something's going on in that gorgeous head of yours," Jesse said as we were lying in bed.

"Between the case and you know everything else, sometimes I just want to escape."

"You're not built that way, but that doesn't mean there aren't times when you can't have some diversions to take your mind off everything, at least for a little while."

"Though I'm not a fortune teller, I think I can read your mind right now."

***

After a lovely breakfast Sunday morning, we drove home. I was quiet on the ride back, my mind trying to process everything I had learned about my mother and my grandparents.

CHAPTER 31

When Jesse left on Monday morning, I was looking forward to sinking my teeth into the case. I wanted a diversion to block out what I had learned about my birth mother since it was too painful knowing what she had to endure.

As I was having breakfast, I went over in my head what I had found out in the past two weeks. I wasn't sure if Claire's lover was the key to the case but I needed to find him.

Paula Frankel had said something to me that was interesting. What was it she said? Someone Claire had an affair with had been harassing her. Most likely it wasn't her current lover. So who was this person, and did they have anything to do with Claire's death? The shop owner mentioned Claire being dropped off in town by someone who had an old car, maybe a classic. That could be a million people. Who might know?

I picked up the phone and called Howie.

"Hi, Maddie. Any news?"

"Nothing yet, but I have to tell you, Howie, none of this looks good for you. Did Claire find out about your affair and decide this was it? She was going to divorce you, so you killed her."

"That's crazy. I didn't kill Claire. I know this looks bad, but you have to believe me, I would never hurt my wife, no matter what!"

I didn't know if I was buying Howie's story. I wanted to believe him, but it was getting harder and harder. I changed the subject. "Would you happen to know anyone in Claire's life who might have a car that would be considered a classic?"

"Not that I can think of. Why do you ask?"

"Just curious."

"My partner has a very old two-seater Mercedes, but I'm not sure you would categorize it as a classic."

"Any more problems with the police?"

"Not at the moment."

"Okay. Remember what we talked about. Stay away from your girlfriend."

As I was rummaging in my bag for my car keys, I pulled out the photo of my birth mother I had forgotten Janie Miller had given me. The photo was of a young Lydia, maybe right before she became pregnant. The resemblance was striking. She looked happy. I couldn't help but wonder if I was the cause of so much pain in her life.

The phone startled me.

"What did you find out from the friend?" Annie said before I even had a chance to say hello.

"She didn't know who the father was but she gave me the name of a boy who liked Lydia. She also told her parents she had been raped because she felt so guilty for having sex. She was both ashamed and afraid of her parents. Lydia knew her parents wouldn't report the rape because they looked upon it as a sin on their daughter and probably a scandal in their community. Pretty sick, huh?"

"So who knew the truth?"

"Just Lydia and her friend. No one else. Lydia's parents told everyone Lydia was sent to live with her aunt because she had been acting out and needed outside guidance."

"Wow, you can't make that shit up. What a terrible secret for both her and her friend to keep for all those years."

"I lived with what I had imagined for my entire life. Now I have to live with what my mother went through."

"You can't blame yourself. None of this was your fault. Don't forget that."

"I gotta go."

"I'll talk to you later. Love you."

I was sitting in my office contemplating what to do next on the case. I was drinking coffee hoping to stimulate my brain. No luck so far. What the hell, one last ditch effort.

I got out the number for Linda Crawford, the owner of the boutique where Claire worked. She answered on the second ring.

"Ms. Crawford, this is Maddie Landon. We spoke regarding Claire Stevenson."

"Of course. How can I help you?"

"You mentioned you had seen Claire in town getting out of an old car. Can you tell me anything more about the car?"

"I really don't remember?"

"Can you recall if it was a two-seater?"

"I believe it was now that you mention it."

"You said the color may have been silver."

"Yes, but I'm not definite. It could have been a convertible, but again, I can't be sure."

"Thank you."

I took a flashlight from my cabinet and headed up to Westchester. I parked down the block from Gavin Stone's house and sat there for a few minutes. Though I didn't see any cars in his driveway, I knocked on his door just to be sure. There was no answer after several knocks. I stood in front of the garage on my tippy toes and turned on my flashlight. The car in the garage looked like a two-seater convertible. It was hard to make out the color. I was trying to figure out how I could take photos when I heard a voice from a few feet behind me.

"Whoever you are, turn around slowly and drop whatever you have in your hand."

I did as I was told. When I turned, I was looking into the face of a police officer. A neighbor must have gotten scared and thought I was a burglar. I guess in rich neighborhoods the police come quickly.

"Stay where you are."

He was tall, with a hard look on his face. He did not look friendly. Cops always have their game face on. He was walking toward me.

"What are you doing here?" he asked in a stern tone.

"I'm a private investigator. I'm on a case."

"Do you have any identification?"

"It's in my backpack on the floor." I started to open my bag when the officer stopped me.

"Do you have any weapons in your bag?"

"No, sir."

He opened it and found my wallet. He gave it to me, and I pulled out my NYS Private Investigator license.

"Tell me what you're doing here."

"Like I said, I'm working on a case."

"You're trespassing. Why were you snooping around?"

"I wasn't going to break in. I just wanted to look into the garage."

"Did you find what you were looking for?"

"Maybe. I'm not sure."

"You know the neighbor might tell whoever you're investigating that you were here."

"I guess I can't do anything about that now."

"Leave now."

"I'm on my way."

I saw the officer go across the street and knock on the door of the neighbor who probably called the police. He was most likely going to tell the neighbor they needn't worry. Whether that person says anything to Gavin Stone would probably depend on how neighborly they are. I guess I'd find out soon enough.

Is it possible Gavin Stone and Claire Stevenson were having an affair? And if they were, did Stone kill Claire? More questions than answers.

CHAPTER 32

As long as I was up in Westchester, I thought I would take another crack at Gavin Stone. I called his cell number but it went straight to voicemail. I called the real estate office.

"Mr. Stone is out in the field with clients. I can call him if it's urgent?"

"No. I'll leave him a message on his phone. Thank you."

Now what? I decided to hang around and head to Scarsdale. It was lunchtime and I was getting hungry. The weather for the third week of April was seventy degrees. I parked at a meter in town and went to a place called Martine's where I bought a tuna fish sandwich and sat outside on their small patio. I couldn't resist a miniature chocolate babka to take home for dessert later. As I was finishing my sandwich, my phone rang.

"Ms. Landon, it's Gavin Stone returning your call."

"I need to speak to you. I'm in Scarsdale."

"I have to see clients in about thirty minutes. Can't this wait?"

"I'd rather it didn't."

"I can give you five minutes. There's a Starbucks in Eastchester on Route 22. I'll meet you there."

"I'll find it."

I looked up the address and was outside Starbucks ten minutes later. I noticed Gavin Stone getting out of his car. These were always tricky situations. If he was Claire's lover, would he admit to it? We'll find out.

"Hi, Gavin." We found a bench outside and sat down.

"What's going on? Like I said, I only have five minutes."

"Do you want to tell me?" I said.

"What are you talking about? I already told you why I lied for Howie."

"Someone saw you dropping Claire off in Scarsdale in your Mercedes." Gavin cleared his throat.

"Oh, is that all. I may have dropped her off near where she works. Why is that a big deal?"

"Why would you be dropping her off?"

"I was probably at their house and she may have asked me for a ride to her shop. Is that a crime?" he said with a smug look.

"I'll put it simply. Were you having an affair with Claire?"

"That's absurd. Howie is my business partner and my friend."

"Are you sure you want to stick to that story?" I only had a hunch but I was hoping I was right. "If I provide your name to the police, they might decide to open an investigation on you." I saw the fear in his eyes.

"If I tell you what I know, will you keep it between us?"

"I have no obligation to tell the police what I find out." It would certainly help Howie's case if the police had another suspect, but at this point, I wasn't going to assist the police with their job.

"Can we talk tomorrow? I have people waiting at the house I'm showing."

I wasn't happy that I had to wait. He might realize I was bluffing, but I had no choice.

"I want you to be in my office by 10 a.m. If you're not there, I'm going to the police." I had no intention of going to the police, but hopefully that might scare him.

"I'll be there."

At 5:00 p.m. I was sitting in my therapist's office. Usually I sit for a few seconds without saying anything. Apparently, I'm supposed to start and say whatever's on my mind. There are times when I don't feel like talking, like right now. Dr. Goldberg is really good at this and refuses to play my game. I finally give in.

"Over the weekend, I spoke to my birth mother's childhood friend." I went on to tell Dr. Goldberg what she said.

"How did that make you feel?"

"How do you think I felt? I can't imagine what my mother had to live with her entire life. Only her friend knew what really happened until she told her husband right before she died. I know it doesn't make sense but I somehow feel responsible."

"Do you think your birth mother would want you to feel responsible? Yes, it was very unfortunate the way her parents were and the power they had over your mother, but that is not your burden to carry. Now that you know the truth and why she had to give you up, does that change anything for you?"

"I guess I'll have to let go of the things I imagined about her."

"You don't sound very happy about that. Can you tell me why?"

"I don't know."

"Sometimes it's easier to hold on to the anger. It's hard to let it go when it's been with you your entire life. It's like a friend that you needed once but no longer serves you."

"Jesse was with me when I found out."

"How was that for you?"

"He didn't press me to talk about it, for which I was grateful. When we got back Sunday evening, I wanted to be by myself but couldn't bring myself to tell him. I guess I'm so used to being alone, sometimes it's hard to have someone else there."

"Is that how you think of Jesse, as just someone else?"

I teared up.

"What's making you sad?"

"I was actually happy Jesse was with me. It was comforting that he knew too. When I said I wanted to be alone, I didn't mean I wanted him to leave; I just wanted to be by myself for a little while with my thoughts."

"What do you think would have happened if you said that to him?"

"Maybe he would have been insulted and left."

"Maddie, if someone loves you, they don't just leave because you say something that you think might offend them. From what you've told me about Jesse, he would have understood and given you your space. He probably has the same feelings when he's with you from time to time. The best partnerships are the ones that communicate with each other and share their feelings. Why don't we leave this for our next session."

CHAPTER 33

Before driving back, I sat in my car mulling over what Dr. Goldberg said. It was a lot to take in.

When I got home, I was too bushed to eat. I grabbed a yogurt from the fridge and ate it standing by the kitchen sink. I didn't feel like talking to anyone. I got into bed and let the TV lull me to sleep. The next thing I knew, it was 5:45 a.m.

I threw on my running clothes and jogged to the park. As I was on my third loop around, I realized my side wasn't hurting anymore. I was running fast, trying to get out all my pent-up frustrations from the past few weeks. As I was returning to my apartment, I watched parents and nannies walk their children to school.

I barely remember being four or five years old, but I do remember my first day of kindergarten. I was crying because I didn't want to go. My mother thought if she allowed me to pick out my own clothes, I would stop crying, but that didn't work.

I was holding my mother's hand as tight as I could as we were walking to school, hoping she wouldn't let go. My mother was going on about how much fun school was and all the games I'd be playing with the other kids, but I wasn't buying it. When we arrived, a woman approached my mother and they started talking quietly. I couldn't hear what they were saying. When they were finished talking, my mother leaned down and told me she would take me for a hot fudge sundae when she picked me up. I still didn't want her to leave but I reluctantly let go of her hand. My mother kissed me and I watched her as she left, trying to be brave and not to cry. The teacher took my hand and led me into the classroom. Besides the trauma of going to school that day, the only other thing I remembered was the hot fudge sundae with chocolate chip ice cream and mounds of whipped cream.

When I got back to my apartment, I showered and put on a pot of coffee. Gavin Stone was coming to my office at 10:00 this morning. What was he going to say? If he was the father of Claire's baby, did Claire tell him? I could theorize all day long, but in the end, that's all it would be until I found out what really happened.

By 10:15 a.m., I had my doubts whether Gavin Stone was going to show. I was about to give up when I heard the door open. I got up and saw Gavin standing in the reception area. I walked him into my office.

"Can I get you a cup of coffee?"

"No. Why don't we get this over with. What do you want to know?"

Gavin was wearing a dark blue suit with a light blue dress shirt and a gray and blue striped tie. He was definitely easy on the eyes.

"Tell me about Claire."

"There's not much to tell. I'm ashamed to say I slept with her a few times. That was it."

"How did that come about?"

"I had known her, of course, through Howie. The three of us socialized once in a while. It's not like I didn't want to sleep with her. Who wouldn't? She was beautiful and sexy. I envied Howie."

"So what happened?"

"A few months ago, I got a call out of the blue from Claire. She asked if she could come over to my place and talk. I thought she might have been having problems with Howie so I said yes. I know you're not going to believe me but she came on to me."

"I'm not sure if that matters. Apparently, you were a willing partner."

Gavin didn't say anything.

"What was it she wanted to talk to you about?"

"I think she was lonely and she just wanted the company."

"Were you still sleeping with her at the time of her death?"

I could see the wheels turning in his head. What does he admit to?

"No. I broke it off a month before she died."

"Did she tell you about the baby?"

"I had no idea she was pregnant. She never told me. And I'm pretty sure it wasn't mine."

"How could you know? Were you using protection? Because you know it isn't foolproof."

"I was told by a doctor once that I was shooting blanks. Besides, I had no reason to kill Claire. I knew she wouldn't tell Howie and I certainly had no intention of telling him."

That was probably true.

"Whose idea was it to stop sleeping together?"

"Actually, it was mine. I started to feel guilty. And besides, like I said, it was just a few times. It was nothing."

I love it when guys say it was nothing. What does that even mean?

"Do you know if she was sleeping with anyone else?"

"If she was, she didn't tell me."

"Did she ever tell you she was scared of someone?"

"I'm pretty sure I would have remembered if she did."

"Where were you the day Claire died?"

"I was working part of the day and toward the evening, I hooked up with someone."

"I need that person's name."

"It was just one time."

"I still need her name. I promise I'll be discreet."

"Her name is Molly David," he said reluctantly.

"Write down her address and telephone number."

"Are you going to tell Howie?"

"I'll have to think about it."

"Please, it would ruin our partnership and our friendship."

"That's not my problem."

Gavin was probably right about one thing—Claire would have kept their secret. I was afraid if I divulged the affair to Greg, he would tell Howie. I just wasn't sure I should keep the affair to myself.

CHAPTER 34

I decided to pay Molly David a visit where she worked. Gavin mentioned that she was an accountant at an accounting firm in midtown. I grabbed a cab over to her work address. When I signed in, I was told to go up to the eleventh floor.

I opened the door to the offices of Jacob Horowitz.

"I'd like to speak with Molly David."

"Do you have an appointment?"

"No, she's a friend. I'm here from out of town and was hoping to see her." I tell myself lying is okay for a just cause.

"You just missed her. She went down to the cafeteria to have lunch."

As I got off the elevator, I saw the sign to the cafeteria. I had no idea what she looked like, but how hard could it be to find her? I saw a woman sitting by herself. She had long, very curly dark brown hair, most likely in her thirties. Having stick straight hair, I always wanted curly hair. What's that saying, "you want what you can't have" or something like that.

"Excuse me, would you happen to be Molly?"

"Why yes," she said, with a bewildered look on her face.

"I'm sorry to bother you." I didn't see a wedding ring on her finger. "This is a little awkward. Do you mind if I sit?" I sat before she had a chance to say no. "Do you know a guy by the name of Gavin Stone?" The expression on her face gave her away. "I promise I'm not here to cause any problems for you. I'm investigating the death of a woman named Claire Stevenson. Gavin Stone said you were with him the night she died."

"How would I know if I was with him if I have no idea when she was killed."

"You're right. It was March 7th. It was a Friday. Does that help?"

"Gavin Stone and I were together for one night. I don't exactly remember the date."

"How did you meet?"

"He sold me a house and as a thank you, he wanted to take me out for a drink."

It sounds like Gavin had a little racket going—trying to hook up with single women. Maybe this Toni James wasn't crazy after all.

"Were there any problems?"

"No. It was only once and it was consensual. Does that answer your question?"

"Was there a reason you only slept with him once?"

"That's none of your business."

"I still need to know the date you were with Gavin. It's really important. I would appreciate it if you can check. Maybe you marked it on a calendar. Here's my card. If you happen to remember any more details of that day, please give me a call. I'm sorry if I disturbed you."

"This woman who was killed—how did Gavin know her?"

"She was an acquaintance." I didn't feel the need to go into the particulars.

In my book, Gavin Stone was a sleazeball, but was he a killer?

I took an Uber back to my office. Before going in, I stopped at the deli two blocks away and ordered a turkey sandwich with coleslaw to go.

My phone rang as I was turning on the coffeemaker.

"Maddie Landon."

"Maddie, this is Lucy Grainger. How are you?"

"Fine. I'm glad you called. I wanted to talk to you about something," I said.

"I'm in the city for one night and I'd love to take you to dinner. I know it's last minute, but I was hoping you didn't have plans."

"No. I can make it."

"How about if I make a reservation at Café Fiorello for 6:30?" Lucy said.

"That's perfect. I'll see you then."

I had questions I wanted to ask her about Brian Gates, the boy who may be my father. I was also curious why she didn't mention that Lydia had told her parents she was raped. Was she hiding something?

I went home to do a quick wardrobe change, going with a pair of black linen slacks and a gray button-down silk blouse. I changed my short black boots for a pair of black flats and took an Uber over to the restaurant where Lucy was waiting outside for me.

"I'm really glad you were able to meet me," Lucy said, giving me a quick hug.

Lucy was dressed in business attire, a black skirt with a matching jacket and a white blouse. We were shown to our table. The waiter came over and we both ordered a glass of wine. Café Fiorello is an institution in New York. It's right across the street from Lincoln Center. The menu is basically Italian.

"Are you here on a business trip?"

"Yes. I have a client that needs special attention every so often. People who have a lot of money think they're entitled to some hand-holding. I guess they are. So how are you?"

"The case I'm working on is keeping me busy."

"How is your boyfriend?"

"Jesse is fine. I think I told you he lives in Connecticut. We see each other mostly on the weekends."

The waiter came over with our drinks.

"Would you like to order now?"

"Can you give us a few minutes?" I said.

We looked over the menu before we began talking again.

Lucy raised her glass. "To your happiness!"

"And to yours!" I said.

"You mentioned when I called you wanted to talk to me about something," Lucy said.

The waiter came over and we quickly ordered.

"I went to see Janie Berg, though now her last name is Miller. She lives in Wilmington, Delaware."

"How is she doing?"

"She seems to be fine. How come when we spoke you never mentioned that Lydia had told her parents she was raped?"

"How did you find out?"

"Janie told me."

"I'm so sorry about that. I wanted to tell you but I was afraid how you would react. Knowing you were abandoned must have been hard enough, but to know you were the product of a rape, I can't even imagine."

"There's something I have to tell you. Lydia was not raped."

I saw the astonished look on Lucy's face.

"What do you mean she wasn't raped?"

"She made it up because she didn't want your parents to know she had sex. Lydia didn't know how your parents would have reacted knowing their daughter had consensual sex being raised by such religious parents. She thought if she told them she was raped they wouldn't blame her."

"I can't believe this. So Janie knew and never said anything?"

"It was their secret until Lydia told her husband before she died."

"But what if my parents had reported it?"

"Lydia was banking on the fact that they wouldn't because of the shame they felt."

"I don't know what to say. I wished my sister would have told me."

"Janie didn't know who the father was. The name Brian Gates came up. She said Brian liked Lydia."

"It can't be Brian. He's gay."

Now it was my turn to be surprised.

"How do you know that? Isn't it possible he didn't want anyone to know so he pretended to be straight and was sexually active during high school?"

"You can ask him yourself. He lives right here in the city with the man he's married to. He works as a buyer for Bloomingdale's."

Our food came. We were both quiet while we were eating. I was contemplating what Lucy had just told me.

"Would you have any idea who Lydia might have been involved with?" I asked.

"Not really. Well, this might be somewhat of a stretch, but there was one boy. His name was Harris. I'm trying to remember his last name. He was shy, maybe a year older than Lydia. He went to public school. We went to Catholic school."

"What made you think of this guy Harris?"

"One day I was walking to the grocery store. It may have been a Saturday. There was a park across the street from where we lived. I saw Lydia and this boy Harris talking. They seemed pretty friendly. Later, when I mentioned that I had seen them together, there was something in Lydia's reaction that made me think she was hiding something, but I let it go."

As I was taking a forkful of my lasagna, I was absorbing what Lucy just told me.

"I'm glad my sister wasn't raped. I wasn't sure how she was going to get over it. Maybe that was the reason she never had other children."

I decided it wasn't my place to divulge what Scott Reed had told me. As we ate, Lucy talked about her job and a little bit about the time when she was married. She told me that she and Lydia had always remained close.

Outside the restaurant, we shared a cab, first dropping Lucy off at her hotel. We hugged before she left and said we would stay in touch. Though Lucy is my aunt, I didn't feel a strong connection to her. She was really like a stranger I had just met. Maybe over time, if we stayed in touch, I'd feel differently.

As I was falling asleep, I thought about this guy Harris and wondered if he could be my father.

CHAPTER 35

My phone buzzed as I was getting out of the shower in the morning.

"Hello."

"Maddie, it's Greg."

"What's up?"

"That's what I was calling you about. I think we need to meet and discuss the case."

I knew I couldn't put him off any longer.

"Why don't we meet for a drink later?" I said. *As long as it's not at your place.*

"There's a great bar on Eighth Street called Analogue. Why don't we meet up around 5:00 p.m."

I googled the place after we hung up. It wasn't far from where Greg lived. It looked nice from the photos.

As I was eating breakfast, I was debating whether to tell Greg about Gavin and Claire's relationship. He did have a right to know. Would he keep it from Howie? I doubted it. Maybe it was better if the police found out about Gavin's involvement with Claire. It might take some of the heat off Howie. Howie's alibi was Dana Thomas, but how reliable a witness would she make?

I needed to dig deeper into Gavin Stone. Since I couldn't ask Claire about their relationship, I had only Gavin's word for what really went on between them.

I sent an email to the company I employ to access phone records. I gave them Gavin's information and asked them to retrieve three months of cell phone records, the three months prior to Claire's death. Hopefully, there might be something in those records that could help with my investigation.

There was a ping from my phone showing a text came in. It was from Lucy with Harris's last name—Tyler.

Before searching for Harris Tyler, I wanted to speak with Brian Gates. I searched the internet, inputting his name and approximate age. There was only one match that fit with his age. He resided in the Murray Hill section of Manhattan on Second Avenue between Thirty-seventh and Thirty-eighth Street. From what I knew of the neighborhood, it had beautiful brownstones, plenty of restaurants, bars, several small parks, and a path where you can run along the East River. It seems as if Brian Gates had done very well for himself.

I dialed the cell phone number I had found for him.

"Hello."

"Is this Brian Gates?"

"May I ask who's calling?"

"My name's Maddie Landon. I was given your name by Lucy Grainger. She's the sister of Lydia Peterson from your old neighborhood in Philadelphia."

"I was sorry to hear that Lydia had passed away. How can I help you?"

"It's a little complicated. Do you think we can meet later?"

"Right now I'm at work. I'm off at five o'clock. There's a Starbucks between Park and Lexington on Fifty-ninth Street. I can meet you there a little after five."

"I'll see you then." Before hanging up, I gave Brian a brief description of myself.

Oh shit! I just remembered I told Greg I was going to meet him at the Analogue Bar at 5:00. I had no intentions of canceling my meeting with Brian Gates.

"Hey, Greg. I have to change our meeting time to seven o'clock since I remembered I have something I need to take care of," I told his voicemail. Two minutes later, I got a call back from Greg.

"What's going on? Seven o'clock might be a little tight for me. Any chance you can change your appointment?"

"I can't change it."

"I'll see you at seven." He sounded annoyed as he abruptly hung up.

CHAPTER 36

By the time I caught up paying bills, it was time to meet Brian Gates. I was anxious. What if Lucy was wrong about him? What if he was my father?

I arrived at Starbucks a few minutes before 5:00 and sat down. I knew the chances were slim that he could be my father, but what if? Ten minutes later, I saw someone walking toward me. I assumed it was Brian Gates. He didn't look anything like the photo I saw from his high school yearbook. Brian was medium height with a muscular build. He still wore rimless glasses. When I got closer, I noticed he had green eyes. I started to perspire.

"Thank you for coming," I said to Brian, as we shook hands.

"Would you like a coffee or a latte?"

"I'll just stick to coffee." He went up to the counter, ordered, and waited a few minutes until his name was called. My foot was shaking, waiting to hear what Brian Gates had to say.

"So what do I owe the honor of your presence, Ms. Landon?" he said, as he sat down, handing me my coffee.

At least he had a sense of humor.

"This might sound weird as you're listening."

"No weirder than agreeing to meet with a perfect stranger."

I smiled. "That's true."

"Thirty-seven years ago, I was adopted by a family in New York. Unfortunately, when I was twelve, they died in an automobile accident." I didn't mention I was sitting in the back seat at the time. "Without going into too much detail, I never had any interest in looking for my birth parents. It wasn't till very recently I decided to search for them. My parents had told me the name of the lawyer that handled my adoption. When I went to speak with him, he told me my birth mother died five years ago. After doing some research, I found my mother's sister, Lucy Grainger. I also spoke to a childhood friend of Lydia's, Janie Berg." Brian Gates was listening so intently it was kind of making me more anxious than I already was.

"This is where it gets a little weird, so bear with me. Your name came up that you might be my father, but when I spoke with Lucy, she told me you were gay. I know this must come as a complete surprise. I'm sorry if I've offended you in any way, but can you tell me anything you remember about that time?"

"Wow! Where do I begin? I certainly remember Lydia. We were friends but that was about it. I didn't even know she was pregnant and had a baby."

"Apparently the family kept it quiet. They sent Lydia to live with an aunt in South Carolina under the pretext that Lydia was acting out and needed to be in a different environment."

"I'm gay but during that time I kept it to myself. I dated for appearances. I even slept with one girl, but I can tell you for a fact it was not Lydia."

"Are you absolutely sure?"

"I think I would remember since it was the one and only time I slept with a girl."

"I'm sorry I had to ask. Would you happen to remember a guy named Harris Tyler? He went to public school."

"Yeah, I actually do remember him. Good-looking kid. Unfortunately, he wasn't gay," Brian said jokingly, though I imagine there was probably some truth to what he said.

"He lived a couple of streets over. We used to play basketball at a playground in our neighborhood. I believe he graduated a year ahead of me."

"Do you remember what happened to him?"

"He went to college in California. May have been UCLA but I can't be sure."

"Did he come back after college?"

"I couldn't tell you. I came to New York for fashion and never moved back to Philadelphia. I know he was into computers. Maybe he stayed out there and got involved with a tech company. But the truth is, I have no idea. You know you look a lot like Lydia."

"So I've been told. Lucy mentioned you're married. Do you have children?"

"About ten years ago we were thinking about possibly having a baby through a surrogate but we never did."

"It's probably not too late. You hear about men like Anderson Cooper and I think even Elton John that decided they wanted to be parents later in life."

"Can I ask why you mentioned Harris Tyler?"

"It was something Lucy said to me. It's probably a wild goose chase but at this point it's all I have."

"I still can't believe you're Lydia's child. So you never got to meet her?"

"No, I never did."

"She was a very sweet kid. Very pretty, just like you. It's a shame she gave you up for adoption."

"From what I've learned, she didn't have a choice."

"She did come from a very religious family, if I remember correctly. Do you live in the city?" I was glad he switched topics.

"I live on the Upper West Side. I'm a private investigator," I said, giving him my card. "Hopefully you won't need my services."

"Maybe not but you never know who might."

We sat and talked for a while. I liked Brian. When we said goodbye, I didn't know if I would ever see him again. Why did I feel relieved that he wasn't my father? Could it be there is a part of me that never wants to find him?

I grabbed a cab to meet Greg. I wasn't in the mood to talk about the case or see Greg. I wanted to go home and be by myself. Hopefully, a drink would change my mood.

CHAPTER 37

I spotted Greg waiting in front of the Analogue Bar. He kissed me on my lips before I had a chance to turn my head away. Could I have turned away before he kissed me? I couldn't think about that now.

There were high tables and chairs right as we walked in, with a long bar going all the way back, and a seating area on the opposite side of the bar. Also, there was a back room that I stumbled upon when I went for a quick trip to the bathroom.

We sat down at a table near the bar. I ordered a glass of red wine and Greg ordered a beer.

I couldn't keep Gavin's affair from Greg. "I found out some interesting information that might help Howie. Gavin and Claire were sleeping together. He said it was only a few times and then he broke it off out of guilt."

"Wow! Do you believe him?"

"I have no idea, but I ordered his cell phone records to see how often he was in contact with Claire."

"Good work."

"Though I didn't promise Gavin I wouldn't tell Howie, I would rather you didn't. I would prefer it came from the police if they did wind up bringing Gavin in for questioning."

"If it comes to that, Howie will probably go ballistic. I'm not sure the partnership would survive," Greg said.

The waiter brought over our drinks.

"That might be the least of Howie's problems. I still think Howie has the strongest motive to kill his wife, but there are always surprises."

"Do you think it could be Stone?" Greg asked.

"I don't know. The woman he was supposedly with around the time Claire died couldn't verify the date, so he really doesn't have an alibi at the moment. They were only together that one time. Also, according to Claire's friend, there was someone in Claire's life that she was afraid of. I would love to find out who that person is."

For a moment, I thought I saw a strange look on Greg's face.

"I'd concentrate on Gavin for now. Look into his past. Maybe an old girlfriend that you can talk with."

"That's a good idea. By the way, did you get a chance to give the burner phone to your friend?"

"Yeah, I did."

"Hopefully they can do something with it."

"Did you find out anything else?"

"I spoke with Howie's neighbors but no one knew anything about the Stevensons that could help his case. What are the chances Howie will be arrested?"

"I'm actually wondering why it's taking so long."

"Maybe that's a good sign."

"I'm not so sure. Should we order some appetizers?" Greg asked.

"I've had a long day and I really need to get some sleep."

Greg looked disappointed but quickly recovered.

On the Uber back to my apartment, I wondered if all along I wanted Greg to kiss me. Did it mean anything? I didn't want to go there.

***

I spent the next morning looking into Gavin Stone's past. There didn't appear to be any red flags in his history. Howie was the one person who might know about Gavin's relationships, but I didn't think it was a good idea to involve him. It was better if he didn't know I was looking into Gavin. The report I pulled up listed one name that had been associated with Gavin's current address, an Arlene Fielding who resided there between the years 2012 and 2015. Had Gavin been married or was it someone he had been shacking up with? With such an uncommon last name, she shouldn't be too hard to locate.

I found an Arlene Fielding in Westport, Connecticut. She appeared to be the right person. Her age was thirty-four and the prior address listed was at Gavin's current house in Rye. I thought I'd drive to Westport and take my chances that Ms. Fielding might be home.

I arrived in front of her house at 2:30 p.m. The house was a Cape Cod-style home with a sloping roof and dormer windows. I had no idea what I was going to say to her if she was home. I rang the bell and a very attractive brunette with stylish short brown hair with blonde highlights opened the door.

"I'm looking for Arlene Fielding."

"Yes, that's me. What can I do for you?"

"My name's Maddie Landon," I said, handing her my card. "I'm a private investigator looking into the death of a woman named Claire Stevenson."

"Why does that name sound vaguely familiar?"

"Her name may sound familiar because Gavin Stone is partners with Howie Stevenson, the husband of the victim."

"Yes! Of course!"

"Do you think I could come in and talk to you for a few moments?"

"I guess that would be alright. My two-year-old is napping in the living room, so let's go in the kitchen."

"I'll try to make this quick. Were you married to Gavin?"

"I was, for five years."

"I'm talking to everyone who knew Mrs. Stevenson. Did you ever meet her?"

"I believe it was only once. It was when Howie and Gavin first met before they became partners. The four of us went out. I'm sorry she's dead. That's horrible, the poor thing. Was someone arrested?"

"No, not yet. Can you tell me if you saw anything that made you uncomfortable between the Stevensons?"

"Not that I can remember. They seemed fine, though we're talking more than five years ago."

"I understand." This was the tricky part. "As I mentioned, I'm talking to everyone who knew Claire, and that includes Gavin. I know this may be very personal, but can you tell me why you and Gavin divorced?"

"Why do you need to know that? Are you investigating Gavin?"

I didn't feel the need to tell her the truth.

"No, but if there's anything you can tell me, I would really appreciate it."

"I wanted a baby but not with him."

"Why?"

"Gavin could be controlling and he made it difficult at times. To tell you the truth, I was fed up and didn't trust him anymore."

"Can you give me any examples?"

"Why don't we leave it at that."

"Okay. Did he ever hurt you?"

"Never. Gavin was never violent, and I don't believe he would have killed Claire if that's what you're getting at."

"Do you think he had affairs while you were married?"

I saw a slight hesitation. "If he did, I wasn't aware."

"Is there anything else you can think of?"

"Not at the moment."

I heard the baby crying.

"Well, thank you for talking with me. I'm glad you got what you wanted."

Driving back, I thought about what Arlene Fielding just told me about her ex-husband. Gavin said he broke it off with Claire because he had a guilty conscience. Maybe Claire broke it off and Gavin didn't take it that well. But would he kill Claire over that? I didn't think so, but the jury was still out.

CHAPTER 38

I called Greg when I left Arlene Fielding's house and told him what transpired between Arlene Fielding and me.

"I contacted the detective in charge after we spoke yesterday," Greg said. "Of course, he was playing it close to the vest. He wasn't going to tell me anything. In the meantime, see what else you can dig up on Gavin Stone. Do you think he could be the baby's father?"

"Your guess is as good as mine."

I went home instead of going back to the office. When I looked at my emails, there was nothing pressing. It might be a day or two more before I received Gavin's cell phone records.

While I was eating an omelet I had thrown together with whatever I had in the fridge, I opened up my computer and gingerly fingered the keys. I had been stalling in searching for this guy Harris Tyler ever since there was the slightest possibility he might be my father.

I reluctantly put his name into the computer. I was totally surprised when there was only one person with that name in Los Angeles. He was about the right age, fifty-five. I guess there was a part of me that was hoping he would be more difficult to find. I'm not even sure if this was the right person. For all I knew, the Harris Tyler I was looking for could be right here in Manhattan or living back in Philadelphia.

If I call, what do I say? I'm your long-lost daughter that you didn't even know existed. Or do I fly cross-country to surprise him? Neither seemed like great options. I guess, like Annie said, I don't have to make any decisions right this moment.

I was having trouble falling asleep. When I finally did, I dreamed I was on a plane heading to Los Angeles. Harris Tyler was meeting me at the airport when my plane landed. I was nervous and excited at the same time. Then I heard the pilot say we would have to make an emergency landing in Chicago, since there was a problem with one of the engines. When we landed, I was the only person who got off the plane. I thought that was strange. And when I looked around, I wasn't at an airport; it appeared I was on a deserted island. I was stranded and completely alone. All I could think of was that I was going to die on this island, and my father would never know why I wasn't there to meet him. I jumped up, tears in my eyes and my heart pounding. Though I knew it was just a dream, it nevertheless scared the hell out of me.

I got out of bed knowing it was pointless to try and go back to sleep. The clock said 4:45 a.m. I showered and turned on the coffeemaker. After having my first cup of coffee, I went for a run. The cool air was invigorating.

While I was having breakfast and my second cup of coffee, I kept going back and forth on who had a stronger motive to kill Claire: Howie or Gavin. Or what was the likelihood that someone else murdered Claire? What about the person Claire was afraid of? Could he be the killer?

Greg was calling as I was heading into my office.

"What's up?"

"I just found out the police are pulling Gavin Stone in for questioning tomorrow. I wonder if they found out about his affair with Claire."

"Shit. I think you're going to have to tell Howie what's going on. I'd rather he find out from us than from the police."

"You're right. They'll probably want to question Howie again to see if he knew about the affair."

"We don't know what Gavin is going to tell the police. Just because he told me he ended the affair doesn't mean it's true."

"I'm going to call Howie. I want you to meet me at his place when I tell him about Gavin since you might have questions for him. I'll text you the time."

I thought to myself when I hung up that Howie might blow a gasket. I wouldn't blame him, though I don't have much sympathy for him even if he didn't kill his wife. What a complete mess this was turning into. An hour later, I got a text from Greg to meet him at Howie's place at 5:30 p.m.

When I arrived at Howie's house, Greg was just pulling up. I observed the nosy neighbor, Janice Levy, outside. She waved to me. I waved back.

"Who's that?" Greg asked me, as he was exiting his car.

"She's the neighbor who saw Claire and Howie arguing outside."

Howie was standing by the door as we walked up to the house.

"With both of you here, I'm curious if this is good news or bad news."

"Why don't we sit."

"I'm just going to come out and say it," Greg said. "Gavin was sleeping with Claire."

Surprise is way too tame a word to describe the look on Howie's face.

"What the fuck! Are you sure?"

That was my cue to step in and explain.

"Someone had seen Claire getting out of Gavin's Mercedes." I decided not to go into a long explanation. "When I pushed Gavin on it, he told me Claire had initiated the affair, but he only slept with her a few times before he ended it."

"Why are you telling me this?"

"Because we believe the police found out, and they're going to be questioning him," Greg said.

"Did you know about the affair?" I asked.

"No! This is the first I'm hearing of it. I can't believe Gavin would betray me like this. I thought he was my friend. Oh my god! What if he's the father of Claire's baby? I'm going to kill him."

"Howie, get a grip. You're not going to kill anyone. Right now you're upset and you're not thinking straight. Whatever you do, do not get into a fight with Gavin." I decided not to mention that Gavin might be shooting blanks since I only had his word for that.

Howie lowered his head, shaking it back and forth.

"The police are definitely going to bring you back in for questioning again. They're probably going to ask you questions pertaining to Claire's affair with Gavin."

"But I don't know anything," he said, raising his voice.

"Then that's what you'll tell them. I'll be there with you," Greg said.

"What if they think I killed Claire because she was having Gavin's baby?"

"Right now, the police have no idea whose baby it is," Greg said.

"But they know it's not mine. They're not going to take my word for it that I didn't know Claire was pregnant."

"Let's not get ahead of ourselves," Greg said.

If I was Howie, I'd be worried, I thought to myself as we left him sitting on the couch.

CHAPTER 39

Walking toward my car after leaving Howie's place, I saw Janice Levy crossing the street heading toward us.

"I thought since you were here, I'd find out how things were going. Oh hello, who are you?" Janice asked.

"This is Greg Martin. Greg, Janice Levy. She's the nice woman who's been a big help." I could see how flattered she was.

"You look familiar," Janice Levy said to Greg.

"I'm a friend of the Stevensons."

"Oh! Maybe I've seen you at their house."

"That's possible."

"So how are things going?" she asked.

"You know I can't give you any information."

"I promise nothing will get past my lips."

"I'm sure that's true, but I can't divulge anything regarding an ongoing investigation." Hopefully, that should satisfy her.

"Oh well, you can't fault a gal for trying. I'm here if you need me." And with that, she turned and walked back to her house.

"Well, that was weird," Greg said.

"She's harmless. Probably lonely since her husband died and just wants some attention. I think I'll call Gavin and see when the police want him to come in."

"That's a good idea."

I drove back to Manhattan, eager to get home and unwind. I stopped in my neighborhood local seafood place to pick up some cooked shrimp for my salad. While I was getting dinner together, I called Jesse.

"Hey you," Jesse said when he answered. "How's my favorite PI?"

"Nice to know I'm ranked higher than your partner, Mack."

"Always. How are you feeling?"

"Better. I think there's a possibility I found my birth father." I went on to give Jesse all the details. "How can I confirm he's my father without him getting suspicious when I start asking him questions?"

"It might be tricky. What are you afraid of?"

"I'm pretty sure he doesn't even know of my existence. My mother never told anyone she was pregnant."

"Is it possible he might have known?"

"From everything I've been told, no one knew my mother was pregnant except her family and her best friend."

"Okay, let's go on that assumption. I still think it might be better than flying to California and showing up at his doorstep. I would think it would be more of a shock to him than finding out over the telephone. But you have to feel comfortable having that conversation with him on the phone."

"What if he doesn't want to meet with me?"

"Let's not get ahead of yourself. Worst-case scenario, you have a life and you have people who love you. I'm not minimizing that it won't hurt, but it can't be worse than what you've put yourself through."

I was choking up.

"Maddie?"

"I'm here. Tell me something funny?"

"Okay. Let me think a second. Why do we tell actors to 'break a leg?'"

"I'll bite. Why?"

"Because every play has a cast."

"That's funny. Thanks."

"You're welcome. I thought we might take out a boat and do some fishing this weekend."

"That sounds nice and peaceful. I'm not exactly sure what time I'll be there tomorrow. I'll text you if I'm running late."

"Sleep tight."

"Ditto." I decided to skip the minor detail about Greg's kiss.

As soon as I hung up, my phone rang.

"Hello."

"You couldn't wait to tell the police about my affair with Claire," Gavin said in an angry tone.

"What are you talking about?" I said, though I already knew.

"The police want me to come in tomorrow for a chat, as they put it."

"How do you know it's about the affair?"

"What else would it be?"

"I never said a word to the police. I promise you. Did you ever think they found out on their own or maybe it's about the alibi you gave Howie? They could have found out you lied for him."

"If somehow they did find out about the affair, they could think I killed Claire."

"Police need proof. They just don't go around arresting people without physical evidence or a mound of circumstantial evidence."

"I should probably contact a criminal lawyer."

"I can't advise you on that, but it would probably be a good idea."

"Yeah, okay," he said, and hung up.

I wondered what the police were able to find out about Gavin. Would he now be their number one suspect?

CHAPTER 40

The sun was creeping behind the clouds as sunset was closing in on the day. Jesse was pulling up to his place just as I was arriving. I hugged him fiercely, feeling the weight of his body against mine.

"You look tired?" Jesse said when we broke away.

"A way to win a woman's heart."

"You would be beautiful even if you just came through a mudslide and then were caught up in a windstorm."

"Good save."

"Would grilled baby lamp chops and a glass of wine soothe your wounded ego?"

"You had me at grilled." I smiled.

***

Saturday morning, after a lovely time in the bedroom, we had a leisurely breakfast of Jesse's famous blueberry pancakes and crispy bacon. We packed up the car with fishing poles, a tackle box, and lunch, and drove to a lake about five miles from where Jesse lives. We rented a motorized rowboat and paddled out to the middle of the lake.

We baited our hooks and threw our fishing lines into the water. It was very peaceful and I was content not to talk. A few minutes later, I felt a tug and reeled in my line. "Look at that fish, Jesse! She's a beauty," I said, as I carefully took the trout off my line and threw the fish back into the water. "Let's see if you can catch a fish that size," I said to Jesse, gloating. "Hey, no witty comeback?" But when I looked at Jesse, it seemed as if he was somewhere else. "What's wrong?"

"I was remembering when I was five. I almost drowned."

"How?" I asked, taken aback by Jesse's remark.

"My father took my mother and me to the ocean in Maine. It was one of the few times we went on a holiday. We were at the beach and I wandered down to the water. My parents must not have realized I was gone. It was the first time I had been to the ocean and all I wanted to do was go into the water. The next thing I knew I was grabbed up by an undercurrent and went under. I was fighting it, but I had no idea what I was doing. I was so scared. I kept swallowing water and the undercurrent kept taking me further out. The next thing I knew, I was lying on the beach and someone was standing over me. They had given me CPR. There were people all around staring at me, but the only person I saw was my mother sobbing. I didn't know why she was crying.

"I found out later that someone had seen me go under and yelled for the lifeguard. Neither my father nor my mother knew how to swim."

"Did you think you were going to die when you were in the water?"

"I'm not sure those thoughts were going through my mind. I didn't know what was happening to me."

I pulled myself close to Jesse. "I'm glad you didn't die."

"Me too," he said, kissing me gently on the lips.

***

Monday morning on the way back from Jesse's I was eager to know what happened when the police questioned Gavin Stone. I was very interested in finding out what they asked him and what he told them. I called Gavin and left a message in his voicemail.

I went straight to my office, put on a pot of coffee, and turned on my computer. As I was looking through my emails, I saw an email with an attachment. It was Gavin Stone's cell phone records. I printed it out and poured myself a mug of coffee. I was mainly interested in any calls in the two months prior to Claire's death between Gavin and Claire. Looking through the telephone numbers, I noted there were several calls between Gavin and Claire leading up to the time right before Claire's death. Gavin had told me he had broken it off with Claire about a month prior to her death. So why were they still in contact?

I heard my phone ringing. "Hi, Gavin. Thanks for getting back to me."

"What do you want?" he said in an irritated voice.

"I was wondering how it went with the police."

"Why should I tell you? It's your fault they brought me in for questioning."

"Gavin, I don't think that's entirely true. It was just a matter of time before they questioned you again."

"Well, somehow they found out about my affair with Claire."

"What did you tell them?"

"I told them it was casual, mainly a physical relationship. Neither of us wanted to be romantically involved."

"Did they ask for a DNA sample?"

"They did but I declined. The attorney I spoke with said that unless I'm a suspect not to provide a sample. They did ask me if I knew anything about Howie's gambling problems. I told them exactly what I had told you."

"You mentioned that you ended your affair with Claire about a month before she died. I have reason to believe that you were still calling her up until the time of her death."

"Are you accusing me of something? I think this conversation is over."

That went well, I thought to myself, as the phone went dead in my hand. He still hadn't answered my question. I thought I would do a little more digging into Gavin Stone.

I punched in Greg's number.

"I just spoke with Gavin Stone. He said the police were questioning him about Howie's gambling debts."

"That means they might be thinking Howie killed Claire for the insurance money. If he got in over his head and these people threatened to kill him, maybe he got scared and felt trapped. What else did he tell you?"

"They inquired about Gavin's affair with Claire. They asked him for a DNA sample, which he declined. He said if he became a suspect he'd give it up."

"That's interesting. I'm wondering if he's hiding something?"

"At this point, I have no idea what's going on," I said.

"What's going on with us?"

"What are you talking about?" I said, knowing full well what he meant.

"I feel like you're always avoiding me, yet when I kissed you, you didn't pull away."

"I didn't pull away because I didn't have a chance to. But it's your imagination that I'm avoiding you."

"Really! Is that why every time we're in the same room together, you can't wait to leave? Are you still angry at me because I ended our affair?"

"No, of course not. Look, I'm not interested in continuing this conversation. I gotta go."

Maybe Greg was right. I just didn't want to admit, even to myself, that I still might be mad at him for exactly that.

CHAPTER 41

Focusing on the case was all I cared about at the moment. I didn't want to think about Greg.

Right now Howie had the stronger motive, though I still couldn't rule out Gavin Stone. And what about this mystery man who Claire was allegedly afraid of?

I went across the hall to see Larry Banks, the criminal attorney who occupies one of the suites on my floor. When he first came on board, I kept my distance, since he seemed overly friendly and I was afraid things could get sticky. I'm not great at handling situations where I feel uncomfortable. I tend to run the other way. Lately we kind of have an understanding.

"Anyone here?"

"Come in, Maddie. How are you?"

"You got a few minutes. I need to brainstorm."

"Shoot."

I gave Larry the rundown on what I had learned. "I feel stuck," I said when I finished talking. "At the moment, the police don't have enough evidence to charge Howie. I'm hoping he had nothing to do with his wife's murder, but I have my doubts."

"Maybe you need to dig further into the wife's past. You said she grew up in foster care."

"She did. I spoke to the person she was closest to at the home where she grew up. She told me Claire was very guarded."

"I'd take another run at this woman. See if she remembers anything else."

I got up to leave. "Thanks."

"Not sure I helped much. Good luck."

I went back to my office. I had nothing to lose by speaking with Sarah James again.

My phone rang as I was about to call her. I noticed it was Greg.

"What's going on?" I said, when I answered the phone.

"Howie just called me. The police are at his place. They have a search warrant. I'm on my way over there now."

"Do you want me to come up?"

"No. There's nothing you can do. I'll call you later."

This can't be good news for Howie. I wondered what changed. Was there enough circumstantial evidence that a judge would sign off on it, or was there something else? I couldn't worry about Howie right now. I had to continue with my investigation. I picked up the phone and called Sarah James.

"Sarah, it's Maddie Landon. Give me a call when you get this message."

I sat at my desk nibbling on a muffin, wishing I knew what was going on at Howie's place. The fact that the police had a warrant to search his house was not a good sign for Howie. It's possible they think they have a better case against him than Gavin. The buzzing of my phone interrupted my thoughts.

"Ms. Landon, it's Sarah James. Did you find out anything?"

"That's why I'm calling you. When I spoke to Paula Frankel, she told me that Claire was afraid of something or someone, and it didn't pertain to Howie. Can you think of anyone she might have been afraid of? Maybe someone from her days at the foster home? Anything you can remember?"

"I need to think a minute. There was this one kid, Billy Jenkins. He was kind of a geek and Claire used to tease him all the time. I remember he had this toy soldier that he carried around with him. One night when Billy was sleeping, Claire went into his room and took the soldier. The next day when he found the soldier in her room, he had a fit. He said he would get even with her one day."

"How old were they when this exchange took place?"

"I'm not sure exactly, maybe ten or eleven."

"I can't imagine after all these years he had anything to do with Claire's death."

"There's more. Maybe about three or four months ago, he just showed up at her house. He asked her if he could borrow money. When she told him no, he didn't take it very well. His presence made her feel very uncomfortable. Though he didn't actually threaten her, she was scared of him."

"How come you didn't mention this to me the last time we spoke?"

"To tell you the truth, I forgot about it until you just started asking me questions now. It probably slipped my mind."

I can't imagine something like that slipped her mind. Was there a reason she didn't mention it to me earlier?

"Was that the only time she heard from him?"

"If he contacted her again, she didn't say."

"What do you know about him?"

"Just rumors that he's been in trouble, stealing, maybe drugs."

"Do you know where he is now?"

"I believe before he came to the foster home, he lived in Mount Vernon. If he's not in jail, maybe he still has connections to that area."

"Thanks, you've been a big help. One other thing, would you happen to remember what he looked like?"

"Let me see. He was a skinny kid, small for his age with blond hair. He had these big eyes that were so dark, they looked almost black. I thought it was kind of weird that this kid who was fair-skinned with blond hair had such dark eyes."

"When was the last time you saw him?"

"He left when he was around fourteen. I think he got into some trouble and had to leave the home."

"Thanks again."

"Do you think he could have killed Claire?" Sarah said.

"At this point, I have no reason to believe he did. I just want to be thorough."

I had no idea if Billy Jenkins had anything to do with Claire's death, but on the off chance he might have, I had to try and locate him. I doubted whether I was going to find Billy Jenkins in any of my databases, but I did have an idea of how to locate him.

I knew someone from my days on the police force, a guy named Felix, who I could ask to run a criminal check on this guy. Though I didn't have Billy Jenkins' exact year of birth, if he was close in age to Claire, I could approximate. I called my friend and gave him the information, telling him to check under both William and Bill Jenkins.

My phone rang. It was Greg. "What happened?" I asked anxiously.

"They arrested Howie. He'll be arraigned tomorrow and there's no way he's getting bail, not with the charge of first-degree murder. Howie looked so despondent."

"Did they find anything?"

"They must have. I'll make a couple of calls. We need to find out who killed Claire; preferably before this goes to trial."

CHAPTER 42

I didn't mention my possible lead of Billy Jenkins to Greg in case it didn't pan out.

"I'll arrange it so we can see Howie at the jail as soon as possible," Greg said.

"Where will he be arraigned?"

"At the Westchester County Supreme Court, located on Martin Luther King Boulevard in White Plains. This doesn't look good."

"Do you think he's guilty?"

"It doesn't matter what I think. We just need to make sure the jury doesn't."

"Don't take this the wrong way, Greg, but this would be your first murder trial. Maybe we should bring another attorney on board who has trial experience."

"Thanks for the vote of confidence," Greg said before ending the call.

I called Gavin and got his voicemail. "Call me, Howie's been arrested."

"What happened?" Gavin said when he got back to me twenty minutes later.

"I'm not sure. The police searched his house and we don't know what they found, if anything. Are you sure you didn't say something that would have given the police reason to search his house?"

"How would I know? It seemed as if they were asking me questions they already knew the answers to. I think they were fishing to see how much I knew and if I was hiding anything."

"That makes sense. Did they ask you about his alibi again?"

"I needed to tell them the truth. I'm sorry," he said, sounding apologetic. "I knew they would eventually find out, and it would look worse for me if I didn't tell them. Do you think that's why they got the search warrant?"

"Maybe. You need to get in touch with Howie's clients, and make sure they know that you'll be working with them instead of Howie. Also, you never answered my question about why you were still in contact with Claire after you had told me you had ended the affair a month before her death."

"She was worried about Howie. She was afraid for him because she knew about his gambling debts and that he had received some late-night calls. Though he didn't say anything to Claire, she knew those calls frightened him."

"Why you? She had two close friends to confide in."

"Because I was close to Howie. I saw him every day. Though she didn't come out and say it, I think she wanted me to keep an eye out, make sure he was okay."

I had no way of knowing whether Gavin was bullshitting me or telling the truth. For now, there was nothing I could do about it.

"If you think of anything else, call me."

I couldn't fault Gavin for what he told the police, though unfortunately it hurt Howie.

***

I met Greg at the Westchester County Department of Corrections the following day. The Department of Corrections is located in Valhalla, a few miles north of Scarsdale. Inmates are incarcerated there while they're awaiting trial. At his arraignment, Howie was denied bail.

After going through protocol, we were brought to a private room where we waited for Howie. When he walked through the door, I couldn't believe how he looked. His face was haggard and pale.

"How could this be happening? I had nothing to do with Claire's death," Howie said, shaking his head as he sat down.

"As far as I know, most of the evidence is circumstantial. There must have been something they found in the house that caused them to arrest you," Greg said.

"Please, you have to find out who killed Claire."

"Howie, is there anything you haven't told us?" I asked.

"You know everything. What about Gavin? He had an affair with Claire."

"That's true, but I guess they felt they had a stronger case against you," I said.

"What about my business, my clients?"

"Gavin will contact them, and he'll make sure they're taken care of. I know you hate him, but right now you have to think of yourself."

"And how do you expect me to do that in here?"

"Read, exercise, whatever it takes. I don't pretend to know what you're going through, but I'm doing everything I can to find out who killed your wife," I said.

Greg and I stayed for a while trying to pump Howie up. Walking to our cars, I asked Greg again if we should hire another attorney to help with the trial. Maybe it was none of my business but I wanted to make sure Howie got the best defense he could afford, and I just wasn't sure Greg was that person.

"No one's going to work harder for Howie than me, even if I don't have as much experience as some other lawyer."

"I'm not asking you to recuse yourself. I just think it would be prudent to have another attorney at Howie's trial with experience."

"Just do the job I hired you for and let me worry about everything else."

There was no point in continuing our conversation. Greg was adamant about defending Howie without additional counsel.

"Keep me apprised of what you find out," Greg said in a harsh tone, as he got into his car.

I thought Greg was being a real jackass, and I didn't want to see Howie getting screwed. My phone vibrated.

"Hello."

"Maddie, it's Felix. I got that information you wanted. I'm emailing it to you now."

"Just getting into my car. Can you give me a brief summary?"

"Your guy has been in and out of jail a few times: possession of cocaine, petty theft, and two DWIs."

"The guy sounds lovely."

"Yeah, a real choir boy."

"You wouldn't by any chance know where I can find the guy?"

"That would be too easy, but I do have the name of his last public defender. Maybe he'd be willing to help you."

"Thanks, Felix."

When I got back to the office, I opened up the email Felix sent me. It appeared Billy Jenkins had been in and out of trouble his whole life. I'm pretty sure being in foster care couldn't have been easy. When my parents died, I was really bitter. I can't imagine what would have happened to me if I had wound up in the foster care system.

I found the telephone number for Jason Crandall, Billy Jenkins' public defender. Now I had to come up with a story as to why he should give me any information on Jenkins. It's always best to stick close to the truth. I left a message in his voice mail, hoping he would call me back. About an hour later, my phone rang.

"Hello."

"This is Jason Crandall. How can I help you?"

"My name's Maddie Landon. I'm a private investigator in Manhattan investigating the death of a woman named Claire Stevenson. I believe you defended someone named Billy Jenkins not too long ago. It turns out Mrs. Stevenson and Mr. Jenkins were in the same foster home growing up. I'm talking to several people who knew her from the home, and I thought you might happen to know where I could find him?"

"That's the woman who was killed in Scarsdale. Is that correct?"

"Yes."

"I don't live far from there—Yonkers. There's no current address for him, but I believe he hangs out in Mount Vernon."

"Do you have a telephone number for him?"

"I might but I can't give it to you."

"I see. Any particular place in Mount Vernon?"

"There's a bar called Maggie Spillane's Ale House. Maybe you can catch him there."

"Thanks. I appreciate it."

I didn't know if this was going to be a wild goose chase but I was running out of options.

CHAPTER 43

It was only three o'clock. There would be no point in going up to Maggie Spillane's until later tonight. I was getting hungry, so I grabbed my bag and stopped at a coffee shop near my office. I plunked myself down in a booth and waited for Dolores to take my order.

"You want your usual?" Dolores said.

"I guess I'm pretty predictable. Makes life simple." Dolores laughed.

While I was waiting for my tuna fish sandwich and fries, I called Annie.

"Hello, stranger," Annie said when she answered.

"I'm so wrapped up in this case I'm losing track of time. They arrested Howie. He's up in the Westchester County Department of Corrections."

"How's he holding up?"

"Not good. The police must have found something at his house. That or they thought they had enough circumstantial evidence to arrest him. Either way, he's there for a while."

"Any leads?"

"I wish. I'm following up on a guy that was in foster care with Claire. Apparently, he threatened her when they were kids, and about three months ago he just showed up at her house asking her for money. It appears he wasn't too happy when she refused."

"It turns out he got into trouble when he was around fourteen and was removed from the home. Since then, he's been in and out of jail most of his adult life. Maybe he's the guy Claire was afraid of. The only lead I have is a bar in Mount Vernon. He supposedly hangs out there."

"I know you can handle yourself but when you're on your way home, text me."

"Really?"

"If you don't, I won't be able to sleep."

"Will do. Love you."

Dolores brought over my sandwich and fries. My phone buzzed right after I hung up from Annie.

"Hi there," I said to Jesse, as I was dipping a french fry into a mound of ketchup.

"Are you keeping yourself out of trouble?"

"I hope not." I updated Jesse on what was going on.

"You might be right. It could be a long shot but you have to follow up anyway."

"I told Greg he should probably bring another attorney on board who has trial experience."

"I take it he wasn't too pleased."

"You take it right. What do you think?"

"It was the right call, though it probably hurt his ego."

"Screw his ego. Howie needs someone with experience. Greg says no one is going to work harder for Howie than he will."

"He may be right, but I'm not sure it makes up for his lack of experience. Anyway, it's not your problem."

"But if I don't get some evidence to help Howie, it may become my problem. If this lead doesn't pan out, Howie could be in trouble."

"Something else will turn up."

"Aren't you the optimistic one. What are you up to?"

"Trying to track down this guy who appears to be eluding me."

"You've been at this a lot longer than me. Do you ever get burned out?"

"Not as yet. Hopefully, not for a while. If you get stuck, let me know. Be careful."

"I will. Miss you."

After I finished eating, I went back to my office, got my laptop, and locked up. I was dying to go for a run since I hadn't exercised for a few days. When I got home, I changed, grabbed a bottle of water, and jogged to the park.

At 9:00 p.m. I drove up to Mount Vernon, which is just north of the Bronx in Westchester County. It's considered a median-income city. It has its share of seedy areas and a higher rate of crime compared to other places in Westchester. I found a parking spot a block away from the bar. I was surprised when I walked in. The place was huge with an outdoor patio.

The bar was crowded. I squeezed my way in and asked the bartender if Billy Jenkins was around. I figured if he was a regular, the bartender would know him.

"Haven't seen him yet. Can I get you something to drink?"

"Sure. I'll have a glass of Sauvignon Blanc. If you do see him, can you let me know?" I cornered the last stool and parked myself. I figured I'd stay about an hour nursing my drink waiting to see if he showed up.

About thirty minutes later, I thought I recognized Billy Jenkins at the far end of the bar. He looked like an older version of what Sarah James had described to me, except his blond hair was stringy looking, as if he hadn't washed it for a while.

I got off my stool and walked to the end of the bar.

"Hi, I'm Maddie. Are you Billy?" His dark eyes were chilling.

"Who's asking?"

"Do you remember someone by the name of Claire Matthew? You were in foster care together."

"What about her?"

"She was recently killed. I'm talking to people who knew her."

"Are you a cop or something?"

"Private Investigator." He gave me the once-over.

"Claire was a bitch. She thought she was hot stuff—better than me."

"Have you seen her since you left the home?"

"Why are you asking?"

"Like I said, I'm talking to everyone who knew her."

"Nope. Haven't seen her. I'm not even sure I'd know what she looked like if I fell over her."

"Well, Billy, that's not what I heard. Why don't you try again."

"Oh yeah!"

"That's right. I know you were at Claire's house about three months ago, uninvited. Were you angry that she wouldn't give you any money? Was she still the same bitch you remembered when you were in foster care?"

"So I went to see her. Is that a crime?"

"Only if you killed her. Did you?"

"If I did, do you think I would admit it to you?"

"Being a wiseass hasn't served you all that well. Here's my card in case you have a change of heart."

He took it and put it in his shirt pocket.

"Thanks again," I said, and walked out.

As I was opening my car door, a hand grabbed my shoulder. Instinctively, I turned and pushed as hard as I could. I was staring down at Billy Jenkins. His face was red.

"Are you fucking crazy," he said as he got up off the ground.

"What the hell you doing sneaking up on me? You're lucky I just pushed you."

"Think you're a tough guy," he said.

"What do you want? I'm busy."

"If you don't want to hear what I have to say, well, goodbye."

I didn't know if he knew anything about Claire, but I couldn't take the chance.

"Wait up," I said as I walked toward him. "What do you want to tell me?"

"Buy me a beer."

"Are you kidding me?"

"You got a problem having a drink with me?"

"Let's go."

I ordered two beers at the bar, and we sat down at a booth inside.

"Okay, what's on your mind?" I said, hoping I wasn't being jerked around.

"I have some information about Claire, but the information is going to cost you."

"I don't think you're in any position to negotiate with me. Maybe the police might be interested in your visit to Claire."

"Your loss," he said with a holier-than-thou look on his face.

I got up and started walking toward the door.

"Hey, stop," Billy yelled.

I stopped and turned toward him. "Don't waste my time."

"Sit back down. I'm pretty confident we can work something out."

I wasn't sure what he meant by that, but I had nothing to lose by listening.

"Okay, talk," I said as we both sat down again.

"I got in touch with Claire maybe three months ago."

"Why was that?"

"You know, for old times' sake. Just wanted to know how she was doing."

"Look, don't bullshit me. I know what went on at the foster home. She treated you like shit and you threatened her."

"We were kids. You can't take what I said back then seriously."

"If you were an upstanding citizen maybe you'd be right, but that's not the case. I think you got in touch with her for another reason, to harass her."

"Look, you want to know what I have to say or not?"

"Continue."

"Yeah, you're right. I went there to borrow some money from her. It's not like she couldn't afford it, living in that expensive house in Scarsdale. She turned me down, but the conversation took a different turn."

Now he had my attention.

"So what are you going to do for me?"

"What do you want?" I figured I'd go along for the ride.

"What about if I need your services, say, free of charge."

"That would depend on what you need them for. I can't promise you anything."

"Of course. I would never ask you to do anything illegal."

"Of course not," I said with a straight face.

"Claire wanted me to rough up some guy for her. Said he was harassing her and wanted to get him off her back. I figured it was an easy job and she was going to pay me; more than I had originally asked for."

I could feel the hairs on my arms stand up.

"What else did she say? Did you ask her why?"

"She didn't go into details. She said she would call me back the next day with all the particulars."

"How much was she going to pay you?"

"Enough, and that's all you need to know. But when she called me back, she had changed her mind. She said she would handle it."

"That probably made you really mad. You thought you were going to get your money and now you weren't."

"Okay, maybe I was mad, but I didn't kill her."

"Did you have any further contact with Claire?"

"No."

"So you didn't want to get even with Claire after she had tormented you when you were kids? Then she further stuck it to you by reneging on the job she was going to pay you for. What was going on in your mind? Didn't you want to teach that bitch a lesson? Can't screw with Billy Jenkins anymore."

"Maybe I did want to teach her a lesson, but I never wanted to kill her."

I didn't know whether I believed him or not, but I wasn't going to get the truth out of him.

"Did you speak to her buddy, what's her name, Sarah," Billy said.

"Yeah, why?"

"I guess you don't know. Sarah pretended to be best buds with Claire, but she was really jealous of her."

"Why was that?" I said.

"Claire was beautiful, even as a kid, and though she treated people like garbage, everyone wanted to be her friend, including Sarah."

"Is that it? Doesn't sound like someone who'd hold a grudge and wait to get revenge years later."

"I guess Sarah didn't tell you about the time Claire stole money out of Mrs. Mason's purse and let Sarah take the blame for it. But Sarah still wanted to be friends with Claire."

"Who's Mrs. Mason?"

"Ruth Mason was our foster mother. Sarah was almost removed from the home because of that incident."

I was surprised to hear what Billy just told me.

"Well, you have my card if you think of anything else. Oh, one more thing. Do you remember Mrs. Mason's address?"

"It was off Fordham Road in the Bronx. I can't remember the exact address."

"Thanks."

"I'm sure we'll be in touch," Billy Jenkins said.

I have no doubt, I said to myself, walking out. I'm not sure why, but I got the feeling he was telling me the truth and had nothing to do with Claire's murder. If what he said about Sarah James was true, would she be that angry and wait more than twenty years later to kill Claire? Was she pretending all this time that she was Claire's friend, waiting for the right opportunity to kill her?

CHAPTER 44

As I was getting into my car, I noticed a missed call from Greg.

"What's going on?" I said when I called him back.

"They found poison in Howie's house when they searched it."

"Shit. So that's why they arrested him. But what doesn't make sense is why Howie would have kept the poison. Wouldn't he have gotten rid of it? He had to have known he'd be a suspect."

"Apparently, they found it behind some paint cans under the kitchen sink. Maybe he didn't think that far in advance."

"Or maybe the person who killed Claire planted it and Howie had no idea it was there. I need to talk to him face to face. Also, I just spoke to someone who Claire knew from her time in foster care. It turns out he's not such an upstanding citizen. He showed up at her house about three months ago, asking her for money. Instead, Claire told him she wanted to hire him to teach someone a lesson who had been harassing her. In the end she didn't go through with it, but it confirms what Claire's friend told me—Claire was being threatened by someone."

"That might be something. Do you think this guy would testify if we needed him to?"

"Maybe, though I'm not sure he would make a great witness. He's been in and out of jail most of his life."

"Remember how good we were together when we were partners?"

I had no intention of going down memory lane with Greg. All I wanted was to finish the job I was hired to do and never see Greg again.

"It was until it wasn't," I said.

"I really cared about you but I had no choice. If my wife hadn't been pregnant, I would never have gone back to her."

"You really don't have to explain yourself to me. It's water under the bridge."

"It would be great if we could be friends. I still care about you."

This is not what I wanted to hear. Why do I let him get to me? I had no answer at the moment, or nothing I wanted to admit to myself.

I texted Annie that I was still alive and did she have time for a drink the following night. She texted back: Hi-Life Bar and Grill at 6:30 p.m.

***

The next morning, I went for an early run. I decided to work at home for a while and then go up to see Howie.

I was looking through my emails as I was biting into a sesame bagel but I didn't see anything important. I wondered if Billy Jenkins was Claire's stalker. For all I knew, he could have made up the whole story about Claire wanting to hire him and then Claire changing her mind. At this point, we didn't know how the poison was administered. It just occurred to me that I'd been assuming it was a man who killed Claire, but what if it was a woman.

What if Dana Thomas, Howie's girlfriend, killed Claire? She had reason to get rid of Claire, but why would she leave the poison if she loved Howie?

***

I went through security at the Westchester County Department of Corrections, and waited for Howie in the same room as the last time I was there. When Howie walked in, he looked as though he had lost weight since I last saw him.

"I could use some good news," he said, as he sat down.

"I wish I had some. Do you remember if Claire ever mentioned a guy by the name of Billy Jenkins?"

"Doesn't sound familiar. Should it?"

"He was at the foster home when Claire was there. From what he told me, he contacted Claire about three months ago. She told him she wanted to hire him to rough up someone who had been harassing her, but then changed her mind. Whether that's true or not I have no way of knowing."

"I never knew she was being harassed. I wish she would have told me."

"It seems that it was someone Claire might have slept with a few times and didn't want it to end."

"That's why she didn't tell me. You don't think it was Gavin?"

"No. The timeline doesn't work. I think it was someone else."

"I don't understand what possessed her to have these affairs. I guess I didn't know my own wife."

"I wouldn't be too hard on yourself. Claire didn't have an easy time of it growing up. First losing her parents at such a young age and then knowing her aunt didn't want her. That must have been hell for her."

"I still can't believe I had no idea what was going on in Claire's life. How could I be so blind?"

"She didn't want you to know. I think the person who killed Claire was someone she knew. When your house was searched, the police found a bottle with poison under the kitchen sink behind some paint cans."

"What? That's not possible."

"So you had no idea it was there?"

"Of course not. I wouldn't even know where or how to get it. Is that why I was arrested?"

"Probably, plus all the other circumstantial evidence they had."

"You mean the fact that it wasn't my baby. I swear I didn't even know Claire was pregnant."

"Please think. Is there anything that Claire might have said that seemed odd or didn't seem important at the time?"

"I just don't know," he said, looking defeated.

"Okay. Don't worry about it. I'll come up with something."

Driving back, I kept wondering how Claire was poisoned. According to the police report, there wasn't any sign of a struggle, so there's a good probability she wasn't forced to drink the poison. Could the person have poured it into something he or she knew only Claire would ingest. That

person would have to be fairly close to Claire to know that
particular detail. The question is who?

CHAPTER 45

Annie was sitting at a table when I arrived at the Hi-Life Bar. It's a vintage art déco restaurant serving American food. I noticed a glass of wine in Annie's hand.

"Starting without me?" I said as we hugged.

"I just finished up with a client that drove me batty. She gave me her whole life story, besides the fact that she was definitely not playing with a full deck. It's terrible to say, but if I was married to her, I would have jumped off the nearest bridge."

"And I thought I had a flair for the dramatics."

I snagged the waitress and ordered buffalo wings and a glass of Pinot Noir.

"I'm anxiously waiting to hear all the mouthwatering details," Annie said.

"Oh boy! Where to begin." I caught her up to date on everything that had happened in the last couple of days.

"Right now I'm more interested in Harris Tyler," Annie said. "So what do you know about him besides that he may live on the opposite side of the country?"

"Not much. I'm not even sure he's my father."

"What are you waiting for?"

"I'm still figuring out if I should call him."

"How the hell will you know if you don't? If you're not sure what to say to him, I can help you with that."

"No doubt you can, but I think I have to do this all on my own. It's delicate. I don't want to scare him. If he has no idea that my birth mother had a baby, I would be ambushing him."

"I'm sure you can find a way to handle it tactfully."

I gave Annie my "are you kidding me" look.

"Okay, maybe I give you too much credit, but I still think you can handle it."

"What if he isn't my father?"

"Then at least you'll know for sure. If he is, I'll be happy to fly out with you to California."

"As tempting as that sounds, I'll think about it."

"Okay, no more pressure."

The waitress brought my drink and my order of buffalo wings.

"Now can we talk about the case?" I said, after the waitress left. "There's so much circumstantial evidence against Howie. And finding the poison under the sink, the prosecution is going to have a field day."

"I don't know Howie, but why would he leave poison where the cops can find it? If he did kill his wife, it doesn't make sense."

"I thought the same thing. Even if the poison was hidden in the back of the sink, would he be that stupid to keep it? He had to have known the cops would do a thorough check. If someone wanted to frame him, that person could have planted it in the house. I have doubts whether Howie killed Claire, even though there's still so much evidence against him."

"So you think he might be innocent?"

"He just seems so clueless about Claire. And I really believe he loved her."

"What about his affair?"

"I think he started the affair because Claire was excluding him from her life, not because he didn't love her."

"Keep your focus on finding out who else had a motive. As you said, it has to be someone who knew them pretty well. Make a list of all their close friends and maybe something will pop out at you."

"I'll give it a try. How are you and Matt getting along?"

"Great so far. He's easy to work with and definitely knows his stuff. Business is really picking up. At this rate, we might need to hire an associate in the next few months, though we're being cautiously optimistic."

"Do you think you and Doug can make it up to Jesse's next weekend?"

"I'll check with him. Hopefully, he has nothing pressing going on at work. By the way, any problems working with Greg?"

"I have a feeling he wants more than a working relationship."

"Why do you say that, though I'm not surprised?"

"Just the things he says to me. At first, I thought you were being cynical about Greg. But now I'm thinking your intuition may be correct. I would have had some indication by now if he did have a girlfriend. It's just that every time we talk, he's either trying to get together or alluding to the fact that I'm avoiding him."

"Well, aren't you?"

"That's beside the point. I see no reason to have to explain myself to him."

"You don't, but your reaction to him says something is going on."

"I can handle it."

"I'm sure you can," Annie said, amused. "Has Jesse been giving you any flack about Greg lately?"

"No, but I'm always afraid I might say something that would provoke a reaction from him."

Walking to my car, I knew Annie was right. I needed to figure out why Greg pushes my buttons. If I still have feelings for him, where does that leave me and Jesse? I didn't want to think about it.

***

Sitting at my kitchen table the following morning, I started making a list of people who were close to the Stevensons and might have a reason to harm Claire. I was coming up pretty much empty. Nobody I've spoken with fitted except possibly Gavin Stone. He knew their habits and had a motive, especially if the affair didn't end well.

I thought about Billy Jenkins. After all this time, would he know Claire's habits? If he did kill Claire, I'm pretty sure her death would have been more spontaneous and more brutal.

There was someone I wanted to talk with, but at the moment the name was escaping me. I poured myself a cup of coffee, hoping to get some inspiration. My phone interrupted my thoughts.

"Hello."

"Maddie, this is Scott Reed, Lydia's husband."

"Of course. How are you?"

"I'm fine. I just wanted to say hello and see how you're doing."

"I'm okay. I'm in the middle of a murder investigation and I haven't had much luck so far."

"That must be frustrating. The only thing I know about catching murderers is what I watch on TV. So I guess I can't be of much help."

I laughed.

"That's where I get all my ideas from, but don't tell anyone." It was Scott Reed's turn to laugh.

"Your secret is safe with me."

Neither one of us spoke for a moment.

"I wasn't sure if you wanted to hear from me," Scott said. "I didn't really have anything in mind, I just wanted to say hello."

"I'm glad you did." I wanted to say something but I was debating. "I'm sorry I didn't get to meet my mother. It must have been hard on you when she died so unexpectedly."

"It was. It still is. When she finally told me about the baby, about you, I was angry at her. I know she had no choice at the time, but she kept that secret from me throughout our entire marriage. She didn't trust me enough that I would understand. Intellectually I know why she hid it from me, but emotionally I wish for her sake and mine, she would have told me."

"Maybe on some level she blamed herself for not fighting harder to keep me."

"I never thought of that."

"Do you think she was happy?" I asked.

"I think as happy as she could be considering the burden she carried around with her."

"Can I ask you a personal question?" I said.

"Only if I can ask you one. You go first."

"Do you date?"

"Occasionally. I actually went on one of those singles' websites. It's like navigating a minefield. I hope I'm not being too nosy, but I was curious if you found out anything about your birth father?"

I didn't know if I should tell him what I had learned. Would he be hurt if he knew I may have found him?

"I have a possible lead but it might be a long shot." That was true.

"Well, I'll let you go," Scott said.

"Good luck dating. I'm rooting for you."

After speaking with Scott Reed, my concentration was completely shot. The conversation threw me for a loop. Maybe looking for my birth parents was a big mistake. It was too painful to find out how my birth affected my mother and Scott.

I decided to go for a run to clear my head. When I got back, I took another look at the notes I had written. I needed to push Sarah James. See if I could get a better read on her. If she did poison Claire, maybe she'd crack.

I was running out of suspects and maybe time. Besides Gavin Stone, I had no other viable candidates. Maybe if I gave it a rest, something would miraculously come to me.

CHAPTER 46

I opened up my computer. Though I had a possible address for Harris Tyler in California, that's all I had on him. I had been avoiding looking any further since there was a part of me that didn't want to know if he was my father.

I gingerly entered his name and address into my database. There it was. I just had to click on the report and open it. I forced my finger to cooperate. Harris Tyler was listed as fifty-five years old. It appears he was married to a woman named Jennifer. His relatives listed were Adam, twenty-eight, and Andrew, twenty-five. I'm guessing that those are his sons. His parents listed were Jonathan and Grace, both deceased. What jumped out at me was where his parents were from. It listed Pennsylvania. My heart sped up. Could it be a coincidence that both Harris Tyler's parents and my birth mother were all from Pennsylvania? I doubted it. It still didn't mean he's my father. It was only a guess on Lucy Grainger's part that my mother and Harris Tyler were more than friends. I wasn't ready to make that call.

I changed gears and decided to pay Sarah James a visit. I arrived shortly before 1:00 p.m. As I was ringing the doorbell, a blue Audi pulled into the driveway. Sarah James stepped out of the car.

"Ms. Landon, is that you? Did we have an appointment that I forgot about?"

"No. I was in the area and I thought I'd pop in. Do you have a few minutes?"

"Sure, come on in. Why don't we sit on the back patio since it's so nice out. Can I get you anything to drink?"

"No, I'm good. Unfortunately, I don't have that much time. Why don't we just sit inside." I wasn't sure how the conversation was going to turn out. I thought it was better if we didn't get too comfortable.

"How is the investigation going?" she asked, as we were seated in the sitting room with the hanging plants.

"That's what I wanted to talk to you about. Maybe you can help me." That always puts people at ease.

"I was thinking that the person who killed Claire had to have been fairly close to her and was aware of her habits."

"I guess."

"By the way, I tracked down Billy Jenkins. It turns out you were right about him. He's had a few run-ins with the police. Actually, he was in jail for a while."

"Really? I wasn't sure."

"Why would you be? You haven't been in touch with him since he was kicked out of the foster home. He admitted he was in contact with Claire and said that Claire wanted to hire him to hurt someone who was harassing her but changed her mind."

"That must be the person who killed Claire or maybe it was Billy."

"Maybe. Billy also mentioned that Claire stole some money from Mrs. Mason." I looked at Sarah's face to see if there was any reaction. I saw her biting her lower lip.

"Wow! I had forgotten all about that. Yeah, it was so long ago."

"Did you get blamed for what Claire did?"

"I did but in the end it was fine. Claire apologized and we were good."

"So you didn't resent Claire that she treated everyone like dirt, including you?"

"I'm not sure what you're getting at, but no matter what, I loved Claire. I would never have harmed her. I think you better leave now. And by the way, instead of wasting your time with me, maybe you should be looking for the person who really killed my friend."

CHAPTER 47

I couldn't tell after speaking with Sarah James if she was lying. It didn't seem to make sense she would wait so long to kill Claire. Was her resentment and hatred of Claire so strong that she had been biding her time for the right moment? I didn't think so, but I couldn't rule it out.

Since I wasn't in a hurry to get back and had nowhere else to go, I parked my car down the street from her house. Thirty minutes later, I saw her Audi coming out of the driveway. I decided to follow her, giving the Audi plenty of room between us, hoping I didn't lose her.

After following for about twenty minutes, we wound up by the beach in Larchmont. Sarah got out of her car and walked over to a bench looking over the water. I followed but kept a safe distance. A few minutes later, a man sat down next to her. There wasn't any way I could get a photo of the guy with their backs to me.

They appeared to be deep in conversation. It was hard to tell if they were lovers. For all I knew it could be her husband, but somehow I doubted it. Fifteen minutes later they both stood up, embraced, then kissed before he turned and left. I watched as he walked to his car. I snapped two quick photos of him.

As I turned back to Sarah, she was sitting down again. If I was going to get the truth out of her this was my chance. I approached Sarah and sat down next to her. She looked at me, her eyes glossy. I was surprised I didn't get more of a reaction.

"I thought we were done talking. Why are you here?" she said in a flat tone.

"Are you having an affair?"

"That's none of your business. You didn't answer my question."

"I didn't think you told me the truth and I needed to know."

"You want to know the truth. Here's something. I hated Claire. Billy was right. She treated everyone like she was better than us. She didn't care who she hurt."

"Then why were you friends with her?"

"I needed her. She was all I had growing up in that crappy foster home."

"So you pretended to be her friend all those years?"

"When I was older, what happened back then didn't seem to matter so much. Yeah, there were times when she could be self-absorbed, but I realized that she was hurting too. So before you ask me, I did not kill Claire. I loved her."

Again, I asked, "Are you having an affair?"

"I was, but it ended."

"How come?"

"I decided I needed to try and make my marriage work. As you can probably guess, growing up in foster care I didn't have very much. I told you the truth when I said I was jealous that Claire's aunt sent her presents. Do you think I live in a four-million-dollar house by accident? I went after Jonathan. You could say I married him for money, but as we learn when we get older, money doesn't buy you happiness. At one time, I would have done anything to have money. It was Claire who said I should give the marriage a chance. I don't know if it'll work out between us, but I want to at least give it a try. If not, well, I'll go down that road when the time comes."

"Thank you for being honest with me. Do you think Billy Jenkins could have killed Claire?"

"Like I told you, I haven't seen Billy since he left the foster home. I can't say one way or the other. You might have a better guess than I would."

I started to get up. "Good luck. I hope you get what you want."

Driving back to Manhattan, I was completely surprised at what Sarah revealed to me. Either she was a great actress or she was telling me the truth. I opted for the latter. Maybe I was being gullible but I believed her, knowing firsthand what losing parents can do to your psyche.

It was time to go back to the beginning, the foster home where Claire spent most of her young life. Maybe her foster mother could give me some insight into Claire. I didn't know whether it could help with my investigation, but I was stuck.

CHAPTER 48

When I got back to my office, I conducted a database search for a Ruth Mason residing in the Bronx. There was one match. The report listed her age as eighty. It appears she had lived in the same house for more than forty years. Since it was only a little past 5:00 p.m., I thought I would pay a visit to Ms. Mason today.

I drove to the address in the Bronx where Ruth Mason lives. I stayed in the car for a few minutes, observing the house Claire grew up in. It was a white clapboard ranch. The house looked worn as the paint on the wooden frame was chipping and the lawn was overgrown.

I rang the doorbell. A moment later, I heard someone shouting, "I'm coming, I'm coming." When the door finally opened, there was an elderly woman leaning on a cane. "Can I help you?"

"Are you Ruth Mason?"

"Yes," she said warily.

"My name's Maddie Landon. I'm a private investigator. I wanted to talk to you about a former foster child who was in your care many years ago, Claire Matthew."

"Please, please come in. Don't mind the mess. I don't get around like I used to. Bum knees and my eyesight is not so good anymore. Please sit," she said, pointing to a sagging couch in the living room.

"Is Claire alright? Did something happen to her?"

"Unfortunately, she was killed about two months ago. The police believe someone poisoned her."

"How dreadful. Was it her husband?" I was surprised at her question.

"Why would you say that?"

"On TV they always blame it on the husband."

"Oh, I see. Would it be alright if I ask you a few questions about Claire?"

"Well, what would you like to know?"

"Why don't you tell me what she was like as a child?"

"Claire was a beautiful child. She was also very mischievous. She thought she could get away with everything because she was so pretty. But there was another side of her that was begging for attention, yet she kept to herself most of the time. It's not easy on these kids who are abandoned in one way or another. We do the best we can to help them."

"I'm sure you did. I was wondering if Claire kept in touch with you?"

"No. I hadn't seen Claire since she left the foster system when she was eighteen. Yet a few months ago, she just showed up at my door. I had a sense something was wrong but I didn't want to pry. I figured she'd get around to telling me if she wanted to."

"What did she talk about?"

"To tell you the truth, not much. She mentioned she wasn't sure if her marriage was going to last."

"Did she say why?"

"No, but I could tell she was anxious. Most of these kids never have an easy time of it. They're always chasing something."

"Did she mention anything else that was troubling her?"

"She did say she had a feeling someone may be trying to hurt her. But she didn't sound very sure."

"Why do you say that?"

"She was talking out loud but wasn't making any sense. It was as if I wasn't even in the room."

"Did she mention anyone's name?"

"I don't think so. I'm sorry I'm not being much help."

"Don't worry about it. Did she get along with the other children?"

"Claire could be very rebellious at times and picked fights with some of the kids."

"Was there anyone in particular that had a grudge against her?"

"If you're thinking one of my children could have hurt Claire, you're wrong. I brought my kids up better than that." I knew she wanted to believe what she said.

"I heard that Billy Jenkins had it in for her."

"They were just children."

I knew I had hit a sore spot and decided to leave it alone.

"Why do you think Claire came to see you?"

"I don't know. Maybe it was nostalgia."

"If you remember anything, please call me," I said, handing her my card. "Thank you for seeing me. Take care."

"I hope you find out who killed Claire. I wish I could have helped her more."

I thought it was odd that out of the blue, after all these years, Claire went to see her foster mother. Something was definitely upsetting her. If she thought someone was trying to harm her, why didn't she confide in anyone? Did she have a premonition that something was going to happen to her?

CHAPTER 49

I overslept in the morning and quickly showered before Jesse showed up. I just finished drying my hair when the doorbell rang.

After pulling Jesse in, I closed the door behind him.

"I missed you."

"How much?"

"Enough to make you very happy for a while."

"Lead the way."

"You know what I'm thinking?" I said, snuggling close to Jesse after we were both fully satisfied.

"I'm guessing I'll soon find out," Jesse said, caressing my hair.

"I think we should run away together."

"Don't you think we're a little too old to run away?" he said, smiling. "What's going on?"

"I'm completely screwing up this case and getting nowhere. Howie's in jail and I haven't the foggiest idea after talking to basically everyone connected to the case who killed her."

"Rome wasn't built in a day. From what you've told me, you've uncovered more than the police have."

"The police work slowly."

"That may be so, but you've covered a lot of ground. You know something always turns up."

"There's always the case I won't be able to solve."

"That's true, but I wouldn't be focusing on that. It sounds, from what you've told me, you think Howie is innocent, yet the police have so much evidence against him. So why do you think he's innocent?"

"I know you're going to laugh. Call it intuition. Also, it doesn't make sense if he did kill his wife, he would leave the poison in the house."

"You'd be surprised how stupid people can be."

"There's got to be someone in her past that I'm overlooking, or maybe she got involved in something I'm not aware of."

"I have a suggestion."

"Oh, goody."

"How about breakfast or another go at it."

"You are such a tease."

A half-hour later, we were sitting down to eat.

"I thought we might go to the Whitney Museum downtown and soak in some culture. Also, it's a really neat place to walk around. Very trendy area. What do you think?"

"I'm game."

"And here I thought I'd have to talk you into it."

"Though I'm a simple man, being exposed to the culture of your city gives me great joy," Jesse said, grinning.

"That's one of your endearing qualities, your sense of humor."

We spent a few hours at the museum and then walked into Greenwich Village looking for a place to eat. As we were about to cross the street, I heard my name being called. I knew right away who it was. I wanted to keep walking, but Jesse would have wondered why.

"Hey, Maddie, I thought that was you."

"Jesse, Greg," I said, hoping that would be it and we would go on our merry way. No such luck.

"Glad to finally meet you," Greg said. I could see they were giving each other the once-over.

"Where are you guys headed?" Greg said.

"We're looking for a place to have a late lunch. Would you like to join us," Jessie said.

I couldn't believe he just said that. I wanted to kill him. Knowing Jesse, he probably thought this was very amusing.

"Sure. I know a place called Da Andrea on Thirteenth Street. It has outdoor seating."

"That sounds great," Jesse said. "Lead the way."

When we arrived, the waitress seated us and left menus. Neither Jesse nor Greg looked uncomfortable. It appeared I was the only one irritated and wanted to be anywhere else.

"So how do you like being a lawyer? It must be quite different from when you were with the police department," Jesse said.

Thankfully, the waitress came back and we ordered drinks. My wine couldn't come fast enough.

"In truth, in some ways, I miss working as a detective. And having Maddie was a bonus. She was a great partner."

I had no idea if Greg was being sincere or if he was trying to get Jesse jealous.

Our drinks came. "Would you like to order now?" the waitress asked.

Jesse and I both ordered a burger and salad. Greg ordered the seared tuna. I took a big gulp of my wine.

"I see you're still eating meat," Greg said, looking at me.

I decided not to reply. It was Greg's way of telling Jesse that he knew me intimately.

"So you're a private investigator," Greg said to Jesse.

"That's right. I work for two criminal attorneys in Connecticut."

"That must keep you busy. How do you guys manage the long-distance relationship? I know if Maddie was my girlfriend, I'm not sure I'd like her so far away from me."

"Then it's a good thing she's not your girlfriend," Jesse said.

Greg was being an ass and he was trying to get under Jesse's skin. I didn't think Jesse would show any signs of being bothered by Greg's remarks, even if he was burning inside.

"So how did you meet your girlfriend?" I said, wanting to shift the conversation.

"We actually met at a neighborhood bar," Greg said.

"What does she do?"

"She's a physician's assistant."

"That's interesting. Where?"

"For a doctor in Manhattan."

"Oh, I was thinking of switching doctors. What's his name?"

"I don't know offhand," Greg said, looking a little uncomfortable.

"Well, maybe you can give me his name when you get a chance."

"Sure," he said, clenching his jaw.

I didn't believe what he said for a second.

"Maddie tells me this is your first trial coming up. Are you nervous?"

"Not really. With a crackerjack PI by my side, I have no doubt we'll win."

What the hell's his problem?

Our food came and I dug in. It was obvious that Greg was trying to get a reaction from Jesse. The back and forth between them was getting on my nerves. I finished my glass of wine and was debating whether to have another. I decided against it since I might say or do something I'd regret.

The banter went on for a little while longer when I asked the waitress for our check. When it came, Jesse insisted on paying for Greg.

"I'm glad we finally got to meet. You're a lucky guy to have Maddie," Greg said, shaking Jesse's hand as we were leaving.

Though Jesse wouldn't have picked up on it, I knew from the look on Greg's face he wasn't being sincere.

"Maddie, I'll talk to you on Monday," Greg said.

I was angry at Jesse. "What the hell. You invited him on purpose," I said to him when we were out of earshot of Greg.

"I did. I was curious about this guy."

"And?"

"He still has the hots for you."

"I think he made up this girlfriend."

"You may be right."

I knew this was not going to be the last time Greg was the subject of our conversations.

CHAPTER 50

Monday morning, I kissed Jesse goodbye and drove to my office. I was feeling anxious sitting at my desk. My leg was shaking and my heart was thumping. I was worried about the case. Nothing was going right.

When my parents died, I started having anxiety attacks. At first, I didn't know what was happening to me. I was only twelve. I'd have trouble breathing and I felt like I was going to pass out. Initially, I didn't want to tell my aunt, but they were getting worse. She took me to see my family doctor, who was able to diagnose what I was experiencing. He explained to me what to do when I'd have an attack. The most reassuring thing he said to me was that I wasn't going to faint even though it felt like it. Eventually, they became less frequent. I haven't had a full-blown attack in years, but at times my anxiety level can go through the roof. I got up and walked around, trying to control my breathing. Then I called Annie.

"Hey, Annie," I said when she answered. "I think I may be losing my mind."

"Can you be more specific?" I knew Annie thought I was being dramatic.

"This case is driving me crazy. I'm so anxious my heart is racing a mile a minute. I'm afraid I'm going to have an anxiety attack."

"Breathe. Even if you do have an attack, nothing is going to happen to you. Just keep breathing."

"If I'm going off the deep end, please don't put me in the psychiatric ward of the state hospital."

"I promise," Annie said, laughing.

When I hung up, I took a walk around the block, hoping it would help alleviate some of my anxiety. I wanted a cup of coffee desperately, but I knew my nerves couldn't take it. Instead, I went inside Barnes and Noble and picked up the latest John Grisham book.

When I got back, I felt a little calmer. I was curious, what, if anything, Greg's source found on the burner phone.

I picked up the phone and called Greg. He answered on the first ring.

"What's going on, Maddie?"

"It's been a while and I was wondering if your source found anything on the burner phone?"

"My contact said it was clean."

"How come you didn't tell me?"

"I just found out." There was something in the way he said it that made me doubt that he was telling the truth.

"What if you give it to me? I have someone who's a whiz at this stuff."

"If my guy couldn't find anything, no one can. By the way, I just heard the judge set the trial for June 30. That doesn't give us much time. We need to find something that will give us a fighting chance. At this point, there's too much evidence against Howie."

"I agree, but unless we can find out who was harassing Claire, I'm at a loss. I'll keep at it. Hopefully, something will turn up."

"I'm counting on you, Maddie."

I wanted to tell him to go fuck himself, but I just hung up instead. I was already pissed that he didn't want to give the phone to me to have it checked out. At some point, we may have to turn the phone over to the prosecution. Hopefully, Greg's contact was correct, and there was nothing on it that could hurt Howie.

Thinking about Claire, I couldn't make sense of what was going on in her life prior to her death. Why didn't she tell anyone about this person who was harassing her? Was she afraid? According to Howie, he was in the dark about what was going on with his wife. When I looked at the time, I needed to hustle to make my therapy appointment.

I was sitting in Dr. Goldberg's waiting room by myself. Every once in a while, I'll see a patient who has a session before me leaving her office. I watched as Dr. Goldberg's door opened. A man, probably in his forties, with his head down, came out, never making eye contact with me. Maybe he was embarrassed being in therapy.

I sat down in my usual chair opposite Dr. Goldberg. I was trying to quiet my leg, hoping Dr. Goldberg wouldn't notice. We played the waiting game for a minute or two until I caved.

"I feel like my head is being squeezed."

"What does that mean?"

"Nothing is going right. The trial is coming up soon and unless I find something that can help with the client's defense, he's going to be spending the rest of his life in prison. And I know what you're going to say and it doesn't bring me any comfort."

"What drives you, Maddie?"

"I don't know what you mean."

"I understand you want to do everything possible to help the people you represent, but I think there's something else going on."

"Like what?"

"From what you've told me about your parents, they were very loving. Unfortunately, you lost them at a very important time in your life, just before you were entering your teen years. At the time, it may have been the worst thing imaginable. Maybe even a fear you've lived with growing up, knowing you were abandoned at birth. Is it possible that every time you work on a case, you have to solve it, or you'll think you're worthless? Does it mean that failure is not an option and that's what drives you?"

I didn't know what to say. Could she be right? I know I can get tense and frustrated when a case isn't going my way. The pressure can get to me.

"I need some time to think about it. Can we change the subject?"

"Of course. What would you like to talk about?"

"Jesse and I were in Greenwich Village over the weekend and we bumped into Greg. I quickly introduced them, hoping Greg would go on his merry way. But Jesse had other thoughts and invited him to join us for lunch."

"How did that make you feel?"

"I was kind of pissed at Jesse. I think he wanted me to squirm a little, since he's probably still mad that I'm working with Greg."

"That could be true. Do you think he wanted to get a sense of this guy?"

"I guess. He told me afterward he thought Greg still had the hots for me."

"How did the lunch go?"

"It was a disaster. Greg was definitely trying to get under Jesse's skin, making remarks that were intended to get Jesse jealous."

"We've never really talked about your feelings for Greg. At one point in your life, he was very important to you."

"I guess he was. Annie thinks he took advantage of me. Though we were partners, he was definitely the senior partner. I was a rookie and he took me under his wing. I did look up to him."

"Is that how you saw it?"

"At the time yes. I was infatuated with Greg. He seemed so powerful and I felt taken care of."

"I'm sure that felt wonderful. Maybe when you see Greg now, you tap into those feelings you once had, but you have to remember you're not the same person you were then. Why don't we stop here and pick it up next week."

CHAPTER 51

As I was driving home exhausted from my session, I noticed a missed call from Annie.

"Hey, I just got your call. I was in therapy. Do you think I'm driven?"

"Is that a trick question? You just called me hours ago in a complete state of anxiety. You're the most obsessed person I know when it comes to your cases. Why are you asking?"

"Dr. Goldberg seems to think I'm compensating because of my abandonment issues. I have to prove myself over and over."

"Do you think there's any truth to it?"

"I always feel pressure to solve my cases. I thought everyone felt that way."

"I think some people do, but others try their best and whatever happens, happens."

"Is that how you feel?"

"I give it my all. Sometimes it doesn't turn out the way I want it to, but I don't beat myself up over it."

"I just don't know how to stop?"

"Maybe realizing why you're doing it will help. It probably won't happen overnight."

"By the way, why were you calling me?" I asked.

"I wanted to know what to pack for this weekend."

"Right. I forgot you guys were coming up to Jesse's. Do you have any boots you can wear for hiking?"

"I was born and bred in Manhattan. What do you think?"

"Probably not, though I know you'll run out and get the most expensive hiking boots. You are such a fashionista."

"It's important to look the part."

"I would expect nothing less," I said, laughing. "Thanks for sharing," I said and clicked off.

When I arrived home, all I could muster up to eat was a peanut butter and jelly sandwich. I topped it off with chips and got into bed after I undressed. I turned the TV on and watched *Jeopardy*, even though I can rarely answer any of the questions. "How can people be so smart?" As I was concentrating, I was interrupted by the phone.

"Hey, Jesse."

"How's my girl?"

"Isn't that a chauvinistic remark?"

"I take it back."

"No, you can't. I like it even if it is. Did you remember that Annie and Doug are coming up this weekend?"

"I did. I'm planning our menu for the weekend."

"You are my hero."

"Anything food-wise I should know about?"

"Nope. They're not as picky as I am. Annie will now be adding hiking boots to her wardrobe. By the way, I learned in therapy today that I'm driven."

"I could have given you that advice for free."

"It means more when you pay for it," I said, grinning.

"So now that you know, are you going to stop?"

"We'll see."

"Good answer."

"I miss you."

"You know we can rectify the situation," Jesse said.

"I know." Wanting to quickly change the subject, I said: "Well, I'm going to dig into my delicious peanut butter and jelly sandwich and finish watching *Jeopardy*."

"Sounds yummy. I'll talk to you tomorrow. Love you."

"Right back at you."

CHAPTER 52

My phone rang as I was walking to my office the following morning.

"What's up, Greg?"

"I wanted to talk to you about something I've been thinking about. You have a minute?"

"Go ahead."

"I realize you were skeptical about us working together because of our past and I understand that. But I think you're making a mistake by not giving us another chance. The circumstances are different now, and I know we're good for each other."

"I'm not clear what we're talking about here. Is it working together or being together?"

"I guess both. I'm sure Jesse's a great guy, but he's not right for you."

"How would you know that? Don't you think your judgment is just a little impaired?" I said sarcastically.

"Please, Maddie, just think about it."

"It's not going to happen. We are not going to happen. Right now, the only reason I'm continuing on the case is because of Howie. I'll do everything I can to try and help him. Don't bring up the subject of us again."

I hung up angry at Greg and angry at myself for letting him get under my skin. I needed to calm down. Instead of going directly to my office, I stopped at the Coffee Cup to pick up a latte and something sinful to eat to take out my frustrations on. I was waiting in line when

I turned and saw this woman who looked vaguely familiar, but I couldn't place her. As I was leaving, the woman stopped me.

"Is your name Maddie?"

"Do I know you?"

"My name's Beth Carter. I worked at the same precinct as you but I was in the administrative department."

"Of course, how are you?" I remembered Beth's beautiful long, thick, curly red hair.

"I'm good. Do you have time to chat for a moment?" Beth said.

"Sure. Why don't I grab us a table." Actually, I was glad about the distraction.

"So what are you doing now?" Beth said when she sat down.

"I'm a private investigator. Are you still with the police department?"

"Yes. It's going on ten years. Also, I recently got engaged. He's not a police officer, thankfully."

I wasn't exactly sure what she meant by that remark, but I decided not to ask her.

"Congratulations."

"How about you? Are you seeing anyone?"

"I am. He's also a private investigator."

"Working on anything interesting?"

"I don't know if you remember a guy named Greg Martin. He's an attorney now, and I'm investigating the death of his friend's wife. What's wrong, Beth?" She looked upset, wringing her hands.

"It's nothing."

"Beth, it can't be nothing. You seem agitated. You can tell me."

"I had an affair with Greg while he was married. I can't believe I fell for his poor me story."

"What are you talking about?"

"He told me that the marriage had been over for a while, and he was getting a divorce. I subsequently heard rumors that he had several affairs. I probably wasn't the only one he used that line on."

Shit. That bastard. I wanted to kill him. All his bullshit that he's never cheated on his wife before. I was such an idiot.

"I broke it off with him because he was too possessive. He didn't take it well," Beth said.

"What do you mean by that?"

"He kept calling me, trying to persuade me to get back together with him. I'm sorry, I shouldn't have told you. Please don't say anything to him. I have to go."

"Wait, were you scared of him?" She was gone before I could get an answer.

I sat there, not wanting to believe what she just told me. But I knew from the look on her face she wasn't lying. All the women who I thought were so stupid because they got duped by a man. And now I was one of them. I phoned Annie.

"Hey, I just went boot shopping," Annie said. "I'm going to look great on the hiking trails."

"Wonderful. Listen." I went on to tell Annie about the conversation I had with Beth.

"That son of a bitch. Are you going to say anything to him?"

"I don't think so. What would be the point? As soon as this case is over, I'll never see him again. I'm just curious about what he said to her. She definitely had a strong reaction to him."

"You could try and talk to her again if you really want to know."

"I don't think so. He'll soon be out of my life. And please don't mention it to Doug or Jesse. I feel so stupid that I fell for him."

"You can't keep beating yourself up. How could you have possibly known? He was good at it. He had a lot of practice, and he was charming to boot."

"I thought that could never be me. I was smarter than those other women who fell for those jerks. But I guess I was wrong."

"You have nothing to be embarrassed about. He's the dirtbag who should be ashamed of himself."

"Let's drop it. So you mentioned something about boots. If anyone could find a pair of hiking boots that are gorgeous, that would be you. I'll try not to stand too close when we hit the trails, so I won't feel like little orphan Maddie next to you."

"Very funny. Love you."

"Ditto."

I couldn't get the look on Beth Carter's face out of my head when I mentioned Greg's name to her. Was I so blind that I couldn't see the real Greg Martin when we were together? I needed to try and let it go or else it would consume me.

I sat at my desk and closed my eyes, trying to relax in order to think more clearly. I needed to focus on the case. For some reason the police cleared Gavin Stone, though I wasn't sure why. Maybe his alibi with that woman checked out. I ruled out Billy Jenkins, since he wasn't close enough to Claire to know her everyday routine and habits.

There was so much circumstantial evidence against Howie. Though I find it hard to believe Howie would be stupid enough to keep the poison, obviously the police disagreed. *Someone knows something about this guy who was threatening Claire. But who?*

A thought occurred to me. I needed to talk with Howie again.

CHAPTER 53

The following day, I pulled into the Westchester County Department of Corrections parking lot. I went through their usual procedures and then waited for Howie in another small, windowless room.

When he came in, I hardly recognized him. His eyes were bloodshot and he looked like he had lost twenty pounds. The thought of telling him that I had no leads had my stomach in knots.

"Hi, Howie. I didn't know what books you liked so I bought a few different authors."

"Thanks," he said, showing no interest.

"You have to keep positive."

"Why? Did you find the person who killed my wife? Someone is framing me. I did not poison my wife and I have no idea how it got into my house."

"I believe you, Howie. If you didn't do it, then someone else brought it in. Someone who knew Claire's schedule and her habits. If she wasn't forced to drink the poison, the person probably put it in something they knew she would drink but you wouldn't. I need to know what Claire did every day, who she might have seen, and anyone who may have been in your house in the days leading up to Claire's death."

"I already told you I don't remember."

"Try again. It's important."

"In the morning before work, she usually went for a run. If she didn't get a chance to run in the morning, she ran when she came home from work."

"Did she run with anyone?"

"I think she usually went alone but sometimes our next-door neighbor went with her."

"You mean Margo Beck?"

"No, it was her husband, John."

"You never mentioned that Mrs. Beck's husband went running with Claire."

"I guess it never occurred to me."

"Okay, continue."

"When she wasn't at work, she may have been with one of her friends."

"You mean Paula Frankel or Sarah James?"

"And don't forget Gavin. She could have been with him," Howie said.

"What about the days leading up to Claire's death?"

"It was so long ago how could I possibly know who was at our house? I usually left before Claire went to work."

"Okay. Let's think this through. How about the guy she ran with?"

"It's possible John was in our house, but I don't know for sure."

"Who had a key to your house?"

"As far as I know, no one did, but maybe Claire gave a key to someone."

"Do you have a cleaning person?"

"We do, but Claire was always there to let her in."

"Is there anything Claire ate or drank that you didn't?"

"The only thing I can think of is something she drank before she went running. It's called kombucha. It boosts your energy and I think it helps rid the body of toxins. It tastes horrible, but Claire liked it."

"Who would know that?"

"I don't know. Do you think that's how she was poisoned?"

"Possibly, but I can't say for sure. What can you tell me about John Beck?"

"He's a nice guy. Why?"

"Just curious. It seems as if he spent quite a bit of time with Claire."

"I never thought about it. Do you think he had something to do with her death?"

"Without investigating him, I can't answer you."

"How well do you know Mr. Beck?"

"We were friendly, but not close. The four of us went out socially a few times a year and we always had an enjoyable time."

"Did he talk about himself?"

"He talked about his work, but basically we spoke about what was going on in our lives currently."

"Did you get the feeling Mr. Beck was interested in your wife?"

"Not that I was aware of. If he was attracted to Claire or if they were involved, I had no idea. Did you get anything off Claire's burner phone?"

"Unfortunately, no." Howie's face dropped.

"Please keep the faith. I know it's hard and if you think of anything else, call me. You have my cell number."

I got up to leave when Howie said, "Wait! I just remembered something. I completely forgot that Claire and I have a summer place, well it's more like a cabin, about two hours north of here. It's in the town of Valatie, right off the Taconic Parkway, in a pretty remote spot. We used to spend weekends up there."

"How come you never mentioned it before?"

"It didn't occur to me since we hadn't been there in such a long time."

"Do you think she might have gone up there by herself or with someone?"

"Apparently, I'm clueless when it comes to my wife."

"Was she friendly with anyone up there?"

"Not that I recall. We pretty much kept to ourselves."

"Do you know if the police were there?"

"I didn't mention it to them, but they could have found out about it."

"Thank you. Please take care of yourself. We need you to be strong for when the trial starts. Call me or Greg if you want us to bring you anything."

On the way back to my car, I was processing what Howie had told me. I was curious about John Beck, and why this was the first I'd heard he went running with Claire. Could she have confided in him?

CHAPTER 54

At the office, I did a search on John Beck. He had a marketing company in Manhattan. I copied down the address and took an Uber over to Park and Thirty-eighth Street. I walked down the three steps to the entrance of the brownstone and walked in. I opened the door that had the names Stabler and Beck engraved on it.

When I walked in, there was a receptionist behind the desk. Her name plate read: Amy Stewart.

"Hi, Amy," I said.

"Can I help you?"

"I'd like to speak with John Beck." I handed her my card. "Can you tell him it's regarding Claire Stevenson. He'll know who I mean."

"Yes, of course. Please take a seat."

While I waited for Mr. Beck to see me, I casually picked up a car racing magazine and thumbed through it quickly, since I had never followed the sport.

"Excuse me," Amy said. "He'll be right out."

A few minutes later, John Beck was walking toward me. The first thing I noticed was his welcoming smile. The next thing I noticed was the way his suit hugged his body. He definitely had some serious muscles under there.

"Ms. Landon, nice to meet you. Come this way."

I followed him into his office. Mr. Beck motioned for me to sit down. He sat opposite me, behind his desk. I noticed a photo of him and his wife on a credenza behind his desk. They looked happy.

"My wife mentioned she had spoken to you. I was shocked to hear about Claire. I can't imagine Howie had anything to do with her death."

"Why do you say that?"

"The times we socialized with them, he seemed very devoted to her. I feel terrible the police arrested him."

"Do you know how Claire died?" I asked.

"No, I don't."

"She was poisoned."

"That's horrible. Who would do such a thing?"

"That's what I'm trying to find out. I was told you sometimes ran with Claire in the mornings. How did that come about?"

"Quite accidentally. One day, as I was leaving to go to work, I bumped into Claire. I mentioned to her that I see her running in the mornings and asked her if she'd like some company."

"What did she say?"

"She said fine, but that I'd have to run on her schedule. Since the time suited me, I agreed."

"Did you find that a little weird?"

"If you knew Claire, you wouldn't think so. She was actually very shy and kept to herself. I don't think she was exactly looking for a running partner, but it was okay as long as it didn't interfere with her timetable. I didn't take it personally, as I'd rather run with someone than alone. I started running about seven months ago since my doctor thought it was a good idea that I get some exercise. Between running and the gym, I feel better than I have in a long time."

"How long were you two running together before Claire died?"

"I'd say about five months, maybe twice a week."

"You must have gotten pretty friendly with her."

"Claire wasn't a big talker."

"Can you tell me what she did talk about since the slightest detail might be important?"

"Let me see. Everyday stuff, her job. Sometimes she would tell me about her customers. Some of it was quite funny."

"Did she talk about Howie at all?"

"I feel kind of uncomfortable saying anything about him."

"I understand, but Claire's dead and her killer is free."

"She did mention that Howie had gotten into some financial trouble, but she didn't go into details and I didn't ask." Why is it that people don't like to pry? What a shame.

"Did she tell you if she was planning on divorcing Howie?"

"I would have remembered if she did."

"Don't take this the wrong way, but were you having an affair with Claire?"

"Absolutely not."

It's nice to know there are men out there who have principles if what he said was true. This conversation was going nowhere. Either he really knew nothing or he wasn't being honest with me. I had to push him.

"Are you telling me that you ran together twice a week for five months and neither of you talked about anything personal? To tell you the truth, I find that hard to believe."

John Beck didn't speak for a few moments. I waited him out.

"She told me she was pregnant and wasn't sure if Howie was the father."

"What else did she tell you?"

"She said she had an affair with someone a while ago, but he couldn't seem to let go. According to Claire, this person called her several times threatening her."

"What did you say when she told you this?"

"I told her she should go to the police or at least tell Howie. I don't think she did either. Maybe she was afraid to tell Howie since then she would have to admit she had cheated on him."

"Did you mention any of this to your wife?"

"No. I didn't think it was right since Claire told me this in confidence."

"Why do you think she told you?"

"I don't know. Maybe she trusted me."

"Do you know what kombucha is?"

"Sure. It's one of those energy drinks. Why?"

"Claire drank it before she ran. Did she mention that to you?"

"She may have."

"Would you be willing to testify in court to everything you just told me?"

"Absolutely."

"I'm curious why the police never questioned you."

"I believe the day the police came to my house, only my wife was home. Maybe they decided they didn't need to question me or it slipped their mind."

"Thank you for talking with me."

I had no clue whether John Beck was telling me the truth. Could he have murdered Claire? Anything's possible. What I've learned from my days on the police force is that everyone lies and everyone has secrets. He had been in Claire's house, and he did know that she drank kombucha. Yet, I didn't get any vibes from John Beck that he was Claire's killer.

CHAPTER 55

The case was snowballing, and still, I was no closer to finding out who killed Claire. I thought Mr. Beck would make a good witness for our case, since it might put doubt into the jurors' minds that there was someone out there who was threatening Claire. What I needed was something to happen to shake up the case; preferably before the trial.

In the morning, I decided to check out the cabin Howie and Claire owned. Howie said I could find the key underneath one of the large planters. If I had trouble locating the place, he gave me the name and number of the person who checked on the cabin from time to time.

I was up in the area by 10:00 a.m. and going around in circles until I realized the cabin was not registering on the GPS. I pulled into a small mom-and-pop grocery store and called Butch, the guy whose number Howie gave me.

"Yeah, who is this?"

"My name's Maddie. Howie Stevenson said you're the person to call if I can't find his cabin. Is there any way you can help me out? I'm sitting in front of Mama's Grocery store."

"I don't know you from Adam. For all I know, you could be there to rob the place."

"I'm a private investigator. Did you know Howie's been arrested for his wife's murder?"

"Damn! You don't say."

"Why don't you just meet me and we can talk about it."

"I'll be there in ten."

Was this person for real? Twenty minutes later, a guy who looked like an ax murderer with a beard and bushy dark hair came out of a black pickup truck. He was tall and stocky.

"Are you the lady I just spoke with?"

"Yep. I'm Maddie Landon." I gave him my card.

"I never pegged Howie for a killer. Shame about his wife. She was a real looker."

I had to hide my disgust. "Can you give me directions to the cabin?"

"I can do better than that. I'll lead the way."

I wasn't happy about the fact he was coming along, but it didn't look like I had much of a choice. We stopped in front of a small stone house. This would not be my idea of a cabin. I noticed a pile of wood stacked on the side of the house. It appeared there were no other houses around for several miles. Howie was right when he said it was in a remote area. No wonder my GPS couldn't locate it.

"Well, thank you for the escort. I can take it from here. By the way, when was the last time you were in the house?"

"Now let me see," he said as he played with his beard. "It could have been about two weeks ago."

"Were you here to check on anything?"

"Just making sure everything was alright. No leaks, no pipes that burst."

"I see. Well, thank you again. Actually, one more thing. I was wondering when you last saw Claire Stevenson?"

"Why are you asking?"

"That's what private investigators do. We're nosy."

"Well, don't get too nosy, if you get my drift."

Is this jerk serious? Playing the tough guy.

"Can you answer my question?"

"It was a while ago."

"Do you think you can narrow it down a little?"

"Three or four months ago is the best I can do."

"Was she here with anyone?"

"Don't you mean was she here with someone other than her husband?"

"That's another way of putting it."

"Could be. It was dark. I didn't see the guy's face. I only saw the back of him."

"But it wasn't her husband?"

"This guy had lighter hair. I could tell because the porch light was on."

"Did you notice what kind of car it was?"

"I believe it was Mrs. Stevenson's, but I can't guarantee it."

"Did you happen to notice if they were still here the following morning?"

"If I recall, I didn't come back the next day, so I couldn't tell you when they left."

"So you weren't curious whether they stayed the night?"

"It's none of my business what people do. I look after their house, not them."

There was no way this guy wasn't curious when they left. I wondered if he knew.

"Well, thanks for everything. I can manage from here."

"Don't forget to lock up."

I waited till he left before I went searching for the key. I found it underneath the third planter I looked under. When I opened the door, I was surprised to see how modern it was inside. For some reason, I thought it would have more of a rustic feel to it. As I began my search, I wasn't quite sure what I was looking for. If the police found out about this place, they may have already searched it.

I went room by room. I checked every drawer, not knowing what I was looking for. Howie and Claire didn't seem to keep much here. The medicine cabinet had a razor, shaving cream, and some women's toiletries. It appeared neither of the Stevensons had been here for quite some time. Except for coffee that was in the freezer, the refrigerator was empty.

Butch said someone other than Howie had been here with Claire. Was this the guy who was threatening her or was it someone else?

I saved the bedroom for last. I opened closets, looking over every inch, including the top shelves. Nothing. I opened up the nightstand drawers that were on each side of the bed, pulling them out and turning them upside down. Except for a few magazines and a box of tissues, they were empty.

It was time to get down and dirty. I pulled up the bottom of the white bed skirt and got down on the floor, stretching my hand underneath the bed along the gray carpet. I couldn't see or feel anything. I picked myself up and walked to the other side of the bed. Reaching with my hand as far as I could, I touched something that was so small I might have missed it if wasn't hard. I picked it off the carpet, but I wasn't quite sure what I was staring at. It was an extremely small, flat piece of plastic. It appeared to be a dried-up contact lens, but I couldn't be absolutely sure. I knew just the person to ask.

CHAPTER 56

Two and a half hours later, I was back at my office. I went straight across the hall to Cousin Will. Mary wasn't at her desk, so I knocked on Will's door.

"Hey, I was just thinking about you. Sophie was asking me if I've seen you lately. Where have you been hiding?" Will said.

"This case is keeping me busy. I just came from the town of Valatie. It's a few hours from here off the Taconic. The husband whose wife was killed has a stone house up in that area and I was checking it out."

I took out the Ziplock bag I had placed the piece of plastic in. "What does this look like to you?" I said, handing him the bag.

After looking at it for a few seconds, he said, "I believe it's a contact lens."

"Are you sure?"

"Yeah, why?"

"I found it underneath the bed at the house in Valatie."

"Do you think it belongs to the killer?"

"I have no idea. I first have to eliminate the husband and his wife. Even then, it doesn't mean it was left by the person who killed her."

"Any more news on your birth father?"

"There is a possibility I may have found him, but I'm not certain."

"Are you afraid it might be him?"

"Probably."

"Why don't you come for dinner soon? Noah keeps asking for you."

"I'll call the little guy and I'll let you know when I'm free for dinner."

"He'll be thrilled. You know he's crazy about you."

"Nice to know someone is, even if it's only a two-year-old. I gotta go."

"Be careful."

"Always."

I took a peek into the small refrigerator I have in my office, grabbed the remaining half of a leftover turkey sandwich from the other day, and made a fresh pot of coffee.

I needed to find out if Claire or Howie wore contacts.

"Anything new?" Greg asked when he answered the phone.

"Did you know that Howie has a house a few hours from here?"

"He did mention it a couple of years ago, but I had forgotten all about it. Why are you asking?"

"I was up at that house earlier today. Apparently, Claire was there with someone other than Howie."

"How do you know that?"

"I spoke to the caretaker. He had seen Claire entering the house with a man who he said wasn't her husband."

"Did he get a good look at him?"

"He only caught the back of him. The porch light was on so he could tell his hair was lighter than Howie's."

"So he never saw his face?"

"That's what he said."

"That's too bad. Did you find out anything else?"

"No," I said quickly. "By the way, can you ask Howie to call me."

"Anything I can ask him?"

"No. I just had a quick question."

"I'm going up in the morning. I'll tell him to call you."

When we hung up, I wasn't quite sure why I hadn't mentioned the contact lens I found. Between what I now know about Greg and the fact that he didn't want me to have the burner phone checked out again, I was really pissed at him. Anyway, chances of someone's prints in the system besides mine were a long shot. I'd cross that bridge when I come to it.

My next call was to Gavin Stone.

"I'm busy. What do you want?"

"Do you wear contact lenses?"

"No. Why are you asking?"

"No reason. Just curious. Thanks."

One last person I needed to ask besides Howie.

"Mr. Beck's office."

"Amy, this is Maddie Landon. We met yesterday. Is Mr. Beck in?"

"One moment please."

"Ms. Landon, how are you?"

"I'm fine. I have a quick question. Do you wear contact lenses?"

"No, though I did try them at one time but couldn't get used to them. Why are you asking?"

"Just checking. Sorry to bother you," I said, and I hung up before he had a chance to ask me any more questions.

That basically eliminated everyone associated with the case, except Howie and his wife. Almost back to square one. Who the hell was this phantom person who was harassing Claire? Maybe the killer was already sitting in jail. I didn't want that to be the case.

I was getting ready to pack up and go home when my phone buzzed.

"Hey, Annie."

"I have bad news." My heart skipped several beats.

"Doug has the flu or something horrendous, and we won't be able to go up to Jesse's this weekend."

"You scared the crap out of me."

"Sorry, sweetie."

"How bad?"

"Fever, chills, throwing up. All that good stuff."

"Poor guy. Don't worry, we can do it in a couple of weeks."

"I was really looking forward to wearing my new hiking boots."

"Why don't you break them in and wear them around the house?"

"You're hilarious. When are you leaving?"

"At some point tomorrow. Listen, can you meet me for an early breakfast? I found out a few things today that I want to talk to you about."

"Is 8:30 a.m. okay at our usual?"

"I'll see you then."

***

Annie was already seated at the French Café when I got there in the morning.

"Coffee is on the way," Annie said to me as I sat down.

A minute later, the waitress brought over our coffee and we ordered.

"So what did you find out?" Annie said after the waitress left.

"When I went up to see Howie, he mentioned a cabin that he and Claire own. Apparently, it had slipped his mind. I went up yesterday and spoke to the charming guy who takes care of the place. When I say charming, I'm being facetious. He was harmless enough, but not what you would call the friendly type. I think he gets his jollies off on being a hard-ass. Anyway, he told me that Claire had been up there a couple of months ago with someone who wasn't her husband. Though he didn't get a look at the guy's face, he was definite it was not Howie. Also, I found a contact lens under the bed. If the police were already there, they either didn't check under the bed or missed it. I told Greg what the caretaker said but I didn't tell him about the lens."

"Why not?"

"I'm still angry at him because he wouldn't give me the burner phone to get a second opinion, not to mention all the lies he told me."

"What did he tell you?"

"If his connection couldn't find anything, there was no point in anyone else looking into it. I figure I'll have the lab that Jesse's firm uses check the lens out first and see what they come up with, if anything. Hopefully, they can get a fingerprint off the lens, though who knows if the person is even in the system."

"I guess there's no harm in someone else testing it first."

"That's what I was thinking. How's Doug feeling?"

"I left him throwing up, poor guy. I'm glad I have a client coming in this morning. It's the lesser of two evils."

The waitress brought over our food and refilled our coffee cups. After breakfast, we parted outside the restaurant.

While driving up to Jesse's, my phone rang.

"Maddie, you wanted me to call you?" Howie said.

"I have a quick question. Do you, by any chance, wear contact lenses?"

"No, why?" I ignored the question.

"Did Claire?"

"No, what's going on?"

"Probably nothing. Did Greg tell you that someone had been at the house with Claire?"

"No. Is there any way we can find out who it was?"

That's weird. Why didn't Greg mention it to Howie? Maybe he didn't want to upset him.

"I don't know. I'll try. Listen, I have to go. I'll be up to see you after the weekend. Remember to keep the faith and take care of yourself."

I was hoping that Howie would forget I asked him about wearing contact lenses since I didn't want him to mention it to Greg.

I opened Jesse's front door and called out to him.

"What the hell happened to your face?" I said when I saw Jesse.

"It looks worse than it feels. I got sucker punched when I was handing a subpoena to some guy."

"Did you report him to the police?"

"Nah! He's harmless. He was probably having a bad day and I just added to it. But there is something you can do to make it feel better."

"I bet there is."

"Feeling any better?" I said as we were lying in bed about forty minutes later.

"All cured."

"I brought you a present. It's wrapped in plastic, but don't get too excited."

"I know you, Madds, and you're up to something."

"You got me. To make a short story shorter, I found a contact lens at Howie's cabin and I need a favor. I want your lab to analyze it for fingerprints."

"Why not give it to Greg?"

"I want to check it out first. Nothing came up on the burner phone. When I suggested to Greg to have someone I know take another look, he declined."

"Did he say why?"

"Yeah. He said if his source couldn't get anything off it, then there was no point."

"That's a little weird."

"I think he's mad at me."

"Why's that?"

"Does it matter? Let's just say it might not be working out the way he wants it to." The look on Jesse's face told me he wasn't too happy with my answer. I think it was time to have wine.

CHAPTER 57

While we were sitting outside on the patio enjoying our first glass of wine waiting for the grill to heat up, I began telling Jesse what I recently found out about Billy Jenkins.

"I think I mentioned to you that Claire and Billy grew up in the same foster home. According to the foster mother, Claire was a big tease and liked to pull pranks. I guess Jenkins had enough and vowed to get even with her one day. I'm not sure exactly what Billy did, but something got him kicked out of the home. He's been in trouble most of his life, in and out of jail several times. About three months ago, he showed up at Claire's house asking to borrow money. She refused, but then offered him money to rough up someone who was harassing her. He agreed to do it, but when Claire contacted him the following day, she called it off."

"What's your sense of him?"

"I believe him. If he was going to kill Claire, I don't think he would have waited and taken time to plan it. He's not that smart."

"From what you've told me about this guy, you're probably right."

***

The weekend flew by. We went hiking at a state park near Jesse's place on Saturday, and on Sunday we took a ride to a few of the neighboring towns and spent the day exploring the shops in the area.

When I left on Monday morning, Jesse promised to try and put a rush on the contact lens. Depending on how backed up the lab was, it could take a while. I was hoping that wasn't the case. Driving back to the office, my phone rang.

"Hi, Lucy," I said when I saw the number.

"Am I interrupting you?"

"No, how are you?"

"I'm fine. I was thinking about you, so I thought I'd give you a call. How are you doing?"

"I'm okay. Busy, trying to solve a case I'm working on."

"Well, I won't take up too much of your time. I was wondering if you ever got in contact with Harris Tyler, the boy I mentioned to you?"

"I did track down a Harris Tyler, who is most likely the boy you knew. I believe he still lives in California. I also spoke to Brian Gates. You were right. He is gay and definitely is not my father."

"Do you plan on calling Harris?"

"I will when I'm ready."

"Will you let me know what happens?"

"I promise I'll call you."

"I'm glad. Maybe we can meet again next time I'm in New York, and you always have a place here. I'd love to meet Jesse."

"I'm sure he would love to meet you."

"Bye for now. Take care."

I felt torn about my feelings toward Lucy. I kept thinking about my parents, the people who raised me and loved me. Though it made no sense, it felt like I would be disloyal to them if I decided to have a relationship with my aunt. The sound of a loud beeping horn startled me, and I realized I was wandering over into the middle lane, almost hitting a car. My whole body started shaking. Breathe, Maddie, breathe. For the remainder of the ride, I concentrated on the road.

CHAPTER 58

In the morning, I wasn't in a rush to go into the office. I went for a run and when I got back, I watched the news while I was eating breakfast. The trial was getting closer and still no concrete leads. What didn't make sense was why Claire Stevenson didn't tell anyone the name of the person who was harassing her. What was she afraid of? Did this person threaten to harm the people close to her? Why didn't she just go to the police? None of it made sense.

I decided to work from home. I had been so focused on Howie's case I was neglecting my own clients. I spent most of the day working on a few locate searches that I had put aside but could no longer ignore if I wanted to keep my clients.

That night, I turned on a Netflix movie, hoping to distract myself from thinking about the investigation. Instead, my thoughts turned to the conversation I had with Lucy Grainger. I knew I had been making excuses to myself about why I hadn't called Harris Tyler yet. After all these years of not allowing myself to care that he existed, I had to acknowledge that there was a part of me that wanted to know about this man. It's very likely that he had no idea I even existed. How would he react knowing he had a daughter? Would he hang up on me, or would he want to meet me? What if he rejected me? *Is that what I'm afraid of? It's not as if he ever played a part in my life. I've lived without knowing him for thirty-seven years. Why would I care if he didn't want me in his life now?* I fell asleep without any answers.

***

A week had passed and it was getting nearer to the trial date. I still couldn't get any traction on who killed Claire Stevenson. As I was walking into my apartment building, I saw Louis.

"Miss Maddie. There's a package that was left for you."

"Thanks, Louis," I said, as he handed me a FedEx envelope. I noticed it was from the lab in Massachusetts that Jesse sent the lens to.

"Louis, keep your fingers crossed. What's in the envelope could break the case for me."

"I certainly will."

As soon as I got into my apartment, I quickly opened the envelope. My first thought when I saw the name on the page was that it must be a mistake. I kept staring at the name but it didn't change. I couldn't believe it.

I picked up the phone quickly and dialed Annie. "Are you still in the office?"

"Yes. Why?"

"Can you meet me as soon as you're done?"

"I'm leaving now. I just need to call Doug and let him know I'll be late. I'll meet you in thirty minutes at The Dead Poet."

As I was walking over to The Dead Poet, I kept thinking about what the ramifications of this development would have on the case. I waved to Annie as I saw her approaching the entrance to the bar. The hostess seated us and we each ordered a drink when the waiter came by.

"I'm almost afraid to ask what's going on."

"Here, look at this. At first I thought it couldn't be true, but I knew from speaking with Beth Carter that it was. And then I remembered when we were partners Greg told me he wore contact lenses since he could see better with them than when he wore his glasses."

"Are you thinking that Greg had an affair with Claire?"

"At this point, all I know for sure is that Greg was at the cabin with Claire. Chances are, since the contact was found in the bedroom, they were most likely having an affair or at least a one-night stand."

"Boy oh boy, this guy really gets around. Sorry, babe. That didn't come out exactly the way I meant it."

"No apologies necessary. At this point, I don't want to say anything to Greg."

"You have to. It's a conflict of interest. He needs to recuse himself and Howie needs to get another lawyer."

"You're right. I was so shocked with the results from the lab, I wasn't focusing on the fact it would be a conflict of interest."

"When you confront Greg with what you found out, he's going to have a fit. I wonder if he'll still want to stay on the case, even though he absolutely can't."

"Poor Howie. I'm not looking forward to telling him what's going on."

"I suggest you contact a criminal lawyer. I could give you the name of someone, or maybe you can talk to the attorney on your floor."

"Now I'm going to have to investigate Greg. This is a nightmare."

"Before you say anything to him, speak with an attorney first. Maybe he'll give you some guidance."

"Good idea."

We stayed for only one drink since Annie promised Doug she'd be home for dinner.

"I'll keep you posted," I said to Annie as we left the bar.

"Don't worry, it'll work out."

I wasn't so sure Annie was right this time.

CHAPTER 59

In the morning, I stopped in to see Larry Banks.

"Are you free for lunch? My treat." I could see by the surprised look on his face that he wasn't expecting my invitation.

"I'm assuming this is a business lunch, since I know you're not big on fraternizing."

I smiled. "Do you have any place in mind?" I asked.

"You pick it."

"There's a little Italian place a few blocks from here. Is one o'clock okay?"

"I'll knock on your door when I'm ready," Larry Banks said.

"I never knew this place existed," Larry said when we were seated.

Larry is my height, maybe an inch shorter, with a stocky build. I'd say he's probably in his early fifties.

"It's a great neighborhood restaurant. Nothing fancy, but the food is good and everyone is very friendly and accommodating."

"Can I get you anything to drink?" the waiter asked.

"I'll have a glass of Chianti," I said.

"I'll have the same."

"It's impossible to have Italian food without a glass of wine," I said.

Larry chuckled.

We ordered and I got down to business. I explained what I found out and my dilemma. Larry listened intently.

"I need your advice." I didn't go into my history with Greg.

"He needs to withdraw as counsel for Mr. Stevenson. It's a definite conflict of interest and he doesn't have a choice. He could be disbarred."

"I was hoping you'd be willing to represent Howie if he agrees. Since I'm the investigator on the case, you'll have access to whatever I've found out."

"First talk to Greg and then to Howie. If he's willing to hire me, I'll take on the case."

"Great. Actually, I'm glad Greg won't be able to represent Howie since he has no trial experience. I did ask him to bring a second attorney on board, but he refused."

"Can I ask you why you left the police force?"

"You just did. It's complicated. After my partner left, it wasn't easy. None of the guys wanted to partner up with me. Though my captain teamed me up with someone, it wasn't working out. I decided that I had no future as a police officer, so I quit."

"That's too bad."

"It worked out, and I really love what I do."

When we got back to the office, I told Larry Banks that I planned on speaking with Greg today, and then I was going up to see Howie tomorrow.

I called Greg as soon as I walked into my office. I was debating where we should meet since I didn't want to give him the news on the phone. Then I remembered a park not far from where Greg lived.

"Any news?" Greg said when he answered the phone.

"I need to speak with you as soon as possible."

"What's going on?"

"I'll explain when I see you."

An hour later, I saw Greg waiting at the entrance to the park near his apartment building.

I spotted a bench where no one was sitting close by. "Why don't we sit here."

"What's with all the cloak and dagger?"

"When I went up to Howie's cabin, I found a contact lens under the bed in the master bedroom." I may have been imagining it, but I thought Greg looked a shade paler. "I sent it to a lab to check it for fingerprints. Do you have any idea whose fingerprint it was a match for?"

"How come you didn't tell me about the lens?" he said, raising his voice.

"That doesn't matter. Please answer my question."

"It's not what you think."

"Enlighten me."

"We went to bed once and that was it."

"Who ended it?"

"It's none of your business."

I was getting really pissed at him.

"Did she mention anyone that might be harassing her?"

"No."

"Well, is there anything she did say that could help Howie's case?"

"If she did, I would tell you."

"At this point, you can no longer represent Howie. You could be disbarred. How did you ever think this was a good idea to represent Howie when you knew you had an affair with his wife?" He didn't respond at first.

"This is what you wanted all along. You wanted me to step out of the picture."

"That's nuts. I just thought you were too inexperienced if Howie's case went to trial. Right now, you need to withdraw as Howie's attorney, and you need to do it immediately."

"And what would I give as a reason?"

"I don't know. You'll think of something. I'm going up to see Howie tomorrow and explain what's going on. It's not wise for you to see him again. I'll make sure he has a really good criminal attorney with trial experience."

I doubt if Greg was listening anymore. In truth, if we did go to trial, we would most likely call Greg as a witness and that meant giving his name to the prosecution along with our other witnesses. I hoped it didn't have to come to that.

CHAPTER 60

My head was swirling as I left the park. I didn't know what to think. Now that I knew Greg was involved with Claire, things changed. Though I didn't believe Greg had anything to do with Claire's death, I had no choice but to look closer at him. What was I going to tell Howie? Two people who he thought were his friends slept with his wife. What just dawned on me is that there may have been other lovers who came and went. Could one of them have killed Claire?

After dinner, I called Jesse and decided to tell him everything that was going on.

"A penny for your thoughts," I said after I finished.

"Give me a minute. I'm trying to decipher everything you just told me."

"I have to figure out what to tell Howie."

"Just tell him the truth. He has to know why Greg is withdrawing as his attorney. I know it's going to be hard on him, but now he'll have a more experienced lawyer to represent him."

Jesse could have gloated at the fact that Greg was a real bastard, but he didn't.

"I know you're right, though I don't want to see the look on Howie's face when I tell him about Greg."

"Did you have any inkling that Greg was having an affair with Howie's wife?"

"Absolutely none, but now that I'm thinking about it, I wonder if the burner phone had phone calls on it from Greg. Maybe he never had it checked; he just told me he did. I'll have to get it back from him."

"Are you okay with all of this?"

"It doesn't matter if I am or I'm not. I have to keep investigating."

"You need to be careful. If it's Greg, you don't know what he's capable of."

"Don't worry. I have no intention of getting killed."

"I'll still worry."

"Nice to know."

***

I was up at the Westchester County Department of Corrections by 10:30 a.m. the following morning. I went through the usual procedures and waited for Howie in another small, windowless room.

When he walked in, Howie didn't look much better than the last time I saw him.

"I wasn't expecting you."

"I brought you a deck of cards and some more books."

"Thanks."

"Are you doing okay?"

"What do you think?"

I didn't have an answer, and now I had to give him the news about Greg.

"I have to tell you something and I don't want you to freak out. Actually, it might turn out to be a good thing."

"Just tell me. At this point, there's not much you can say that will shock me."

Oh boy! "Greg is removing himself as your attorney."

"I don't understand. Why?" Howie looked dumbfounded.

I was hoping I could get the words out. "The reason he can't represent you anymore is because there's a conflict of interest. Remember when I asked you if you or Claire wore contact lenses?"

"Yeah!" he said, hesitating.

"I found a contact lens up at your cabin in the bedroom. When I had it analyzed for fingerprints, it turned out there was a hit. It was Greg's." I stopped to see Howie's reaction, but quickly continued. "I asked him about it, and he didn't deny that he had slept with Claire. He told me it was only once."

"I'm not sure I understand. So all along he was acting as my friend, but he slept with Claire?"

"I know it's a lot to take in. I'm so sorry. But the good news is I spoke with a criminal defense attorney, and he's willing to take your case. His name is Larry Banks and I can get him up to speed with the investigation."

"Why did Greg agree to take my case if he slept with Claire?"

I had my theory but I wasn't willing to share it with Howie at the moment.

"I'm not sure."

"Wait! How do we know that Greg didn't kill Claire?"

"We don't, though I'm not sure what his motive would be." That wasn't entirely true but Howie didn't have to know that. I was concerned that Greg may have been the one threatening Claire but I had no proof.

"I just can't believe this. How could Greg do this to me? If I wasn't in jail, I'd kill him."

I wanted to kill him, too. "You need to put aside all your hatred for him at the moment. I know it's hard but the most important thing right now is focusing on yourself. Can you do that for me?"

"Do you think this guy Banks is good?"

"I do. He has a very good reputation. I can have him come up tomorrow and talk with you."

"Okay."

"Great. The sooner he gets on record as your counsel, the better. I think you'll like him. By the way, have you had any visitors?"

"A few. Dana's been coming."

"I'm glad. I'll see you in a couple of days. And Howie, please take care of yourself."

When I left Howie, he seemed despondent, and it worried me. On the way back to the office, I called Larry Banks and told him what was going on, emphasizing Howie's state of mind. He agreed to see Howie the next day.

I grabbed a sandwich at the deli before going into the office. Sitting in front of my computer, I was thinking of how little I really knew about Greg. We were partners for two years, but I couldn't even tell you anything about his childhood. Most of our conversations revolved around the job and the fact that he was unhappy in his marriage. Maybe that was intentional on his part. From what I now know, he could have been with other women while he was sleeping with me. But was he a murderer?

CHAPTER 61

I didn't want to believe Greg had anything to do with Claire's death, but unfortunately, there was no way I could leave it at that. I had to know for sure one way or the other, and I had an idea where to start.

I conducted a search on Greg's ex-wife, Stacey Martin, though I didn't know if she had remarried or gone back to her maiden name. I immediately found her in one of my databases and pulled up the report. It appeared her last name was now Weinberg, and she was residing in Ridgewood, New Jersey. Ridgewood is a fairly affluent neighborhood in northern New Jersey. I wanted to talk with Stacey today. Since Greg had told me that Stacey had found out about our affair, I wasn't sure how receptive she would be when I showed up at her door. If she wasn't willing to be cooperative, I would have to persuade her.

Stacey's house was on a dead-end street. It looked like a farmhouse with a wraparound porch. I didn't see any cars in the driveway. I got out and knocked on her door. No answer. I looked in the garage and it was empty. I could sit in my car and wait, but who knew when she'd be back. When I looked at the time, it was only three-thirty. I decided to drive into the town and walk around for a while.

I found a metered parking spot right in town. After feeding the meter, I went looking for a place to get a coffee. The town was bigger than I had imagined, with lots of shops and places to eat. I stopped at a coffee place and ordered a cappuccino and a croissant, and sat at a corner table. I started thinking about my relationship with Greg. When he told me he had separated from his wife, I remembered feeling a little guilty because I was happy he had separated. I had wanted to sleep with him ever since we partnered up. When he told me he had to give his marriage another chance because his wife was pregnant, I was angry and hurt.

At the time, I assumed when he told me why he was going back to his wife, that was the truth. Now, I'm not so sure what the truth is.

I was parked in front of Stacey Weinberg's place by six o'clock. There was a gray Toyota in the driveway. I knocked on the door. I had met Stacey a few times back when I was partnered with Greg. When she opened the door, she looked the same as I remembered her, very attractive with dark brown wavy hair down to her shoulders, and a runner's body.

We looked at each other. At first, I wasn't sure if she remembered me, but then I saw the recognition on her face.

"You have a hell of a nerve showing up at my house."

"You're right, and I'm sorry, but it's important that I speak with you. I'll only take up a few minutes of your time."

I can see she was debating what to do.

"Come in," she said in a matter-of-fact tone.

We sat in a lovely kitchen that looked recently remodeled with subway tiles as a backsplash, a state-of-the-art gas range, and wide plank gray wood floors. She didn't offer me anything to drink. Who could blame her.

"So why are you here?"

"A woman named Claire Stevenson was murdered. Her husband was arrested, and in the course of my investigation, I learned that Greg slept with her at some point."

"That's not surprising."

"I want you to know that when Greg and I started our affair, he told me he was separated. I never would have slept with him if he wasn't. He also told me I was the only woman he slept with since he was married. I've come to realize he may have lied to me."

"Why are you telling me all of this?" she said, with an annoyed look on her face.

"Because I'm trying to find out if Greg had anything to do with this woman's death."

"How would I possibly know?"

"You may not, but the more I know about Greg, it might help with my investigation."

"Why should I help you?"

"Look, I can understand how you feel, but now it's about a dead woman, not me or you. Anything you can tell me."

"I knew he was cheating on me. It's why I finally left. He was so full of himself that it never dawned on him that I knew about his affairs."

"Was he ever violent?"

"Never, but he was controlling."

"Do you think he would harass someone if they broke off their relationship with him?"

"His ego would be bruised and he might not take it well. But capable of killing someone, I doubt it."

"What if he found out she was pregnant and she threatened him? Would that tip the scales?"

"I don't know."

"Is there anything else you can tell me?"

"As you know, Greg can be very charming. Did he play big brother to you when you were partners?" I was feeling a little uncomfortable. "Did he make you feel special? I can tell by the expression on your face he did. I'm not sure what you want me to say. The Greg I knew was a pompous ass, but I can't imagine he would kill anyone over an affair."

I got the feeling she was still annoyed at me, or maybe it was Greg she was still angry at.

"I'm sorry about the baby," I said.

"What baby?"

Did Greg lie to me? Oh shit!

"What baby are you talking about?" she said, now clearly upset.

I was stuck. "I don't know what to say. When he broke up with me, he said it was because you were pregnant and had decided to give the marriage another try."

"If it wasn't so sick, it would be funny."

"Again, I'm sorry." It was time to make my exit. "Thank you for talking with me."

I felt like an idiot. I was so angry at Greg I wanted to punch his lights out. I put my car in gear and left. Stacey wasn't much help, though she did think Greg might be capable of harassing a woman if she rebuffed him, but not capable of murder.

The picture I was getting of Greg was not the Greg I thought I knew. Another side of him was emerging, one that I never knew existed. I still find it hard to believe he could have killed Claire, even if she ended the affair.

CHAPTER 62

I had to speak with Beth Carter again. When we last spoke, she left looking scared when I asked her what had happened between her and Greg. Though it was after 9:00 p.m., I called her anyway.

"Hello."

"Beth, this is Maddie Landon. I'm sorry to disturb you so late but it's important that I speak with you about Greg."

"I thought I made it clear I didn't want to talk about him."

"Things have changed since we last spoke. I wouldn't ask if it wasn't important. Just hear me out when I see you, and if you still don't want to talk to me, I'll back off."

A few seconds later she said: "There's a coffee shop a block from 1 Police Plaza. I'll meet you there tomorrow at 12:30 p.m."

I knew exactly what place she was talking about. "Thank you."

***

The following day, I saw Beth walk into the coffee shop and I waved to her. She slid into the booth.

"Thank you for coming, Beth. I appreciate it."

The waitress came over and we both ordered coffee.

"So what did you want to tell me?" Beth said in a cold manner after the waitress left.

"I found out that Greg slept with the woman who was murdered. He had to recuse himself from the case. So you see, he's now a possible suspect."

"But I thought her husband was arrested."

"He was, but my job is to try and prove someone else did it."

"Here you go, ladies. Let me know if there's anything else I can get you."

"Beth, I need to know what Greg did. He'll never know you talked to me." I was hoping I didn't have to go back on my word.

"I'm not sure I feel comfortable talking about him."

"Please, it's very important."

"Greg and I had a relationship, if you could call it that. We slept together."

I knew exactly what she meant. It wasn't any different from my relationship with Greg. I couldn't think about that now.

"You told me that you broke it off with him. What happened when you did?"

"At first nothing, but then he started calling, wanting to get back together. I told him I wasn't interested and to stop bothering me. But then he tried to intimidate me."

"Can you explain what you mean?"

"Once, when I was leaving the office, he followed me till I got to the subway station. He didn't actually do anything, but just his presence made me uncomfortable and that was his intention."

"How long did it go on for?"

"Maybe a few weeks. It was mostly phone calls pressuring me to go back with him. Can I ask you something? Did he harass you?"

"What do you mean?" I said, totally surprised by her remark.

"I knew about you and Greg."

"How?"

"I was curious since you were partners. One day, I followed both of you to a motel and saw you and Greg go into a room together. It didn't look like you were there on police business."

I didn't comment.

"Do you know if there were other women he slept with that might have similar stories?" I asked.

"I don't."

"Do you think Greg is capable of killing someone?" Beth said.

"I didn't think so, but I guess we never know what someone's capable of."

CHAPTER 63

I took the train back to the office and knocked on Larry Banks' door, but there was no answer. I left a voice message since he hadn't hired a receptionist yet.

As I was opening up my office door, my phone buzzed.

"I'm just leaving the courthouse now. Why don't we meet in my office in an hour and we can discuss the case."

"Did you get a chance to see Howie?"

"I did. I'll see you soon."

An hour later, I was sitting in Larry Banks' office.

"How did it go?" I asked.

"He vehemently denies having anything to do with Claire's death."

"Do you believe him?"

"It doesn't matter whether I believe him or not. It's the jury that we have to convince. As soon as I get the files, I'll go through everything and see exactly what they have on him, and what we need to do next."

I gave Banks a brief account of what I'd learned so far with my investigation.

"I can't believe I was partners with this guy, yet was clueless about him," I said.

"There are people who show the world one face to hide who they really are. Keep digging and I'll see what I can find out. What about this guy Gavin Stone?"

"I think he can actually be helpful for Howie's defense. If the prosecution doesn't call him, we can. The fact that he was having an affair with Claire and originally told me he was Howie's alibi might put some doubt in the jurors' minds."

"What are the chances he killed Claire Stevenson?"

"Unfortunately, I have no proof. If what he told me was true, I don't see a motive."

"What about Greg?"

"What about him?"

"I'm going to have to subpoena him. He may or may not have anything to do with Claire's death, but the jury needs to see him as a possible suspect."

"Is there any way we won't have to call him?"

"I know he was your partner, but my priority is Howie."

"I understand."

"Anything else?"

"At this point, I've pretty much ruled out Billy Jenkins since he wasn't close enough to Claire to know her habits, and he doesn't strike me as the sort of guy who would plan a murder. And poison would definitely take some planning."

"What about the loan sharks that Howie still owes money to?"

"They could have killed me when they had the chance. I don't see them going to all that trouble to poison Claire."

"Fair enough."

"We still have some time before the trial. Get the burner phone back from Greg and I'll have someone check it out."

I called Greg as soon as I left Banks' office.

"Why do you need the phone back? I already had it checked."

I thought I would try some diplomacy since I didn't want to get into a pissing match with him.

"It never hurts to have someone else take a second look." At this point, I wasn't sure if Greg was hiding something or was just really upset that he was off the case. I didn't feel sorry for the guy since he only had himself to blame.

"If you want the phone, you can pick it up at my place."

He wasn't going to make it easy for me. "I'll be there by 8:30 a.m. tomorrow." The next thing I heard was a loud click.

I didn't want to believe Greg was guilty. More to the point, I didn't want to believe the man I had once slept with was a killer.

CHAPTER 64

I was ringing Greg's buzzer at 8:30 a.m. sharp. No answer. I buzzed again, but no luck. Was he playing games with me? I saw someone leaving the building, so I quickly grabbed the door before it closed. I was thankful this wasn't a doorman building.

I took the stairs to the second floor and knocked on his door. At first, nothing. I knocked louder and heard footsteps.

"I was buzzing you from downstairs," I said when he finally opened the door.

"Sometimes the buzzer doesn't work."

I wanted to say to him, "You're full of shit" but decided against it. He didn't invite me in, he just handed me the phone.

"I thought we were friends. You're making a big mistake," Greg said.

"You made the mistake when you slept with Claire and then represented Howie. Is that why you hired me, to keep close tabs on the investigation?"

"You give yourself too much credit, Maddie. I wouldn't waste any time looking at me."

"Thanks for the warning," I said facetiously.

When I got back, I stopped by Larry Banks' office, gave him the phone, and then went straight to my office. I wasn't sure what to do next since I didn't think one contact lens belonging to Greg would be sufficient to get Howie acquitted.

Then something occurred to me. I picked up the phone and dialed Janice Levy's number. She answered on the first ring.

"Mrs. Levy, this is Maddie Landon. How are you?"

"I'm fine. I'm so glad you called. I've been thinking about poor Claire. How is your investigation going?"

"That's why I was calling. I was wondering if you weren't busy today, I could come up and talk with you?"

"That would be wonderful. I just finished baking banana nut bread. It'll be fresh and warm for you."

"Thank you. How about noon?"

"That's perfect. I'll have coffee ready too."

It was going to be a long afternoon.

Traffic up to Scarsdale was light. Mrs. Levy opened the door just as I was about to ring her bell.

"Come in. Why don't we make ourselves comfortable in the living room. I'll just be a moment while I pour us some coffee."

"This looks absolutely delicious," I said as she placed a big slice of banana nut bread down in front of me. Then she went back for the coffee. Finally, she sat down. If I wanted to get any information from Janice Levy, I knew I couldn't rush her.

"So how can I help you?"

"You remember when I last saw you, I was with a gentleman named Greg Martin. You mentioned he looked familiar."

"Oh yes, I rarely forget a face. What about him?"

"Well, I was curious when you might have seen him at the house?"

"Hmm, I believe it was a few months back. I was going to the store when I saw Mrs. Stevenson by her front door, arguing with this man. I wanted to make sure everything was alright, so I waited till he left. That's when I got a good look at him. As I said, I never forget a face."

I didn't know if she was making it up or actually saw them arguing.

"How could you tell they were arguing?"

"Their voices were raised and she appeared to be gesturing with her arms."

"Could you hear what they were quarreling about?"

"I'm sorry, they were too far away."

"Do you recall how long he was there?"

"I'd say a few minutes, maybe longer. When he left, she slammed the door shut."

"How come you never told me about the argument?" I said, exasperated.

"I must have forgotten until you just mentioned him again."

"Was that the only time you saw him at the house?"

"Yes, but he could have been at her house other times. Maybe I shouldn't say anything since I really liked Claire, but I think she entertained quite a few men, if you know what I mean."

"Oh really! You never said anything during our conversations."

"The poor thing was dead. And poisoned. How terrible. I didn't see any reason to say anything bad about her."

"Did you get a look at any of these men?"

"I really didn't. At the time, I didn't pay much attention. It wasn't until much later that I realized what may have been going on."

"How do you know why they were there?"

"Oh please! Isn't it obvious?"

I decided not to mention what Howie said about Janice Levy, since I didn't want to embarrass her.

"Thank you for your hospitality. You've been a big help."

"Come back anytime."

As I walked out of her house, I wasn't sure how much credence I should give to her remarks. How much of what Mrs. Levy told me was fictional and how much was real? I didn't know what to make of any of it. Maybe Howie was right and she was crazy with too much time on her hands. What I knew for sure was that Claire Stevenson was having an affair with Greg and Gavin Stone. I guess it's possible there were other men. I couldn't rule it out, but how did knowing any of this help Howie?

CHAPTER 65

As I was getting into my car, I noticed a woman by her mailbox three doors down from the Stevensons. I walked over to her and introduced myself, handing her my card.

"I'm Carrie Benson. It was so disturbing to hear about Mrs. Stevenson. I can't believe Mr. Stevenson might have killed his wife."

"Did you know Claire?"

"Not really. Just to say hi to. I have two school-age children, so I'm pretty busy with parenting duties. Do you have children?"

"No, I don't. Are you off somewhere? If not, I'd like to ask you a few questions. I stopped by a couple of weeks ago, but you weren't home."

"I'm sorry I missed you. The kids don't get off the bus till three and thankfully there's no baseball or soccer game today. Don't get me wrong. I love watching them play, but there are days when I'd rather skip it. Do you know how boring those games can be? I'd invite you in for coffee, but I have some errands to run before the kids get home from school."

"That's fine. I just came from your neighbor, Janice Levy, and I had coffee there."

"Did she chew your ear off?"

"What do you mean?"

"I don't like to speak ill of anyone but she's one strange bird."

"How so?"

"I think she's lonely since her husband died. There were rumors that her husband died while he was with another woman. I guess I should feel sorry for her, but she makes it hard, since she's always gossiping about the neighbors, especially Claire."

"What did she say about her?"

"She told me she thought Claire was entertaining strange men. I don't think she has anything else to do but spy on people. It's none of our business what Claire did."

"Did you notice any men at Claire's house, maybe when her husband wasn't home?"

"I didn't, but as I told you, I'm pretty busy."

"Is there anything else you can tell me about the Stevensons? Did you ever hear them arguing?"

"I'm sorry, I can't help you. Do you think Mr. Stevenson killed his wife?"

"I'm still investigating."

"If I think of anything, I'll call you."

I sat in my car for a few moments thinking about what Mrs. Benson said about Janice Levy. I felt kind of sorry for Mrs. Levy. It couldn't have been easy for her knowing that her husband was cheating on her and may have died while in the sack with someone else. Did she have emotional problems? I couldn't waste too much time thinking about her. My focus had to be on finding Claire's killer.

Later, as I was lying in bed, I was getting myself worked up thinking about Greg. I picked up the phone and called Annie.

"I can't believe what a complete jerk I've been," I said, before Annie even had a chance to say hello.

"What are you talking about?"

"There was no baby. There never was a baby."

"You're not making any sense."

"Greg. He told me he went back to his wife because she was pregnant. I spoke to his ex-wife. There was no baby. And I wasn't the only one he was sleeping with. How could I have been so stupid?"

"How could you know? He was your partner and you trusted him."

"I was a cop, for god's sakes. I should have had better judgment."

"Maddie, you're being too hard on yourself. You have to let it go."

"I know, but right now, I'm investigating him. It's not like I have the luxury of never speaking to him again."

"Do you still have feelings for him?"

"All I have at the moment is anger. After my parents died, I felt completely alone. I know my aunt did the best she could, but she worked a lot, and even though I had you and Will, I was really on my own. When I first joined the police department, I was naïve enough to think I would be part of a family. It didn't exactly work out that way. I was snubbed by most of the other cops. So when Greg and I became partners, I was thrilled. Greg made me feel special. I realize that none of it was real, but unfortunately, I got caught up in it."

"Did you give any more thought to contacting the person who may be your father?"

"I keep stalling."

"Now might be a good time. Sleep on it."

The last thing I thought of as I was nodding off was the phone call to Harris Tyler, which scared me more than anything else.

CHAPTER 66

In the morning, I decided to get up enough nerve and make that phone call to Harris Tyler. When I looked at the time, it was only 5:30 a.m. in California. It was way too early to call. I was going over in my head what I would say if he answered the phone. I needed a Plan B in case I had to leave a message.

There was nothing on Greg to prove he was involved in Claire's murder. I knew Larry Banks would subpoena him at trial. I was hoping to avoid Greg the embarrassment if he didn't kill Claire, even though it would help Howie.

Why did I care if Greg would be embarrassed? He deserved it. Yet even though I hated him for what he did, he had been my partner and taught me how to be a good cop. No matter what, we had trusted each other, and we always had each other's back.

As soon as I got into the office, I pulled up the report on Harris Tyler to get his cell phone number. I heard a knock on the door.

"Hello, anyone here?" I recognized Larry Banks' voice.

"The DA's office sent over what they have. Can you spare some time now?"

"Give me a minute. I want to print out everything I have on the case."

I gathered all my reports and my notes and walked across to Banks' office.

"Why don't you bring me up to date first, and then we'll talk about what the district attorney's office has sent over."

"I spoke with Howie's neighbor, Janice Levy again. The last time I was up there to see Howie, Greg was with me. As we were leaving, Mrs. Levy approached us. When she saw Greg, she mentioned to him that he looked familiar. Greg said that Howie was a friend. That made sense why he might have been at Howie's house. But thinking about it with what I now know, on the off chance she may have remembered something else, I went up to see her.

"It turns out she saw Greg and Claire Stevenson arguing on Claire's front porch. Unfortunately, she couldn't hear what they were arguing about. That was a few months ago. She wasn't specific when this occurred."

"Anything else?"

"Yeah. Something that she said was a little weird. She thought Claire was entertaining men at her house. When I asked her how she knew why they were there, she told me matter-of-factly, 'isn't it obvious.'

"When I was leaving Mrs. Levy's house, I noticed a woman by her mailbox. I remembered I had knocked on her door when I originally started my investigation, but she wasn't home at the time, and she never responded to the card I left.

"I walked over and spoke to her. She didn't have any information that could help with the investigation, though when I told her I had just come from Mrs. Levy's house she made a comment that Mrs. Levy bad-mouthed Claire, telling her that Claire had been entertaining strange men.

Then Mrs. Benson said there were rumors that Mr. Levy died while he was with another woman. If that's true, I can understand how Claire's indiscretions might have bothered Janice Levy."

"Is that it?"

"Yep."

"Okay. There wasn't a lot in the material they sent over that I didn't already know from what you've told me. She was poisoned with arsenic that they found under the sink in the kitchen. They know about his gambling problems and the insurance policy on Claire. The phone wasn't mentioned, which is good. They know about the girlfriend and the fact that he lied about his whereabouts the night Claire died."

"It sounds as if there's a lot of evidence against Howie. Though I keep asking myself why he would leave the poison in the house."

"I thought the same. We have witnesses that we can call that also had a motive to kill Claire."

"Do the police know how the poison got in her system?" I asked.

"It's not in the report."

"Howie told me that before Claire went for a run, she drank something called kombucha. Howie hated it. I'm thinking whoever killed Claire knew that fact."

"We have to find out who in Claire's life was privy to that information."

"Unfortunately, Howie had no idea. There was a lot that Howie didn't know about his wife, or at least he claims."

"In the meantime, why don't you see what you can find out about this rumor involving Mr. Levy. It may be nothing, but it can't hurt."

I took a ride to the Scarsdale Library to check out the local library newspapers to see if there was an obituary for Stephen Levy. I thought chances were slim to none there would be any mention of who he was with at the time of his death.

The library was old-world in character. I was informed that the library would be closing in the next month or so for a complete renovation. Since I knew when Stephen Levy died, I was able to narrow the dates of the newspapers I needed to check.

I requested the microfiche films for both the *Scarsdale Inquirer* and the *Journal News*, the main paper in Westchester. Under the obituaries in the *Scarsdale Inquirer*, it listed the death of Stephen Levy, a local resident of Scarsdale. It went on to say he left a wife, Janice Levy, and a sister, Judy Stein, residing in Tuckahoe, New York. I knew that Tuckahoe was only a few miles south of Scarsdale. I couldn't find any other articles related to Stephen Levy's death. As I was leaving the library, my phone rang.

"Maddie, it's Larry. Nothing came back on the phone. It was completely wiped."

"That's too bad. Maybe Greg wasn't lying and he did have it checked out. I'm just leaving the Scarsdale Library now. The only thing in the newspaper on Janice Levy's husband was an obituary naming a sister of Mr. Levy living in Tuckahoe. I might as well talk to her while I'm in the area. Maybe she can fill us in on some of the details about Janice and Stephen Levy's relationship."

"Okay, but tread carefully."

"Will do, but we take the chance the sister-in-law might say something to Janice Levy."

"We can't worry about that now."

"I'll let you know what I find out."

CHAPTER 67

Before heading to Judy Stein's place, I grabbed my computer from the back seat and did a search on her. I located an address in Tuckahoe and drove over.

Ten minutes later, I was sitting in front of a Tudor-style home on a small plot of land with similar-style houses up and down the street. It was almost four thirty. I knew there was no use thinking of what to say to Judy Stein, since it rarely worked out the way I planned.

I rang the bell. A woman, maybe around sixty-five, with short gray hair, and wearing running clothes, was standing in front of me. She looked to be in great shape.

"Can I help you?"

"My name's Maddie Landon," I said, handing her my card. She looked at it for a moment. "I'm investigating the death of a woman named Claire Stevenson. You may have read about it in the papers. Anyway, this may be a little awkward. I've been talking to neighbors, including Janice Levy, who's been a big help with the investigation." When I mentioned Mrs. Levy, I swear I saw a weird look on her face.

"Maybe you should come in. It seems this might take a few minutes."

The hallway was fairly dark. We went into the kitchen, which was much brighter. I knew that Tudors could be dark inside.

"Sit please. So what is going on?"

"Are you close to Janice?"

"I'm not. We were years ago but things changed."

"Can I ask why?"

"First, tell me why you're interested in her."

"She's not a suspect, but I found out a few things and I have no way of knowing what Janice told me was the truth."

"Please tell me what you found out."

"At one point, she told me she really liked Claire Stevenson, but then a neighbor said Janice was bad-mouthing her. Mrs. Stevenson's husband mentioned Janice was very nosy and used to come over to their house for no apparent reason." I decided not to mention the rumor about her brother's affair for the moment.

"I liked Janice, and my brother and her seemed very happy together. Eventually Janice got pregnant but miscarried. She was told she probably would never be able to have children. After that, she became very depressed and never really recovered. It was very sad. My brother tried to be patient, but eventually he stopped trying. He confided in me about Janice's mood swings. Though he begged her to get help, she wouldn't go."

"I'm sorry, I have to ask. There was a rumor that when your brother died, he was with a woman other than his wife."

"That's true. Since Janice refused to get help, he knew he couldn't go on the way they were. He stayed but was leading a separate life from his wife."

"Why didn't he divorce her?"

"I think he felt guilty. He didn't want to leave her, but knew he needed to have a life apart from Janice."

"Do you think she's unstable?"

"I don't know what her mental condition is now. I haven't seen her since Stephen died."

"Are you married?"

"Yes. My husband's at work now. Do you think she lied about her feelings toward Mrs. Stevenson?"

"I don't know for sure."

"Why does it matter?"

"I don't know if it does." I wasn't sure what it meant, myself, though Janice could be providing me with information that might be false if she had a problem with Claire.

"Has anyone been charged with Mrs. Stevenson's death?"

"Her husband, but I can't go into any details. I really appreciate you talking with me. If you think of anything else, please call me," I said, as I stood up to leave.

"How does Janice seem to you?" Mrs. Stein asked, as she was walking me to the door.

"I think she's a very lonely lady with a lot of time on her hands. I don't know if she has any friends."

"I think it would be difficult to be friends with her."

"That may be. Well, thank you for talking with me."

After speaking with Mrs. Stein, it became clear to me that Janice Levy was a lonely person seeking attention any way she could, even if she had to make things up.

I was hungry and tired by the time I got home. I still had not made the phone call to Harris Tyler and I was running out of excuses to tell myself. After I changed and ate, I nervously picked up my phone and called Harris Tyler's cell phone number. It went straight to voice mail.

"My name is Maddie Landon. I'm not sure if I have the right Harris Tyler. I'm looking for a Harris Tyler who grew up in Philadelphia. I got your name from Lucy Peterson, who lived near you when you were kids. If I do have the right person, can you please call me back?"

My hands were shaking as I hung up. I had no clue whether he would call back, and I wasn't sure if I wanted him to.

CHAPTER 68

I got up early on Saturday, knowing Jesse would be here shortly. I had given Larry Banks a very quick account of the conversation I had with Judy Stein on my way home yesterday. I told him I was taking the weekend off and would touch base with him on Monday. There was a part of me that wanted to work, but I also knew it was important for my relationship that I didn't let work consume me. If it was necessary to work, I knew Jesse would be fine with it.

I heard the knock on the door and I quickly opened it.

"Hello, stranger," I said as I pulled him inside. "I hope you're hungry, since I'm making you pancakes from scratch."

"That's nice but don't take this the wrong way. I'll starve before those pancakes are made."

"Is that nice to say to the person who's feeding you?"

"I have a better plan. Why don't we get reacquainted and then I'll make you pancakes."

"That's one proposition I won't argue with."

I was pouring the water into the coffeemaker while Jesse was mixing the batter and grilling the pancakes.

"I made the call last night," I said, as we were sitting down to eat. "I had to leave a message. So far I haven't gotten a call back."

"It's only been a short time. Don't use that wild imagination of yours to make up stories about why he hasn't called yet. It's too soon to drive yourself crazy."

"I can always count on you to make me feel better. I thought we could rent bikes and ride around Central Park."

"That's a great idea. Even if cooking isn't your strong suit, your mind is what turns me on."

"You're so full of crap but I'll take it," I said, kissing Jesse on the tip of his nose.

***

We spent a good part of the day riding around Central Park, stopping only to rest on a gigantic rock to take in the views. Though I was having a nice time, I couldn't help but wonder if Harris Tyler would call back.

We wound up at the Boat Basin and had an early dinner. Later that night, when we were lying in bed, I filled Jesse in on what else I found out about Greg and what I learned from Janice Levy's sister-in-law.

"Do you have any viable suspects?"

"Tough question, Jesse Monroe. Can I get back to you on that?"

"Only if you have something else in mind."

I came up with something else.

***

After saying goodbye to Jesse on Monday morning, I went back upstairs to my apartment and showered. I still hadn't heard from Harris Tyler. If he was going to call, he should have by now. He couldn't possibly know why I was calling, or maybe he did. Maybe I had the wrong person. *Stop driving yourself crazy, Maddie.*

About an hour into my emails, the phone rang. It was a number I didn't recognize.

"Hello," I said cautiously.

"Is this Maddie Landon?"

"Yes."

"My name's Harris Tyler. I'm sorry I haven't called you back sooner, but I've been on vacation and basically had my phone off."

My heart was beating like a drum. I could hear the thumping in my ear.

"I was stunned to hear the name Lucy Peterson. It was another lifetime ago. What is this about?"

I was caught off guard and quickly thinking about what to say.

"Do you remember her sister, Lydia?"

"Yes. I kind of had a thing for her. I don't know what happened, but she went away for a few months and when she came back, she never spoke to me again."

"Her parents sent her away because she was pregnant." There was silence on the other end. I continued.

"She was forced to give up the baby. A couple from New York adopted the baby girl."

"I had no idea. I'm so sorry."

"If you slept with her, you may be my father," I said bluntly.

"Wow! This is a lot to take in. Please don't take this the wrong way, but are you sure?"

"I believe you're the only boy she had sex with."

"Can I call you back? I need to take this all in. It's quite a shock."

"If that's what you have to do," I replied and then I hung up.

I was so angry I didn't realize I had dug my fingernails down my thigh and was bleeding. I picked up my phone and called Annie, tears streaming down my face.

"Hi, sweetie, I was thinking about you," Annie said when she answered.

"He called me back."

"Who called you back? Are you crying?"

"Harris Tyler. I just spoke to him," I said through my tears. "I told him he may be my father and he said he had to call me back. It was a shock to him. Do you believe the nerve of this guy?"

"It's been thirty-seven years and this man had no idea he had a daughter. I think it would be a shock to anyone. It doesn't sound as if he was blowing you off."

"So you think I'm overreacting?"

"Let's see what he says when he calls you back."

"If he does."

"I bet he will. How did he sound otherwise?"

"He said that he had a thing for Lydia. He was baffled when she had left without saying goodbye. And when she got back, she never spoke to him again."

"Well, he did admit that he liked her, and he didn't deny that he might be your father. I think he just needed some time to take it all in. You can't blame him for that."

"I hung up on him."

"I'm sure he realized you were upset."

"I guess."

"I'm really happy you called him. I wonder what he looks like. I bet he's very handsome."

"You know you have a warped sense of humor."

"Don't tell me it hasn't crossed your mind."

"Of course I'm curious, but not in that way. I wonder if we have similar facial features or personality traits that we both have in common."

"Call me as soon as you get off the phone with him."

"If he calls back, you'll be the first to know."

CHAPTER 69

When I hung up with Annie, I tried to put my conversation with Harris Tyler out of my mind and drove to the office. I stopped at the deli near me for an egg sandwich and put on a pot of coffee as soon as I got in. I wanted to talk with Larry Banks about what we should do next, but I knew he had court this morning and probably wouldn't be back in the office till noon.

Then I thought about what Jesse asked me the other day—did I have any suspects? Gavin lied to me right from the beginning, and it wasn't till he was backed into a corner that he admitted to his affair with Claire. He explained away the reason why he was still in contact with Claire up until the time of her death, but I only had his word for it.

Both Greg and Gavin were having affairs with her. But who was she getting the harassing phone calls from? If I had to guess, I would put my money on Greg from what I recently learned about him. The phone interrupted my train of thought.

"Hello."

"Can you come by in half an hour?" Larry Banks asked.

"See you then."

"Anything to report?" Banks said as I was sitting in his office.

I went over the conversation I had with Judy Stein in more detail.

"She told me that she hasn't spoken to Janice since her brother's funeral."

"How does this relate to the case?"

"It probably doesn't. My take on Janice Levy is that she's a lonely woman who has too much time on her hands. Plus, she might have some emotional problems."

"How would she be as a witness?"

"It's questionable, though she could help our case since she's the one who allegedly saw these men coming and going from the Stevensons' house."

"If it's true, which we don't know, it's a gamble. If the prosecution looks into her, they're going to portray Janice Levy as unreliable with her history. It might muddy the waters."

"Do we know everything the prosecution has?" I said.

"No, we don't."

"How do we get around the poison found in Howie's house?"

"Anyone can easily get arsenic. You can buy it online. We have to show the jury that Claire slept around. Even if Greg and Gavin both have alibis for the day she died, it doesn't mean that's when the poison was administered. It could easily have been put in her drink the day before."

"What about the fact that Claire was pregnant and it wasn't Howie's baby," I said.

"We have to get the jury to believe that the person who was threatening Claire might be the father. We know from at least two people that she was receiving threatening telephone calls."

"But if we don't know who the father was, it's just supposition."

"We do the best with what we have. It takes only one juror to believe us," Larry Banks said.

"We're going to make Claire out to be promiscuous," I said, not thrilled with the idea. "I'm not sure Howie would be okay publicizing the fact that his wife was sleeping around."

"I'm trying to get Howie acquitted. She's dead."

"I know. I just wish we didn't have to drag her name through the coals."

"Unless we find out who killed Claire before the trial, I don't have a choice."

"What are Howie's chances of getting acquitted?"

"Juries can be unpredictable, so it's hard to know."

"We should prepare Howie so he's not blindsided."

"I agree. Do you want to go up together?"

"I'd like to tell him," I said.

"He has to know this is his only option. We can't give him a good defense if he won't agree to it. It's your job to convince him he doesn't have a choice, unless he wants to be an old man when he gets out of prison, if he lives that long."

I walked across the hall to my office. I knew Banks was right, but I wasn't looking forward to giving Howie the news. Though Claire did have affairs, I knew it wasn't because she was promiscuous. She was the victim of her past and couldn't ask for the help she needed. I knew the feeling.

My thoughts got lost in thinking about the man who may be my father. Was meeting him what I really wanted? I wasn't sure about anything. Were my fears of being left again so strong I wasn't willing to completely commit to Jesse? What if I never could?

Right now, I couldn't think clearly. I packed up and left the office. I went home, changed into my running clothes, and jogged to the park. After I finished my three-mile loop, I sat down on one of the park benches and tried to think about where I went wrong. I couldn't let go of the feeling that I was letting Howie down. He may wind up being convicted of a murder I was fairly sure he didn't commit. Was it possible it wasn't Greg or Gavin Stone? Was there a third person in Claire's life that I wasn't aware of? I couldn't compel Greg to take a paternity test, and I knew Gavin did not consent to a DNA test when he was being questioned by the police. What was I missing?

I wanted to speak with Dr. Goldberg, but she was at a conference in Boston. When I got home, I quickly showered and tried to get up enough energy to eat something. When I looked in the refrigerator, I had some leftover lasagna that I threw in the oven to heat up. I poured myself a glass of wine, trying not to stare at the oven while waiting for my lasagna.

I was eating and watching TV in the bedroom. The next thing I knew, I was in the backseat of my father's car. My mother was sitting next to my father and they were singing a song, though I couldn't hear the words. I kept wondering where we were going since it was late and it was a school night. "Are we going someplace special?" I asked my father. He didn't answer me. It was dark out and I was scared. The singing had stopped. When I looked in the front seat, my mother and father were gone. I screamed so hard I woke myself up drenched in a pool of my own sweat. My heart racing.

I ran to the bathroom, pulled off my undershirt, and splashed cold water over me. This was the second nightmare I had in the last few months. Why were they starting to happen again? When I walked back into the bedroom, the clock read 12:05 a.m. I noticed my plate of lasagna and my glass of wine were on my nightstand, empty. I pulled the blanket up to my chin to stop the shaking. At some point, I must have fallen back asleep since the next time I looked at the clock. it was 6:30 a.m.

***

I was sitting with Howie in a large room with other inmates and their visitors at the Westchester County Department of Corrections. We were at a table by ourselves. I noticed his right eye was twitching every so often.

"I wanted to talk to you about the trial. Mr. Banks thinks we have a good shot at getting you acquitted." Maybe that was a slight stretch. "In order to accomplish this, we have to portray Claire as someone who was promiscuous, though we know that's not true."

"No! No! No! I can't have people thinking that way about her."

I noticed the guard looked our way.

"Keep your voice low," I said to Howie. "We don't have a choice. We want to show that any one of the guys she was with could have killed Claire. We already know she was being threatened. I know this will be hard for you to listen to during the trial, but there's no way around it."

"I knew something was wrong, but she wouldn't talk to me about it. If only I had insisted."

"You can't blame yourself. She was dealt a bad hand and didn't know how to help herself. She did the best she could." Tears were streaming down Howie's face. I couldn't help but feel bad for him.

"Please take care of yourself. We need you to be strong for the trial."

"Are you sure there's no other way?"

"I am. There's still hope we may be able to find the killer before the trial."

"I won't hold my breath."

I would probably feel the same way if I were in Howie's position.

CHAPTER 70

I went back to my office feeling depressed and frustrated. The look on Howie's face when I left haunted me. I knew Larry Banks had a good reputation and a good track record, but I wasn't as confident as he was. Maybe he wasn't either.

"Hi, Mary," I said as I stopped by to see Cousin Will.

"Well, if it isn't Maddie Landon. I haven't seen you in ages," Mary said with a grin on her face.

"I know. I've been so busy with this case I'm working on, I haven't had time for much else."

"How's it going?"

"Not so good. The trial is in three weeks and so far I still have no idea who the murderer is."

"Sorry to hear that."

"Is that my long-lost cousin I hear?" Will said, as he popped his head out of his office.

"Are you busy?"

"Come on in."

"I spoke to someone in California who I think may be my father."

"How did it go?"

"Not as I thought, though it probably was a big shock to him. He said he had to digest all of it and would call me back."

"What do you know about him?"

"He's married with two grown sons. He's lived in California since he left Philadelphia to attend college. And he has his own software company."

"Sounds very successful."

"I'm pretty sure he had no idea I existed. He did admit he was fond of Lydia. He told me Lydia had stopped talking to him when she got back from South Carolina, and he didn't know why."

"If I were him, I'd be in shock as well. He must feel awful."

"Maybe he won't even call back."

"Are those your defenses talking? Please, Maddie, you have to let the good in without feeling the other shoe is going to drop."

"I had another nightmare. The same as all the others."

"I'm still here, Annie is still here, Jesse is still here. We all love you, and I know your parents didn't choose to leave you. I know how much they loved you and how happy you made them. You're going to miss out on so much joy if you let fear rule you."

"Are you sure you're in the right profession?" I asked.

Will laughed and gave me a hug.

Later that evening, I opened up my John Grisham book, hoping to distract myself from thinking about Harris Tyler, when my phone rang. I recognized the number and my hand started to shake as I pressed my finger down to answer.

"Hello," I said carefully.

"Maddie, this is Harris Tyler. I'm sorry I ended our conversation the way I did yesterday morning. I wasn't prepared for what you told me, and I needed some time to think."

"As I said, I'm not sure you're my father."

"Did you speak with Lydia?"

It hit me that he had no idea Lydia was dead.

"You didn't know she was dead?"

"No. I'm so sorry. How did she die?"

"She died of sepsis about five years ago when her appendix ruptured." He was quiet for a moment.

"Do you know why she gave you up for adoption?"

"It's kind of a long story. The short version was that her parents were extremely religious and forced Lydia to give the baby up, to give me up. To them, it would have brought shame to the family."

"No wonder she never told me. Listen, I know we can't be positive that I'm your father, but the odds are pretty good that I am. Lydia and I did have sex, but I can tell you that it was completely consensual. We were very young and maybe it wouldn't have lasted, but we were crazy about each other. Unfortunately, we had to keep it a secret. When she left without telling me, and then never spoke to me again when she got back, I was heartbroken. I think that's why I chose a college in California. I wanted to get as far away from home as I could."

I was trying to make sense of what he just said.

"What would you have done if she decided to keep the baby?" I said nervously, realizing I was afraid to hear his answer.

"I wish I could tell you, but I just don't know. I hope I would have stepped up and done everything I could to support Lydia. I spoke to my wife about our conversation and we would both love to meet you. I'm not sure how we can work it out, but I'd be willing to fly to New York."

I didn't know what to say. "Could we exchange photos?"

"I'd love to. I realize I know nothing about you or your life, though I have to admit I looked you up and you are quite an impressive young woman."

"Maybe we can talk on the phone again."

"I'm sorry if I came on too strong. We can certainly talk on the phone. How about if I call you in a few days?"

"Thank you. I'll send you a photo."

"Maddie, I'm so sorry I wasn't in your life."

I didn't say anything.

"I'll call you," he said and hung up.

I wasn't expecting his reaction. I guess I was thinking the worst. Two minutes later, I was staring into the face of the man who was most likely my father. He was handsome. I had his square chin and his high cheekbones. Though I had my mother's green eyes, I had his large almond-shaped eyes. His wavy brown hair was sprinkled with gray.

I looked for a photo to send and found one that Jesse took of me in Central Park. I got a text back with two words: "You're beautiful." I remembered something my mother had told me: "The more people in your life that love you, the richer you are." After my parents died, I only had Cousin Alan and his parents. I had no other extended family except for my aunt. Maybe that's why she always encouraged me to search for my biological parents. It wasn't until I opened the letter my parents left for me with their wishes that I search for my birth parents that I changed my mind.

It threw me for a loop when Harris Tyler suggested he would fly to New York to meet me. Things were going faster than I expected. I wondered what was upsetting me.

CHAPTER 71

The following morning, I read through my notes on the case again to see if I overlooked anything. It was driving me crazy that the killer was eluding me. What was I not seeing? I was running out of time before Howie's trial. I didn't want to leave it up to a jury to decide Howie's fate. I was racking my brains for anything.

As I was digging into my cereal, something Janice Levy said was rattling around in my head. What was it? Something about Claire being poisoned. I didn't recall telling Mrs. Levy that Claire died of poisoning, and it was never reported in the newspaper. How would she know that?

"Larry, call me as soon as you get this message. It's important."

I was trying to contain myself. I couldn't sit still. Maybe I was jumping the gun. She could have heard it from somewhere else.

I answered the phone as soon as it rang.

"What's going on?" Larry Banks said.

"I remembered what Janice Levy had said the last time I spoke with her. She told me that she felt bad that Claire died of poisoning. I never told Mrs. Levy Claire was poisoned. I think she really hated Claire because she thought Claire was promiscuous, just like her husband was. After Janice Levy's baby died, she never recovered. Her husband had affairs and I don't think she ever forgave him."

"This is all supposition."

"So I'll have to prove it. And I think I know how." I went on to tell Larry Banks my plan.

"Okay. I'll talk to the lead detective on the case."

"Let me know what he says and we'll set it up."

I was waiting on pins and needles, hoping John Vaughn, the detective in charge of Claire's case, would cooperate with us.

Later in the day, I heard back from Larry Banks. He told me that John Vaughn would go along with our plan, though he wasn't thrilled that I was meddling in his investigation. I told Larry to set it up for 5:00 p.m. that day.

I left my apartment at 4:00 p.m. and drove up to Scarsdale, hoping Mrs. Levy would be home. When I arrived, I sat in my car till 5:00 and then rang Janice Levy's bell.

"Ms. Landon, what are you doing here?"

"I was at home thinking about the case and realized I was at a dead-end. I needed some insight into the case and thought of you, since you've been so helpful to me from the beginning of my investigation into Claire's death. Do you have a minute to brainstorm, to help me figure out how to find the person who killed Claire?" I was praying she bought my line.

"Of course, come in. I'll help you in any way I can."

We were sitting in the living room and I was thinking of what to say next.

"This has been a hard case for me. I'm afraid I've lost my objectivity. Normally, I would feel sympathy for Mrs.

Stevenson, but with all her indiscretions, it's been difficult for me. I've never shared this with anyone, but when I was eleven, I saw my father kissing another woman. I never told my mother, and keeping that secret made me feel like an accomplice. Even though this happened over twenty-five years ago, I haven't been able to reconcile those feelings. Situations of infidelity are particularly painful to me." *Please, Dad, forgive me for my lie*.

"I know how you must have felt. My husband cheated on me throughout our marriage," Janice said.

"That's horrible. Did you ever say anything to him?"

"No. I held it in just like you did. You can't imagine how difficult this was for me."

I knew I had to tread lightly so Janice wouldn't get suspicious.

"I'm so sorry you had to endure all that."

"Thank you."

"It couldn't have been easy living across the street from Claire, watching men parade in and out of Claire's house."

"Her husband loved her, and his love meant nothing at all to her. How could she hurt him that way? It just made me so angry."

"If I lived across the street from Claire, I don't know if I could have sat back and done nothing. It must have been heartbreaking to watch what was going on." My heart was racing.

"You have no idea what it was like for me. Flaunting herself with all those men when her husband was so devoted to her. I had to do something. I couldn't allow her to continue to betray him."

"What did you do?"

"I don't know what you mean."

"Why don't you just tell me? You'll feel better."

"She deserved it."

"And is that why you poisoned Claire?"

"I had no choice. You can certainly understand that," Janice said with a blank expression on her face.

"I can. I wish I had the courage to do what you did."

"I said more than I should have. Maybe you better leave now."

"I'm sorry this was so painful for you."

Detective John Vaughn had been listening to the entire conversation and was waiting outside with two other police officers. As I passed him, he said, "Good job, Landon." If it wasn't for the fact that Howie was sitting in jail for a crime he didn't commit, I would almost feel sorry for Janice Levy.

On the way back, I called Larry Banks and told him Janice Levy was being arrested and we needed to get Howie out of jail as soon as possible. I wondered what was going to happen to the relationship between Howie and his partner, Gavin Stone.

CHAPTER 72

I didn't want to call Greg, but he had a right to know what happened. I could sense he felt a great relief now that there wasn't going to be a trial. And I told him never to call me again.

On my way to The Dead Poet to meet Annie for drinks, I called Jesse and explained everything that happened. He was overjoyed that I had closed the case.

"My brilliant private investigator," Annie said, as she gave me a big hug before sitting down. "I can't believe you solved the case, and that you weren't knifed, shot, or hit over the head in the process. Tell me everything."

"The last time I met with Janice Levy, she mentioned that Claire was poisoned. It didn't dawn on me until today that I never told Janice Levy how Claire died. Since we had no physical evidence, I had no choice but to get her to confess. In order for that to happen, I had to sympathize with her since I knew how she felt about Claire's promiscuity. I believe that by murdering Claire, Janice Levy was expressing the rage she had contained toward her husband all those years. Emotionally, she was killing him, not Claire.

"In order for the confession to stand up, I had the lead detective on the case listening in on our conversation."

"Does Greg know?"

"Yes. He was really relieved that the case wasn't going to trial."

"So how did you leave it with him?"

"I told him never to call me again. After examining my feelings toward him, I realized that whatever relationship I thought I had with him at the time wasn't real. He knew I was vulnerable and took advantage of that. He used me like he used all the other women he had affairs with."

"You couldn't have known. Let it go."

I was curious if Greg was the father of Claire's baby. I wondered if Greg knew. I guess I'd never know who was threatening Claire.

We drank to closing the case.

***

A week later, I was getting ready to leave for the Archer Hotel in midtown Manhattan, where I was going to meet the man who was probably my biological father. I was so nervous I was up by 5:00 a.m. and couldn't fall asleep.

I was getting cold feet. Maybe this wasn't such a good idea. *After all these years, do I really want to include this man and his family in my life? I like my world just as it is. Why did I ever agree to meet with him?* It was already twelve noon, too late to call it off.

I walked into the hotel lobby. I recognized him right away. He smiled and I smiled back.

THE END

ACKNOWLEDGMENTS

It has been my great joy to write Murder on Drake Street, the second in the Maddie Landon Mystery series.

I'd like to thank all my wonderful friends who have supported me during the writing of this novel, particularly Ann Spadafora for always lending me her ear. And to my writing group for their encouragement and input. Thank you to the team at BooksGoSocial for their invaluable contributions in connection with this novel.

Finally, my love and heartfelt thanks to my daughter Carrie Lozo and my close friend, Susan Greene, for reading early drafts and providing edits and advice for improving the plot and characters of this novel. I am grateful to everyone who has been instrumental in the creation of this book.

ABOUT THE AUTHOR

As a private investigator with more than thirty years of experience, Ellen Shapiro's professional expertise has brought an authenticity to her characters and the storylines she has created for her novels. She is the author of five mystery novels and has written articles in her field for both local and nationwide newspapers. Ellen is a member of Mystery Writers of America and resides in Scarsdale, New York.